# Gehenna Dawn

# Dawn

## Portal wars I

# Jay Allan

**system 7**
publishing

# Also By Jay Allan

Marines (Crimson Worlds I)

The Cost of Victory (Crimson Worlds II)

A Little Rebellion (Crimson Worlds III)

The First Imperium (Crimson Worlds IV)

The Line Must Hold (Crimson Worlds V)

To Hell's Heart (Crimson Worlds VI)

The Dragon's Banner

www.crimsonworlds.com

www.jayallanbooks.com

# Gehenna Dawn

Gehenna Dawn is a work of fiction. All names, charac-
ters, incidents, and locations are fictitious. Any resem-
blance to actual persons, living or dead, events or places
is entirely coincidental.

ISBN: 978-0615916972

*"If tyranny and oppression come to this land it will be in the guise of fighting a foreign enemy."*

— *James Madison*

# PART ONE
# A WARRIOR IN HELL

# Chapter One

From the Journal of Jake Taylor:

There are two suns here, and no night. The brightness is constant; it wears you down until you can feel the madness building inside you...a craving, a painful longing, willing in vain for it to be dark. Then the wave of frustration, of anger and bitterness when there is nothing but the light, the unending light. Even when you close your eyes you can still see the hazy orange glow, constant, unceasing.

But it's not the light that's hardest to take; it's the heat. Erastus is a hot world, hotter than the most sunbaked desert back home. When you first get here you can't breathe, and when you do force air into your lungs it feels like fire exploding in your chest. Your instincts conflict...first trying to stop you from taking another searing, agonizing breath, then succumbing to the irresistible need for air. You think you are going to die then and there, to yield to natural forces you were never supposed to survive. But you don't. A world like Erastus teaches you just how adaptable man really is.

On Earth I loved the night, the quiet darkness, the cool stillness, a field of twinkling stars the only light in an inky sky. Now I can hardly remember what it felt like, sitting on the porch breathing the crisp air. I always loved autumn, the first chill of the year that sent me to the closet to fetch another blanket. Now all I know is a hellish perversion of

**eternal summer. Cold? A memory almost faded now. The concept remains, a lingering vestige, but the recollection of how it felt? Gone.**

The FNGs were dying...they were dying like flies. The 213th Strike Force was pinned down on Blackrock Ridge, and they were catching hell. The Machines were attacking from three sides, trying to cut off the only line of retreat. The strategy was predictable - most of their operations were - but that didn't mean it wouldn't work. If they closed the circle, no one from the 213th would make it back to base.

"Sergeant Taylor, get your section into that gap. Keep it open, whatever it takes. The ground's too rugged here for evac." Lieutenant Cadogan's voice was raw. He was trying, without much success, to hide his fatigue. Both suns were in the sky, and the strike force had been fighting on the open ridge for over an hour. Half the troops were almost incoherent with heat exhaustion, and the rest weren't far behind. The Machines felt the heat too, as much as they did anything, but they were less vulnerable to its effects. Which made fighting during midday a big advantage for them.

"Yes, sir." Jake Taylor's voice was gravelly, somber. He hated to see the new guys getting themselves massacred. His people had been in reserve, so he couldn't see everything happening up on the forward line. But he bet himself over a dozen of the rookies were down already, and probably more.

Taylor spent a lot of time lecturing the new recruits when they first arrived, but not many of them listened... and that meant not many of them survived. Not on Erastus. Not against an enemy like the Machines.

"Let's go, 2nd Section." Taylor took a deep, searing

breath. He'd been on Erastus a long time, long enough for his body to adjust to the harsh environment. His was muscular, but lean and wiry, his physique adapted to the constant dehydration. It didn't matter how long you stayed on Erastus, how used to it you became...the air was still goddamned hot. "Follow me...into the gap. We've got to hold the door open."

Taylor's troops snapped into position, following him down the jagged rocks of the ridgeline into the small gully behind. The narrow depression led back toward a small plateau...flat ground where the evac ships could land. The strike force could withdraw that way under cover...as long as the Machines didn't break through and block the route.

Taylor's troops were veterans mostly, though none had been on Erastus as long as he had. Jake had been onplanet five years, a tenure that made him part of an elite group. Men didn't survive that long in the battle lines. The Machines killed them...or Erastus did. Or they went mad from the heat, the thirst, the fear. Not many men could survive that long on the front lines in hell.

He waved a sunbaked arm, worn assault rifle gripped firmly in his hand. "I want two lines. First team left, second team right." His voice was hoarse and scratchy... everyone got that way on Erastus sooner or later. Yelling felt like broken glass on his parched throat, but it was the only way his people could hear him, even with the com implants. "I want 3rd and 4th teams in reserve, ready to move to either flank."

"Blackie, get your HHV set up between those two rock outcroppings to your south. That should give your guys good cover and a nice field of fire." Taylor tended to micromanage his teams. He couldn't help himself. His grasp of the field was extraordinary – as it had been from the day he stepped out of the Portal into the blazing sunlight of Erastus. He was a raw cherry with no military training other than what he'd gotten in Basic...but there was something in him, some hidden talent that suddenly emerged. His eye immediately focused on key positions, and his mind rapidly assessed the strengths and weaknesses of the tactical situation. There weren't many things more important in small unit tactics than a good feel for the ground, and Taylor was one of the best. It was one of the things - one of many things - that made him such a good natural soldier...and leader.

"Got it, Sarge." Tony Black's voice was deep, with a heavy urban accent. "Deploying now." Black was the senior corporal in the section and the longest-serving veteran after Taylor. He was Jake's best friend...and his go-to man for anything difficult or vital.

"I'm counting on you, Blackie." Taylor trusted Black... as much as he did anyone. The corporal was a little shit, maybe 170 centimeters in his boots, but he was tough as nails. Taylor had seen him cornered in a ravine by three Machines and live to tell about it. Black had grown up in the streets of the Philly Metrozone, just about the worst of the urban freezones in the US sector, and his survival instincts were well developed long before he ended up in UN Forces: Erastus. "They're going to come through right below that position. I can feel it. You should be able to wipe the field clean." As long as there aren't too many, he thought, keeping that part to himself.

"I'm on it, Sarge." Black's voice was confident, definitive. He'd served with Jake a long time. If "Mad Dog" Taylor said the enemy was coming through that ravine, it was as good as a guarantee to him. "If they come this way, we'll put 'em down."

"Fuck, it's hot," Taylor muttered to himself, running his hand along the back of his neck, wiping away the sweat.

He grabbed his bottle, and put it to his lips. He was disciplined, only allowing himself a small sip...barely enough to wet his parched lips. Water was precious. In this desert, it was life itself.

He turned and trotted up over a small rise, crouching low as he did. He wasn't sure he was exposed to the enemy's line of sight, but there was no point sticking his head out and taking chances. Carelessness got soldiers killed; that was something he constantly reminded the cherries... and his veterans too. It only took an instant of distraction to end up on the KIA list, and he'd seen experienced soldiers, men who should have known better, make the same mistakes as newbies straight out of the Portal.

He scrambled down into the gully and up the other side, coming out just behind the hulking figure of a man. "OK, Bear, get your boys over to the east. Spread out and grab some cover." Taylor paused for an instant before he added, "My gut says they're going to hit us from the west, over by Blackie's position. But keep your eyes open, just in case they come in from both directions."

The big man turned and looked back, nodding. The commander of Taylor's 2nd team, Chuck "Bear" Samuels was a giant of a man, well over 2 meters tall, with huge shoulders and powerful, muscled arms. Erastus usually finished off the big ones quickly...they just couldn't take the heat. But Samuels handled everything the planet and the Machines threw at him and kept right on going. Another two-striper, he was the best natured guy in the unit, cheerful and boisterous...when he wasn't fighting the Machines, that is.

"On the way, Boss." Taylor was never sure why Bear called him boss, but he always let it go. He got a kick out of the way it sounded in the gentle giant's slow southern drawl. "We got some good cover over there. I'll get the boys situated real good. Just in case." Like Black, Samuels considered Taylor's instincts a sure thing. If the sergeant said the enemy was going to hit the other flank, then that's what they were going to do. But he was a veteran too, and he didn't like taking chances any more than Taylor did. So he wouldn't let his guard drop, not for an instant. Not after all the times Jake had pounded that into his head.

"Get to it, Be..." Taylor's head snapped around. It was fire...HHV fire. The heavy hyper-velocity weapon was a tripod-mounted, rapid fire, infantry support gun firing depleted uranium projectiles at 3,200 mps. In a good position, a skilled HHV crew could sweep whole sections of a battlefield clean, tearing apart anything foolish enough to show itself. It was particularly effective against the Machines. The alien soldiers were far less sensitive to casualties, and they frequently attacked in the open, their dense formations attempting to overrun the human forces with massive waves. Against a few well-placed HHVs, that strategy was the rough equivalent of suicide.

"Get to it, Bear." Taylor turned and jogged down the hillside without waiting for an acknowledgement. He had his other two teams and the support personnel stacked up in the ravine. He slid down the rocky slope and ran along the bottom to where he'd posted the reserves.

"Longbow, grab yourself a vantage point off to the west." Tom Warner was standing closest to Taylor, watching the sergeant scramble toward the position. He was the section's sniper, the deadliest shot Taylor had ever seen. Warner constantly insisted he was even better with a bow than a rifle, and he had a seemingly limitless collection of stories to back the claim. No one was sure what to believe or not, but eventually the name stuck.

"Yes, Sarge." Warner strapped his weapon on his back and trotted off past Taylor. The MZ-750 computer-assisted sniper rifle was a long weapon, and the muzzle extended more than half a meter over Warner's head. In the hands of a well-trained shot, the MZ-750 could hit a man-sized target in partial cover at 4 klicks. Warner was an expert.

Jake stared at the rest of his reserve, 2 eight man teams plus the other 4 section specialists. "The rest of you stay down and wait. If they come in heavy, we'll probably have to extend the line so we don't get flanked." Taylor turned and took two steps before stopping and looking back. "Check your weapons and ammo. I want everybody ready on a second's notice." His 3rd and 4th teams were mostly new guys. Even most of the NCOs had less than a year onplanet. You couldn't remind the FNGs enough, he thought. You could say it ten times, and some fool will still end up in the line with an unloaded rifle.

He turned again and headed back toward Blackie's position. He wanted to scout things out for himself over there, but he glanced back for one last check to make sure his reserves were staying low. The walls of the ravine provided cover against line of sight, but that didn't mean the Machines wouldn't start dropping shells there. Taylor nursemaided the newbs – it was the only way to try and keep them alive. He hated seeing them gunned down like sheep, and he hammered away at his rookies, trying to beat some sense into their heads. It didn't always work, but Taylor had the lowest cherry casualty rate in the brigade. He intended to keep it that way.

He could hear the enemy fire coming in, getting thicker as he came back up to Black's position. The HHV was in place and firing full. "Blackie, how's it look up here?" He was still low in the gully, about 3 meters below the ledge where Black's team was deployed.

"It's hot, Sarge." Black's accent was thicker than usual;

he really sounded like an inner city tough. That told Taylor all he needed to know. Black's accent was the best way to read his stress level…and it only took a quick listen to tell that the veteran corporal was definitely tense.

"Alright, brother…hang on. I'm gonna get some eyes up." Taylor didn't want to commit reserves yet, not unless he was sure the enemy was coming in hard. He put his hand to his helmet, switching the com frequency. The speaker was in his head, an implant inside the ear canal, but the primary controls were external…a small pad on the side of his helmet. "Frantic, I need you to get two birds up ASAP. West flank, north and south trajectories." He paused then added, "Get me one to the east too." Might as well confirm if anything was heading Bear's way. Taylor didn't think so, but intuition was no substitute for solid intel.

It was obvious to everyone how Corporal Karl Young had gotten the name Frantic. The guy was twitchy sitting back at base playing cards. In a close in fight he was batshit crazy. Normally, Jake wouldn't want a loose cannon in his command, but Young was the best fighter he'd ever seen… and the crazy bastard wasn't scared of anything. Plus he'd done one thing no one else on Erastus had. He'd saved Jake Taylor's life.

"On it, Sarge. I'll have 'em up in half a minute." Young commanded Taylor's 3rd team. He was the only real veteran in either 3rd or 4th.

Jake climbed up the embankment and slid into place next to Black. "I've got drones launching. Once they're up we'll have better targeting intel." Taylor and Black had the same com implants, just like every soldier on Erastus, but Jake always preferred to hear with his own ears whenever possible.

Black nodded. "Good." He was prone behind a large

rock outcropping, firing his assault rifle through a slit in the granite slab. "'Cause I think we got another phalanx of these motherfuckers just behind that crest."

There was no way Black could have known what was hidden by the elevation, not until the drones got up and over there, at least. But Taylor had learned to respect his number two's gut almost as much as his own. He hadn't believed in intuition or anything like it before he came to Erastus, but he'd seen it work too many times not to pay attention. And Black's was one of the best.

Taylor's didn't rely entirely on guts, though, his or anyone else's. He'd learned to survive, but he'd done it with his head mostly, analyzing each situation and exercising caution. Most screw-ups happened because of poor planning or recklessness. Taylor was methodical, maintaining his calm deliberation even in the middle of combat.

He pulled his own rifle off his shoulder and slid into position a few meters south of Black. He was extraneous now, at least until he had more intel…and one more rifle in the line could make the difference. He could see out 1,000, maybe 1,200 meters. Beyond that, the ground sunk behind a small ridgeline, cutting line of sight. Black thought there were heavy enemy reserves back there, but they wouldn't know for sure until one of the drones was in place.

"Taylor, I've got evac inbound, but we're looking at maybe 20 before they're here." It was the lieutenant, sounding even worse than he had a few minutes earlier. "As soon as the birds are close, I'm gonna pull the rest of the sections back, through the gully between your two lines. Copy?"

"Copy, sir. Understood." Fuck, Taylor thought, twenty minutes was a long time. A long goddamned time. If there was another phalanx of Machines hidden behind that ridge, things were going to get real hot in a lot less than 20 minutes. He turned toward Black. "Twenty minutes until evac. We must not be the only disaster today."

The UN forces on Erastus didn't have a lot of air support, and what was available was always needed in three places at once. It took enough energy to transport men and supplies. Larger ordnance was sent on an "urgent needs" basis only. And antigrav transports and gunships were way too big to fit through a Portal. They had to be sent through in sections and assembled onsite. The whole process was time-consuming and prohibitively expensive. On UN Central's spreadsheet, it was a better deal to go through a few more men than spend too much on logistical support.

"I don't know, Dog. If they're stacked up behind that ridge out there, we're gonna be fucked up the ass in way less than 20 minutes." The use of handles was widespread in the UN forces, but rarely with a superior. Taylor tended to be casual with his non-coms in base, and Black sometimes reverted when it was just the two of them talking in the field. Taylor didn't really care. He wouldn't let it spread and affect overall discipline, but Black was like his brother.

"No shit, Blackie." He let a tiny smile cross his lips. He and Black were thinking the same thing. Not that it would do them much good. If they were right, they were going to be neck deep in Machines in a few minutes. He tapped the com pad on his helmet. "Frantic, where the hell are those drones?"

"They're up, Sarge." Young sounded half-crazed, as usual, but nothing out of the ordinary. "There's a lot of interdictive fire. I'm trying to bring them around the perimeter…avoid the heaviest spots."

"Understood, Corporal, but I need some intel now." Taylor sighed, but he didn't push any harder. Getting the drones shot down wasn't going to help. Karl Young was one of the best operators in the whole brigade. Taylor knew he'd get the drones around as quickly as he could without getting them blown away. "Do the best you can. I need to know what the enemy has behind that ridge."

"Yes, Sarge." Young was practically screaming. "I'll get you what you need."

There was a long silence, maybe a minute and a half. The line was still open, and Taylor could hear Young breathing hard on the other end. Jake was looking out over the field, his eyes straining, panning across the ridge. He thought he got a quick glimpse of one of the drones, flying low across the field in front of the ridge before it vanished from view. The small aircraft was zigging and zagging wildly, avoiding the heaviest pockets of enemy fire. He knew Young was good, but he hadn't seen much precision flying that could match what he was watching.

"Sarge, I got a drone over the ridge. Feeding you the scans." He paused, sucking in a deep breath, trying to control his edginess. "You better get what you need fast, Sarge…cause this thing ain't gonna last long."

"Thanks, Frantic. Great job." Taylor was slamming down his visor as he spoke, hitting the small button on his helmet that activated the projection system. The inside of his visor flickered with a soft blue light, and then the feed from the drone's camera started.

"Fuck…" Taylor stared as the drone transmitted a panoramic view of the backside of the ridge. A few seconds later there was a flash, then nothing.

"Sarge…did you get what you needed?" Young again, shouting into the com. "We lost the drone. I tried to keep it in a random pattern, but they picked it off anyway."

"Yeah, Frantic." Taylor's voice was grim. "I got what I needed." Now, he thought…what the fuck am I going to do with it?

He tapped his helmet controls, cutting the link with Young and calling up the lieutenant. "Sir...Taylor here."

"Go ahead, Jake." Cadogan sounded exhausted. He was up on the forward ridge with the other three sections. Taylor's people were getting some partial shade at least, but the rest of the strike force had been in direct sunlight for almost 90 minutes. Taylor didn't know for sure, but he suspected they'd already had fatalities from heatstroke.

"We got a drone up over that western ridge. They're massing back there. Looks like battalion strength, at least." The Machines didn't use human organizational structures, but UNFE forces tended to refer to enemy formations by their own force equivalents.

The line was silent for a few seconds. "Alright, Jake. You know you need to keep the escape route open. I'm gonna start sending the worst hit sections back toward the target LZ. You and your boys...hold firm." It was a point-less order, but it was all Cadogan had to give.

"Yes, sir." Taylor took a deep breath, wincing a little as a sharp pain lanced up his side. "Fuck," he grunted. He'd cracked a couple ribs on patrol a few days before, and they were bothering him more than he thought they would. Doc hadn't wanted to clear him for duty, but there was no way he was letting his people go out on a strikeforce level search and destroy mission without him. Especially this one...so far from base. And right after he got six new cherries transferred in.

"Blackie..." He turned to face his number two, shout-ing across the ten meters or so rather than using the com. "I'm going slip Jackson's team in on your flank. The way we're set now, if these guys attack, they'll just swing right around your boys." He paused, thinking for a few sec-onds. The whole situation was bad news. He was sending his least experienced unit commander to hold the exposed flank. But he was only going to have one team left in reserve, and he needed a veteran in command of it...and the only really seasoned guy back there was Young. Barret Jackson was a good soldier, but this was his first mission commanding a team.

"I'm gonna go with Jackson's team." He started sliding his way down the embankment as he spoke. "Frantic's people are in reserve. Be cool, Blackie...we can't burn through them too quickly. But pull them up a pair at a time if you really need them to plug your holes."

"Got it, Jake." Black was still firing through the split in the rock, turning his head back as he shouted after Taylor. "You take care of the south flank. I've got things handled here." It was bravado, but that was Blackie's style.

Taylor scrambled down into the gully and started moving south. He tapped the com controls on his helmet. "Jackson, get your boys up and moving. I want you on the line south of Black's team." He glanced back. He could hear the incoming fire on Black's position, and it was getting heavier. "Immediately, Corporal."

# Chapter 2

From the Journal of Jake Taylor:

What the hell am I doing in a place like this? The bureaucrats back home, they call it Erastus. I don't know what that means or where it came from. Some Admin's daughter probably named the place. But we grunts, the ones who do the fighting and dying here...we call it Gehenna. Literature and myth offer a host of names for the fiery hells conjured by God or man's imagination, but that's the one that stuck.

I was a farmer, and a writer too, or at least I wanted to be. But they made a soldier out of me instead. I didn't have a choice, at least not a real one. The harvest had been bad, the worst I'd ever seen. We went hungry that year, all of us, and there was no crop left to sell. When the inquisitor came, there was no money to pay the taxes.

My father was a good man, but he was never as careful around the monitors as he should have been. He was older, already past forty when he met my mother, and he remembered a time that none of the rest of us did. Before the Consolidation. Before the monitors were installed. Mother begged him to be more careful, and I did too when I was old enough to understand. People disappeared for saying things they shouldn't...the Enforcers came and took them in the night. He tried, but it just wasn't in him to hold his tongue. He hated what our world had become, and he cherished the memories of his youth, when people were free to read and think and speak as they wished.

But misty-eyed memories don't change the harsh present, and his passionate rants only put all of us at risk. A good man, my father, but a fool. He must have been on more than one watchlist, so when he couldn't pay the taxes, there was no chance for leniency, no possibility of an extension.

There was one option, though. I still remember the government man sitting at the kitchen table explaining it to me. His eyes...I don't think I'll ever forget his eyes. They were brown, but there was something else there, something cold, feral. His name was Carruthers. He sat there at our table, wearing a suit so fine, I remember thinking it must have cost more than our tractor. He came right out and said it to me...I could enlist to serve in the off-world military. If I did, the debt would be waived. If I refused, my family would lose the farm. There was no negotiation, no discussion. Either I accept immediately or we'd be put off the land by morning. He laid it all out in brutal detail. My term would be life; if I accepted I'd never come home, never see my family again. He said it all matter-of-factly, without the slightest trace of pity or understanding.

Father begged me not to go, swearing empty promises that we could find another way. Mother cried hysterically when I told her I was going to do it, her grief turning to unfocused rage as she grabbed at me and beat on my chest in a tearful fit. I listened to Father's entreaties, though I knew they were without substance, and I held Mother in my arms until her anger burned itself out into whimpering sobs. But my mind was made up.

What else could I do? Stay and watch my family slowly starve in the urban free zones? See my baby brother grow up a gutter rat, picking through the garbage for food? Let my little sister sell herself for scraps of bread?

No, I didn't have a choice. I was scared, screaming inside, dreaming of days long gone, when I was a child and felt safe, when a mother's hug could make everything better. Memories I'd thought long forgotten came rushing back to me. Simple things...picnics and family dinners and walks by the stream. Experiences I suddenly realized I hadn't truly appreciated. The little joys I took for granted as a child now seemed a distant, lost dream. I ached to go back and relive those days, truly valuing them this time. I was sad and terrified and longing for a life I could feel slipping away...like water through my fingers. But I signed the papers anyway and bonded myself to a lifetime's service.

I was a laughable choice as a soldier, unsuited in more ways than I can easily list. I'd always been a weak, skinny kid, prone to illness and without much stamina. I was gentle by nature and not at all aggressive. Not until the government taught me to hate.

Firebase Delta was built into a rocky hill on the edge of Erastus' biggest desert. The 213th had rotated in a month before, after a year's posting in the jungle belt. They'd gotten used to the steamy humidity of the planet's equatorial zone, no less unpleasant than the desert, but different. They were still re-acclimating to the searing dry heat, and Taylor felt his section's performance was suffering as a result. They'd get used to it eventually, but Taylor wasn't going to wait...he was going to give them a day's rest after the heavy fight they'd just been in, and then they were going to do midday maneuvers. More than anything, winning a fight on Erastus meant staying sharp and alert despite the intense heat.

The battle at Blackrock Ridge the day before couldn't be classified as a win, not by any reasonable measure. They'd inflicted heavy losses on the ambushing Machines, far more than they had suffered, but that was only normal. The Machines were relentless attackers and highly tolerant of casualties. They always lost more. In the end, the human forces were forced to flee the field, and they barely got away at that. It hadn't been the disaster it could have been, but it was nothing anyone was going to write any songs about.

Still, the 213th survived, at least some of it did. For a while that had seemed like an impossibility. Even Taylor had almost given up hope. By the end, he had everyone on the line; he even took most of 2nd Team from the eastern flank, leaving Just Bear and one private to protect against an attack there.

Taylor still had the images fresh in his memory. The Machines looked a lot like humans, especially from a distance. The plain in front of the ridgeline was covered with their dead. They launched two all-out assaults, and the second came close – too close – to breaking through. The 213th had been a hair's breadth from being overrun. For a few seconds, Jake thought they had been. He still wasn't sure how they'd managed to beat back that last charge, and he knew just how tight it had been. Taylor's section had 11 casualties, 3 of them KIA. That was half the casualty rate of the rest of the strikeforce. His people remembered what he'd been telling them, what he'd been pounding into their heads.

The evac finally came – closer to 30 minutes than 20 – and it would have been too late except for the pair of Dragonfire gunships escorting the transports. The big antigrav craft strafed the line just as the Machines were launching their third assault. The heavy autoguns tore into the advancing enemy, massive hyper-velocity projectiles tearing the Machine's flesh and steel bodies to shreds.

Two or three more passes might have shattered the enemy force, Jake thought, but the gunships withdrew after one attack. The fire from the ground was too heavy, and the Dragonfires were too valuable to risk. The 2 gunships were worth more to the high command than every man in the 213th, so one firing run was all they got.

It turned out to be enough. The Machines suffered heavy casualties and were badly disordered. It took time for them to shake back into an attack formation, and by then Jake Taylor and Blackie were mounting up on the last transport. The strikeforce was on its way back to base, battered but not destroyed.

Now it was the day after. Most of the 213th was sacked, trying to catch up on sleep after the grueling fight. A lot of guys had trouble sleeping on Erastus; the relentless heat was just too uncomfortable. But sooner or later, when you got tired enough, you could sleep through anything. And most of the 213th was tired enough.

Taylor was walking slowly down a corridor. The passage had been dug into the solid rock, the walls smooth and wavy, like part of a candle that had been melted and re-hardened. The look was familiar, the tell-tale sign of the plasma drills that had bored out this refuge.

He pulled a small cloth from one of the large pockets on his fatigues and wiped his forehead. It was hot, even in these subterranean passageways. The mind expected tunnels and caves to be cool and damp, but Erastus was a different kind of world, its crust and mantle wracked with geothermal activity. It was almost as warm underground as it was outside, though at least you could get out of the direct sunlight. You could even be in the dark inside, something you couldn't quite manage outside, even with your eyes closed tight. That didn't make it any cooler inside, but it helped somehow. It was an illusion, perhaps, but on Gehenna, you took what you could get.

The mission had been a search and destroy that turned into a trap. The Machines were unimaginative and tactically weak, but they were highly organized and uniquely able to move rapidly to exploit an opportunity. And the 213th had walked right into an ambush. It had been a poorly planned op from the start. Too far from base, inadequate support, and a long march that practically telegraphed the objective. It wasn't Lieutenant Cadogan's fault...it was Battalion that screwed the pooch. They sent a crack strikeforce into an unwinnable situation with insufficient intel...and now it was all shot to hell.

It was without a commander too. The 213th had suffered just under 50% casualties, and those losses included the lieutenant. He wasn't dead, not yet at least. But he was in bad shape...or at least that was the rumor going around.

Taylor was on his way to the infirmary. The pain in his chest had migrated to his back. He was pretty sure he'd broken at least one of the cracked ribs, and he figured he'd have to deal with it sooner or later. He was also hoping to get some info on the lieutenant.

Cadogan was the only man in the 213th who'd been on Erastus longer than Taylor. Jake looked like he'd make a poor soldier when he first stepped out of the Portal into the searing heat of Erastus. The skinny kid almost passed out, and he certainly didn't look like he had what it took to survive. But Cadogan had been the same when he arrived, and he saw something in Taylor, something that wasn't obvious on a cursory glance. Then-Sergeant Cadogan took the shaky new private under his wing, teaching him how to survive, and later, how to lead.

Like most of the guys who'd been around a long time, Cadogan had a nickname...Scholar, though it had largely fallen into disuse as his original peers died or moved on to other units. Taylor certainly never dared to call him that, though Cadogan was fairly tolerant of informalities around base. The lieutenant himself never called any of the men by their nicknames either, usually referring to them by their

ranks and surnames. When he wanted to be more informal, he used first names, but almost never handles.

Cadogan had been a teacher of some sort; Jake knew
that much. He'd been older than most of the recruits
when he first got to Erastus, and highly educated too. It
was a mystery to everyone how he ended up in the off-
world military. As far as Taylor or anyone else seemed to
know, Cadogan had never talked about it. At all. There
were plenty of guesses, but no real facts.

His age was another frequently discussed topic. There
were rumors – never spoken of in his presence - that the
lieutenant was over 30 years old. Most of the recruits who
came to Gehenna were 19 or 20, and some were even 16
or 17. Not many of them survived their first year, and
lasting a decade was unheard of. The UN supervisors and
appointed senior officers were older, of course, but a 30
year old combat soldier was rare indeed.

Jake was 25 himself, which made him pretty old too, at
least on Erastus. He'd picked up the handle Mad Dog not
long after he arrived. No one seemed to know why…it
didn't match his personality at all. But the mystery would
remain unsolved…whoever hung that tag around Taylor's
neck was long dead, and Jake himself wasn't talking.

Except for the lieutenant, no one had been onplanet
as long as Taylor. He was a Five Year Man. He'd been
wounded three or four times and had a few close calls, but
no Machine had been able to put him down for good. At
least not yet.

Nobody could remember how the use of handles and
had become so widespread in the UN forces on Erastus,
but the tradition seemed to date back almost as far as the
original expedition. Sooner or later, nearly all the veterans
picked up nicknames. It didn't take too long, usually just
a couple months. A new guy would survive a few battles,

make a few friends...then someone would pick something out - a personality or physical trait - and pin a new name on him. Most of the time it stuck. It was OK to call someone at or below your rank by his handle, even in combat. In camp you could usually call an enlisted superior by his nickname, though generally not in the field. It all depended on the non-com. Things tended to be much more relaxed among the real veterans, guys who'd been onplanet two years or more. With first year casualties averaging over 80%, that was a small group.

Taylor reached the end of the rough tunnel leading from the barracks area to the infirmary. The field hospital was several levels lower than the main base, in the most secure section of the facility. The 213th was lucky...they shared their HQ with the battalion hospital. The other strike forces had only rough aid stations. They had to get their serious casualties evac'd to Base Delta, which was anywhere from 20 to 50 klicks from the other strike force HQs.

There was a rough metal ladder built into the stone wall, leading down through an opening. UN Forces Erastus didn't waste time on anything fancy. Everything needed for the war effort had to come through the Portal, and it took a dozen nuclear reactors on Earth to power the thing. Casualties brought in from the field came through a larger tunnel that ramped down from the surface, but lightly wounded grunts making their own way from the barracks had to climb.

Taylor reached out and grabbed the first rung, wincing as he felt the predictable pain shoot through his chest. There were 36 rungs leading to the infirmary level, and every one of them was going to hurt.

"I told you to stay off-duty, didn't I?" Doc Evans

had what was generally considered to be the least original handle on Erastus. He'd been there for a long time, so long that no one Jake had ever met could remember a time when Doc wasn't the battalion surgeon. His handle was so ubiquitous, Jake wasn't even sure he'd ever known Evans' first name. If he had, he'd forgotten it.

Jake made a face. "It's a damned good thing I went, Doc." Evans was a captain, an exalted rank that should have precluded a sergeant like Jake from using a nickname. But everybody called Evans "Doc." Everybody. "Somebody really screwed the pooch on that one. We're lucky anybody made it back."

Taylor sat on an examination table, gritting his teeth while Doc slid the bone fuser across his back. The fuser didn't hurt, not exactly. But it was an unpleasant feeling, sort of a cross between electric shocks and bugs crawling across your skin. It was worth it, though. One short session was as good as a month's normal healing.

Jake had been in a lot of pain since the battle, but he'd stayed away from the infirmary for over a day. He'd always believed the first day was for the seriously wounded. He couldn't stand the idea of sitting around the hospital whining about his sore ribs, while his boys where having their guts sewn back together.

"Yes, I know you're indispensable, Jake." Evans smiled. He had a pleasant disposition; even his sarcasm was gentle. He was condemned to spend the rest of his life on Erastus, just like all the grunts he put back together, but it never seemed to bother him. Doc was the most liked guy Jake Taylor had ever known. In five years, he'd never heard a negative word uttered about the battalion's surgeon. "But still, you should listen to your doctor once in a while." He paused, his smile broadening. "Just to be polite."

"OK, Doc." Taylor didn't mention he was dragging his

section out for unscheduled maneuvers in a little over 14 hours. "I'll try to take it easy."

Evans nodded, but he looked unconvinced. He'd known Jake Taylor for a long time, and he didn't expect his suggestion would accomplish much. Still, he figured, at least I tried. Doc had dealt with a lot of the old timers on Erastus, and they were all pretty much the same. He wasn't sure if they thought they were invincible, or they just didn't care. But not one of them listened when he told them to take it easy.

Taylor sat quietly while Doc finished up. The light in the treatment room was glaring, the strips on the ceiling augmented by several focused spots. It wasn't as bright as Erastus' two suns at high noon, certainly, but it was an unpleasant change from the welcome dimness of the rest of the base.

Taylor didn't utter a word about Cadogan until Evans was almost done. Then he worked up the courage to ask what he'd been wondering, what all the guys had been wondering. "How's the lieutenant, Doc?" There was a nervous edge to his voice. Taylor had been hesitant to ask for a number of reasons, not the least of which was that he wasn't sure he was ready for the answer.

Doc let out a long sigh. "He's not good, Jake." His eyes met Taylor's. "There's a decent chance he'll pull through, but even in the best scenario he's looking at a long recovery. At least a year. Maybe more." The surgeon paused again, his eyes dropping, looking down at the floor. "And I doubt he'll ever be 100% again. Without a miracle, he's done in the field."

Taylor sat quietly for a few seconds before he slid off the table and started getting dressed. It just wasn't right. He hated casualties...despised the whole bloody slaughter...the waste of good men. He blamed himself for his own KIAs, reviewing every aspect of each mission over and over, trying to figure what he'd done wrong, or what he hadn't done…why his soldiers had died. It wasn't entirely rational, and deep down he knew it. But it didn't matter. That was just who he was.

Jake was lost in his thoughts, and he almost walked out without another word. He caught himself at the door and turned. "Thanks, Doc." He swung his arm around. "It feels better already." He paused. "And let us know about the lieutenant, will ya, Doc?"

"Sure thing, Jake." Evans' voice was soft…sympathetic and sad. "But I doubt anything will change for at least a few days." Doc was looking down at the table, slowly putting away the instruments he'd used. "But Cadogan's a tough old bird." The lieutenant was old to the grunts he commanded, but Evans was at least ten years older still. "He'll make it."

Taylor nodded and ducked through the door into the hallway. The lieutenant wasn't his responsibility, and he didn't blame himself like he did with his own men. But Steve Cadogan was one of the best combat officers he'd ever known, and it twisted him in knots to think of such a good commander – such a good man - going down because of a botched assignment. He could reconcile with losing someone like Cadogan in a straight up fight, but he knew that's not what the combat on Blackrock Ridge had been. The whole thing had been one administrative fuck up after another, and Taylor knew no one would be held responsible. Cadogan might die, but the planning staff officers would cover for each other. They weren't lifers on Erastus like Jake and Cadogan…or even Doc. They were UN permanent staffers doing two-year rotations onplanet. They had return tickets through the Portal and political patronage and careers waiting back home. None of them were about to let the deaths of a few footsoldiers interfere with any of that.

Jake knew why there were men fighting on Erastus. He hated the pus-sucking Admins from New York and Geneva who treated the combat troops with callous disregard, but deep down he believed in their cause. The Machines, and the Tegeri who built and commanded them, were mankind's enemies, a deadly alien menace who would destroy or enslave humanity...unless men like Jake and his brothers stood in the breach and barred the way. The methods UN Central employed to conscript soldiers or blackmail them into volunteering sickened him. But he couldn't blame them for the war. He even had to acknowledge that, however imperfect the methods had been, the UN Consolidation had saved Earth from invasion, mankind from defeat. The individual nation-states could never have stood against the Tegeri, as a united mankind had done. Wars between nation states were a thing of the past. All the resources and production of human civilization were pooled together against the common enemy.

There were 8 known Portals on Earth...8 transit points to other worlds, and none of these had fallen. Men were fighting and dying on more than three dozen worlds, but not on Earth itself. The Machines were fighting Taylor's men, and thousands like them, on distant Portal Worlds, not in the streets of terrestrial cities and towns. The enemy wasn't rampaging through helpless villages, ravaging farmhouses like the one Jake had called home for most of his life. They weren't murdering civilians and helpless children or destroying the civilization it had taken man millennia to build. And for that, Jake would hold back the anger and the bitterness, the resentment over his own treatment and the tragic fate that had been his lot. He would take his place in the field, pick up the rifle...and he would protect those he'd left behind.

# Chapter 3

From the Journal of Jake Taylor:

We try to help the new guys. Most of them don't last long. Just surviving on Gehenna is hard, and fighting the Machines is like something out of a child's nightmare. They are meticulous, and you need to be cool and deliberative to counter their attacks. Their tactics are mediocre, but there is an inhuman relentlessness to them. If you lose your focus they will tear you apart. It's hard for the rookies to stay cool under fire, and a lot of them hesitate, give in to fear. They panic. And they die.

I was different when I got here...calm, resigned to my fate. I can't really explain why. I was bitter, of course, mourning a life that had been taken from me. All I'd ever cared about had been stolen away – home, family, love, writing. But for all the wrong that had been done to me, I'd always clung to the thought that it was not entirely in vain...that my sacrifice had been made to a good cause. I was protecting Earth, standing between others like me, like I had been, and the doom of a relentless alien horde bent on destruction. That was a powerful salve, one that kept me going for years.

Then there were the vids. They showed them to us when we got to training camp, the records from the first colonies. Peaceful little towns, outposts on new and untamed worlds...and adventurous families blazing a trail into the frontier.  The first expeditions had been before the Consolidation, and the colonists were national heroes, citizens with the courage to leave Earth behind and help build mankind's future.

Then the Machines came.  They swooped down on the tiny settlements, slicing through their meager defenses and slaughtering everyone.  The videos showed it all...the hideous creatures, manlike but grotesquely different too, rending the helpless civilians, feasting on the flesh of the children.  After a few minutes, we all wanted to run from the room, but they made us watch.  They made us watch it all.  By the time we left we were consumed with rage, straining to get at these inhuman monsters...to kill them, to tear them apart as they had done to the colonists.

Our hatred drove us, and our sense of duty...but it was still an odd feeling, fighting to protect something you knew you'd never see again.  This was no old-style war, where the boys would come marching home after a glorious victory.  For us, it was a one-way trip.  We were soldiers for life.  Sending someone through a Portal took an enormous amount of energy, and a return trip was far too costly for us footsoldiers.  There'd be no parades for my comrades and me, no ribbons tied to trees, no sweethearts waiting for us to come walking through the front gate.  We were dead to our loved ones, already mourned and gone forever.

"That was pathetic." Taylor's voice was angry, scolding. He knew the troops were still tired from the fight at Black-rock, but that was no excuse.  Not for such a lackluster effort.  "We're gonna do this again.  We're gonna do it as many times as it takes you to get it right."

He looked out at the downcast faces, dripping with sweat.  Bear stood in front of his team, his drenched fatigues plastered to his massive body.  He looked like he was about to fall over, but Taylor knew the big man was tough as nails.  Chuck Samuels would stand under the heat of Erastus' two suns for as long as Jake told him too.

"I'm hot and tired just like all of you." And my fucking ribs are throbbing too, Taylor thought but didn't say. "But I don't want to watch a fucking Machine put you down, and that's exactly what's going to happen if you continue to let them outperform you in the heat." He was speaking to the new guys, mostly. The vets knew already…and they'd heard it a hundred times before. But a reminder never hurt.

"So I better see some rapid improvement from all of you, or we're going to be out here all day…and all night too." He panned his eyes across the entire assembled section. "You think I'm kidding?" His voice was growing louder, harsher. "Don't fucking try me."

There was a brief pause. It was eerily quiet, not a sound but the wind whipping through the valley. The breeze was a welcome relief from the oppressive heat, but the air felt like it was coming off a blast furnace. It helped, but not much.

Tony Black had been looking at Taylor, but now he turned back toward the massed troops behind him. "You heard the sergeant." His voice was higher pitched than Jake's but his volume was a match any day. "Get your asses moving. I want you reset for the exercise in five minutes or I'll beat the sergeant to it and rip off your heads and crap down your fucking necks. I shit you not." Black had the foulest mouth in the section. Where he'd come from, that little speech would have been a sloppy wet kiss.

The troops moved quickly, scrambling across the sand, taking positions facing each other. The section was split into two forces, and they were fighting a simulated meeting engagement. They were a little over ten klicks from base, and they'd marched the whole way in the blazing sun. They'd be marching back too, but at least it would be closer to twilight then. Erastus was never comfortable, but it was marginally less unbearable when only one sun was in the sky.

Jake stood and looked out at the troops getting ready to run the maneuver again. Black's team, and most of Bear's too, were already in place. They were the veterans, the guys who'd been onplanet awhile and learned to survive. But 3rd and 4th teams were mostly rookies, and they moved slower. If they'd been under fire, he thought, half of them would be dead already.

It wasn't by design that Taylor's veterans and recruits were so segregated. The Machines had accomplished that a month earlier...just before the entire 2nd Battalion was transferred north, out of the steaming equatorial jungle. Denny Parker had been part of Taylor's inner circle and the section's exec before Blackie took his place. A corporal on the cusp of becoming a sergeant, he and almost half the section were cut off by a sudden enemy attack. By the time Taylor and the rest of the men broke through, there were only 2 survivors. Parker wasn't one of them.

Taylor's first thought was to reorganize the section, balancing out the experienced troops. But he didn't do it. The 8-man teams were extremely close knit units. The men of a team fought together, bled together. They shared out their rations, listened to each other's stories. They were families, the only families any of these men would ever have again. When Taylor first arrived on Erastus, scared, angry, and desperately lonely, it was the men of his team that pulled him through it. Some section commanders would have moved names around a roster sheet, but not Jake Taylor. He bumped Karl Young up to team leader and moved him from the 1st Team to the newly reconstituted 3rd, but otherwise he left his guys where they were. He owed them that much.

Young was screaming at his team now, berating them for their sluggish efforts. "What part of move your asses don't you people understand?"

Taylor was too far away to get a good look, but he knew Frantic well, and he could practically see the vein bulging on his neck as he urged his men on. The corporal sounded a little like a martinet, shouting at his soldiers, asking them to do the impossible. Taylor knew better. Young acted like he was crazy, but there was no one you wanted at your side more in a desperate fight. Jake had found that out a few months earlier, when he went down during a routine patrol. Young killed two Machines about to finish him off, and he carried the wounded Taylor 7 klicks in the midday sun. It wasn't until they got back to basecamp that Taylor realized Young had also been hit – twice - and he'd carried his stricken CO all the way back, wounded and bleeding himself.

"Alright, Blackie…" Taylor spoke softly into the tiny mic on his helmet. "…let's do this again."

"I'm going to hear from Battalion again, Blackie." They'd been back a few hours, and most of the section was sacked. Taylor had authorized a double water ration for his troops…in addition to burning through 85,000 practice rounds during his exercise. Water was scarce in the desert zones of Erastus, and even in the jungle belt where it was plentiful, it was so infested with aggressive pathogens it cost a fortune to purify. And ammunition was worse… it had to come through the Portal. Some of the other worlds had onsite production facilities, or at least that was the rumor. But Erastus didn't…not yet. And bringing crates of ammunition through the Portal was expensive.

Taylor took good care of his men, excellent care. That usually translated into issuing them more rations and burning through ammunition on unscheduled training exercises. There had been two formal inquiries about excessive use of supplies, but Lieutenant Cadogan had appropriately "filed" them. One of these days, he figured, UN Command Erastus would get tired of being ignored, and pursue things more aggressively. But it hadn't happened yet. And his boys had earned that extra ration.

"Tell them to suck my dick." Blackie didn't pull verbal punches, especially not when sitting in base shooting the shit with Taylor. "How the fuck do they expect us to keep these little baby cherries alive? Half of 'em don't have hair one on their balls." Black had less respect for rules than anyone Jake had ever met, a vestige of the Philly freezone streets, he supposed. Still, he couldn't understand how someone with no respect for authority could make such a good soldier. And Black was one of the best.

Taylor's background couldn't have been more different than Blackie's. He was from New Hampshire, a small farming town no one had ever heard of. Compared to most of the guys, he'd had it good. Better, certainly than the city rats from the squalid urban freezones...guys like Blackie. The suburbs were pretty bad too, except for the gated sanctuaries...and you had to know somebody to get into one of those. And none of the grunts on Erastus had ever "known" anyone.

The farms, on the other hand, were pretty much left alone. They were just too important, especially to the Admins and other privileged classes. The Blight had taken out at least half the arable land in the world. The masses might subsist on the marginally edible output of the huge sea-based algae fields, but those with some level of wealth or influence wanted real food. And the small farms were the only source of those once common but now precious foodstuffs.

The farmers were an odd breed, and they were held on a looser leash than those in the more populated areas. There were monitors, of course, but only one or two per family. It was rumored – quietly - that a different speech code applied to the Growers, that they could get away with saying things that would get anyone else sent to a reeducation camp. Whether or not there were actually any such formal directives, there was some truth to the innuendo. You could occasionally get something like a little privacy on a farm.

The tradeoff was hard work. Goddamned hard. Not many small farms could afford much automation, not with the heavy taxation and the need to bribe at least a dozen government officials to avoid crippling harassment. UN Central wanted the Growers producing the fresh food the privileged classes demanded...it just didn't want them getting rich doing it. Crop prices were set by the government, and they were usually too low to allow much beyond basic sustenance for the farmers, especially with operating costs so high. It wasn't just the equipment; it was the fuel to run it that was really expensive.

Taylor had never particularly liked farming, though he hadn't realized before how much he enjoyed the perk of eating real food rather than the artificially-engineered products that fed most of the population. It had been hard for him to adapt to army rations. He'd grown up on apples from the orchard, fresh bread baked from newly-milled grains, and the other bounty from the farm. Now he subsisted on things like chemically-enhanced algae protein bars. It was months before he could choke one down without retching.

He'd been born on the farm, and he'd expected to spend the rest of his life working it. But what Jake Taylor had really wanted to do was write. He knew that opportunities to earn a living that way were scarce, but even if he had to work in the fields all day, he still felt the urge to sit at his keyboard nights and create something. Even though he knew he'd probably never earn anything from it.

Writing was dangerous too. It was just about the most regulated trade, and it was easy to run afoul of the myriad rules and guidelines. There were more writers in the reeducation facilities than just about any other profession.

After he got to Erastus, Jake realized how fortunate he'd been to be born on the farm...and how little he'd appreciated it at the time. Soldiers in UNFE tended to come from the lower classes, and the stories of the violent freezones and decaying suburbs made him reconsider his memories of childhood in what he now considered the idyllic countryside.

Tony Black wasn't the first city rat Jake had met and befriended, but he was the one who came from the worst shithole. The Central Philly Core was a decent urban sanctuary, but everything outside its guarded gates was a nightmare. The place was notorious as one of the worst freezones, a vast slum where violence and lawlessness were rampant and social services in short supply. People died every day in Philly. It was considered a good night when only a dozen or so bodies were in the streets come morning.

Black had gotten into some kind of trouble back home, which is why he was on Erastus. He never told anybody what it was, except for once when he got really drunk. Taylor had gotten half the story that night, but he'd never shared a word of it with anybody. Black and Taylor were best friends and, despite the difference in their ranks and backgrounds, they had come to trust each other completely.

Black...and Bear Samuels, Karl Young, Longbow... they had become a very tight group, even more than usual among the fighting men on Erastus. Taylor had been onplanet for five years, and he'd had friends before, but these guys were something different...something special. Denny Parker had been part of that group too, and they were all still mourning him. Taylor wasn't sure it was smart to get so close to guys who were only going to die anyway. And they were going to die; he was sure of that. Everyone died on Gehenna.

# Chapter 4

From the Journal of Jake Taylor:

My father was a vet. It was something I never knew, a part of him he never shared with any of us...not until I was getting ready to leave for my deployment. He just sprung it on me the day before I shipped out. I was stunned at first. I almost got mad that he'd hidden it for so long, but I caught my anger. I didn't want to spend the last few hours I'd ever see my father arguing over nonsense that didn't matter.

He said it was something he hated to talk about, didn't even like to remember. There wasn't time to get into a lot of detail, but it was obvious he still had some open wounds from his experiences. He'd served in the old U.S. Navy, before the Consolidation. He fought in the Mideast War and the Taiwan Intervention, he told me. I'd heard of both conflicts, but only vaguely. They were both quarantined topics. Talking about them wasn't safe, and there was nowhere to get any information anyway. Nothing beyond vague rumors. Certainly nothing worth risking a trip to a reeducation facility.

Never trust the government, he told me...the bureaucrats who moved the pieces around the board. Keep my eyes open. All the time. Think for myself, and don't believe anything I'm told. "Medals, causes, speeches," he said, "They are all worthless. They are as corrupt as the puppet masters who use them to control men." Finally, he looked at me with sad watery eyes and said, "Jake...don't you ever depend on anyone except those guys standing next to you when the shooting starts. They are your brothers...and they are the only ones you can trust."

I understood. Everyone chafed under the regulations, the constant monitoring. We were all a little afraid. Most people knew someone who'd been sent for reeducation. Or knew someone who knew someone. But it was normal to fear the government, just as a child fears upsetting a parent. The average person didn't comprehend, couldn't see the whole picture the way the Admins did. I understood better than my father. My education had been more modern than his...I'd had the chance to study how difficult it was for the common citizen to grasp the complexities of governing a chaotic world. The importance of controlling damaging speech and limiting freedoms that would only be abused to the detriment of all. My father didn't understand any of that...he just lashed out at UN Central, blaming the government for all the world's problems.

UN Central was far from perfect, but they'd absorbed the failing nation-states and defended us against the Tegeri and the Machines for 30 years. In all that time there'd been no war on Earth, no nations left to wage it. All mankind's potential, for so long squandered in internecine strife, was focused to one purpose. To my father's thinking, we'd lost our way, our freedom. No one could convince him otherwise, and I'd long since tired of trying.

He was emotional, struggling to get out the words he wanted to say. That was a hard day for both of us, for obvious reasons. I knew my father. I'd heard his rants before. He hated UN Central, despised what government had become. But that day was different. There was a rawness to what he said, a passionate urgency I didn't pick up on back then. There was too much else on my mind...and so many of the things I would see and learn were still ahead of me. I listened to all he said, feeling strangely that there had been so much about my own father I'd never known. But I discounted most of his advice, wrote it off to an old man's political rants.

That was a mistake.


"I'm afraid Sergeant Lin has been killed in action on Asgard." Gregor Kazan sat, looking uncomfortable despite the considerable plushness of the leather chair. Kazan had an odd demeanor to him, both physically and in the way he spoke. When he was younger, it had been called many things, variations on "creepy" being the most common. As he rose through the UN bureaucracy and his power grew, those types of comments became less and less frequent. Now that he was Assistant Undersecretary for Military Affairs, all he got from most people was obsequious pandering. He enjoyed that.

"That is unfortunate. He was our top prospect." Undersecretary Keita leaned back, taking a long puff on the cigar he held gingerly in his massive hand. Unlike Kazan, Anan Keita looked entirely at ease, with the serene confidence of a man totally assured of his own power. "I presume you have reviewed the remaining candidates and brought me a recommendation." It wasn't a question. People didn't waste Anan Keita's time.

The view behind Keita was extraordinary. The Undersecretary's conference room, and the large adjoining office, had floor to ceiling windows offering a kilometer high panorama across the Arve River to the snow-covered peak of Mont Blanc in the distance. The UN headquarters in Geneva was the largest building ever built, an architectural triumph. No expense had been spared in its design or construction. It was a monument to the government of a united Earth, and it rose almost two kilometers above the mostly low-rise structures surrounding it.

"Yes, Mr. Secretary." The form of address wasn't technically correct. Normally only the Secretary himself would be referred to by title, not an Undersecretary like Keita. But Secretary Patel was old and sick, and his hold on the office was largely ceremonial. Keita was effectively acting-Secretary, and he was almost certain to take over the office when Patel died or formally retired. Besides, Anan Keita was a vain man. Kazan was aware he'd see through the blatant pandering...but he knew he'd like it anyway. Any favor he could cultivate with Keita could only help his position. "I have selected the top six." He slid a small tablet across the table. "Though I feel the first two are substantially better choices than the others."

Keita put the cigar in a large ashtray on the table, knocking off a clump of ash as he did. He scooped up the tablet, scanning the two names at the top. "Sergeant Jake Taylor and Sergeant Pedro Sanchez." He was focusing on the glowing pad, reading the summaries Kazan had written about each man. He stopped after the first two. He didn't have any interest in the secondary candidates. Filtering through the backup choices was Kazan's job. "Do you have a preference?" His eyes were still on the tablet as he spoke. It was hard to tell from his tone if he was really interested in his subordinate's opinion.

"Well..." Kazan paused. He hated being put on the spot. A successful career in government usually meant avoiding as many decisions as possible, at least at his level. He didn't yet have enough patronage or support to withstand a major mistake, but Keita certainly did. Still, he knew he'd get scapegoated for any errors, whether they were his or Keita's. "...Sanchez has a longer service record than Taylor. He's been on Argos for almost seven years." There was a hesitancy in his tone.

"I can sense a 'but' in this." Keita's impatience was

clear, his tone annoyed. "Don't waste my time, Kazan. Just make your point."

"I do not believe this direct comparison tells the whole story." Argos was an ocean world dotted with small islands. It was a difficult planet on which to wage war and manage logistics, but it was nowhere near the hell that Erastus was. "Sergeant Taylor has been on Erastus for five years, which I believe indicates a higher relative degree of resiliency and toughness. The five year survival rate on Erastus is 1.2%." That was the lowest of any world where UN forces were deployed. Casualties were high on all the Portal planet battlefields, but a posting to Erastus was generally considered a death sentence. "Additionally, Taylor came from a farm, while Sanchez grew up in the violent slums of the Mexico City Freezone." Kazan's point was a tricky one, but Keita understood immediately. Taylor had been almost comically ill-prepared for the violence and deprivation he faced on Erastus, yet he had adapted magnificently and survived against the odds.

Keita leaned back in his chair, reaching out and moving the cigar back to his lips. "Yes, I tend to agree with your logic." He glanced down at the tablet again. "Personal toughness and adaptability are primary considerations for the program." He looked up at Kazan. "Have you reviewed the records of the troops under each man's command? That is a perspective we should examine as well, particularly since we are looking for an entire strike force, not just one man."

"I have." He really hadn't, at least not with the thoroughness Keita would want. But he wasn't about to admit to it. "I believe Sergeant Taylor's section to be the better of the two." He was bullshitting, at least in part, but he was pretty confident the troops on Erastus would prove to be tougher than those on Argos.

He's full of shit, Keita thought, amused...he glanced at those dossiers, nothing more. He sat quietly for a few seconds, leaning back in his chair, trying to decide if he wanted to let Kazan off the hook or press him further. "OK, I'm inclined to agree with you that Erastus is a crucible more likely to produce what we want than any other world." He decided he wasn't interested in discussing the trivialities any further, especially not with a brownnosing simp like Kazan. "We could talk this to death, but we need to move forward. Let's put Sergeant Taylor and his people through one final test, and if they succeed...." By which he meant, if they survive. "...they will be our subjects for the program. And I believe I have just the thing." He stared down at the screen, punching keys for a few seconds. "I know I saw an alert about Erastus...yes...there it is." He read to himself for a few seconds before continuing. "We have discovered one of the Machine manufactories on Erastus...the first one, I believe, on that world." The Tegeri defense of each Portal planet was centered around a network of large bases where they produced their biomechanical warriors. Ultimately, the UN forces on each planet were tasked with locating and destroying these facilities.

Keita scrolled down the screen, reading the full report. "Let's make sure that...what is the correct unit?" He looked at his screen again. "2nd Battalion...is assigned to the operation." He hesitated as he continued reading. "It appears Taylor's strike force commander was just seriously wounded, which is perfect for our purposes. Let's put the good sergeant in command and see how he does." He paused then added, "And make sure his troops are placed in the vanguard of the assault."

Kazan nodded. "Yes, Secretary Keita." He slid his chair back slowly, assuming he had been dismissed. "I will send a dispatch at once." He started to get up.

"No." Keita's voice was calm and even…but firm.

"Excuse me, Secretary?" Kazan fell back into the chair.

"You will go to Erastus personally. You will observe the operation and prepare a full report for me." Keita was expressionless, his voice betraying no emotion. But he was enjoying making Kazan squirm. "This is a crucial program for us. Indeed, our ultimate success in the war against the Tegeri may hinge on it. We must be thorough at every step."

Kazan's mind was racing, trying to think of a way out. But there was none. Disappointing or defying Keita would end his career in its tracks. He could feel his head nodding, almost involuntarily. "Yes, Secretary." He swallowed hard. "If that is your wish."

Gregor Kazan much preferred the civilized comforts of Geneva and the upper class lifestyle his political post allowed him to the harsh conditions the UN's soldiers endured. The Portal worlds were battlefields, uncivilized frontiers. And, by all accounts, Erastus was the worst of the lot. He could feel the tension in his stomach. He was going to be sick.

"That's all, Kazan." Keita's voice was dismissive. "You may go and prepare. You leave tomorrow."

Kazan stood up quickly, nodding again. "Yes, Secretary Keita." He turned and moved toward the door as swiftly as his wobbly legs would carry him.

Keita watched with amusement, a thin smile creeping momentarily onto his lips. He spun his chair and stared out over the magnificent vista. Despite the astonishing view, his smile quickly faded. He was privy to far more classified data than Kazan. The war wasn't going badly, at least not to superficial analysis. UN forces were push-ing the Tegeri back almost everywhere. Given limitless resources, the UN forces had a good chance to ultimately defeat the enemy and take control of the entire Portal network. But resources are never without limit, and Keita had seen the projections. The maximum productive output of Earth intersected with the anticipated men and supplies required. The lines crossed far short of the point of victory. They were going to run out of resources long before they beat the Tegeri. Unless something changed the military situation.

"Project Zed," Keita whispered softly.

# Chapter 5

From the Journal of Jake Taylor:

I'm starting to forget. I close my eyes and try to focus, but my mother's face is fainter, harder to see. I know I'm losing what little I have left of her, of home. I try to recall the taste of apple pie or the feeling of the cool water of the swimming hole, but those things are slipping away too. I remember the words, but less and less the feelings and images that give them meaning.

I don't want to lose those last hazy links with home, with the family I left behind. But it's hard. Have you ever really tried to will yourself to remember? It's not an easy thing to do. You try to stay focused, but you get distracted... you fight, you sleep, you work...then, when you remember again, the recollection is that much weaker. No matter how hard you try, you still lose a little each day.

I had a girlfriend back home. Beth. I left her behind, just like I did everyone else. When I first got here I used to think about her back home, picturing her crying for me... for lost love. I imagined the change day by day, as time slowly turned heartbreak to sadness...then to fond remembrance. How long, I've wondered, before she lived a day without thinking of me...before she was free? Before she found someone else, someone with a life of his own to share with her? Where was she now? Settled down with a family? Does she still think of me after all these years?

Sometimes I wonder if she ever walks outside, leaving her husband and children for a few brief moments to stare at the sky and remember her lost love. I'd like to believe she does, but I'm not sure I do. I'm not even sure I should want that. What could it help? What use is there but to cause more sadness...and resurrect pain mercifully forgotten? I have nothing left to offer her, even as a memory. Better she never thinks of me again.

I used to lay awake, slick with sweat on my cot when I couldn't sleep in the relentless heat, thinking of her. I'd close my eyes and imagine the way her hair felt in my hands, the smooth softness of her skin against mine, the sound of her voice whispering gently in my ear. Now I'm forgetting, losing a little of that remembrance with each passing day. I fight against it, trying to cling to every detail, but it is pointless...she is lost to me forever. Perhaps the forgetfulness is a blessing.

Taylor stared wordlessly at the small tablet. He'd been doing the same thing for at least ten minutes, and the orders on the backlit screen still said the same thing.

Taylor, Jacob (Sergeant), commanding Section 2, 213th Strike Force, 2nd Battalion, 2nd Brigade, UNFE is hereby reassigned to: Taylor, Jacob (Lieutenant), commanding 213th Strike Force, 2nd Battalion, 2nd Brigade, UNFE. Assignment effective immediately. Lt. Taylor is hereby ordered to assume command upon receipt of this communique.

He wouldn't have been surprised to be placed in acting command of the strike force. He was the section leader with the most time onplanet, the logical choice to take over while Cadogan was in the hospital. But this was a permanent assignment...and a promotion to commissioned rank. He wasn't sure how he felt about being an officer. From the day he'd stepped out of the Portal, Jake had felt out of place. He never thought of himself as a real soldier, even now, although his troops knew he was one of the best on Erastus.

He was sure what he thought about the formal reassignment, though. Lieutenant Cadogan was still alive in the infirmary, and Taylor wasn't ready to accept that he wasn't coming back. He'd have been OK with covering for the lieutenant, but replacing him? Permanently? It felt wrong. Disloyal somehow. At least until it was certain the lieutenant wasn't coming back.

His rational mind understood, realized such thoughts were foolish. But some things came from the gut, the heart. And taking Cadogan's place was one of them. He'd follow the orders, of course…he didn't have a choice. But he wouldn't feel quite right about it.

He read further down, scrolling through the communique, reading softly aloud as he did. "Lieutenant Taylor is authorized to reorganize the strike force in any manner and is empowered to issue non-commissioned promotions within the command structure." He stopped reading and looked up. That's odd, he thought. The orders gave him a lot of latitude, far more than standard practice. He knew, for one thing, that Cadogan hadn't had the power to issue promotions. He sent recommendations up the chain, often waiting weeks or months for an approval. Strange…

"Hey, Dog." Taylor could recognize Blackie's voice anywhere. His accent was so heavy, it almost sounded like a bad fake. Even after two years, Taylor still wasn't truly used to it. "Some of the guys are playing cards with a crew from the 189th. You wanna come down, help us take their money?" There wasn't any currency on Erastus, not really. The troops did get a form of scrip, which they could use to pay for the few items that passed for luxuries on Erastus. Most of the fake currency ended up in the brigade brothels when the guys got a few day's leave. In between those infrequent breaks, it gave them something to gamble with.

"Take a look at this, Blackie." Taylor was distracted, and he'd mostly ignored what Black had been saying. He reached out, handing the tablet to his friend.

Black took the pad, glancing down to read the orders. "F...u...c...k..." He drew out the word as he said it. "I guess I'm gonna have to get used to calling you sir." He laughed for a few seconds, but then his voice became serious. "Honestly, Jake. No one deserves it more than you. You've kept more of these fool kids alive than anybody I've ever seen." He took a couple steps toward Taylor, extending his hand as he did. "Congratulations, my friend."

"Thanks, Blackie." Taylor reached out and took Black's hand. "I appreciate the sentiment." He smiled for a few seconds, taking the tablet back. "But there's more to it than my great military gifts. Have you ever heard of a lieutenant approving promotions?" He paused, though not long enough for Black to answer. "Something is up, Blackie."

"You're paranoid, Jake." Black smiled. "The strike force needed a new CO..." He paused, his expression becoming more serious. He hadn't considered that Taylor's promotion meant the lieutenant wasn't coming back. No matter what. They'd both known that intellectually, but this forced it to the forefront. The 213th had been Cadogan's strike force, but no more. Now it was Jake Taylor's. "Look, Dog, we're all sorry about the lieutenant, but the strike force needs a leader, and you're the logical choice. Sure, it happened a lot faster than the usual glacial pace. But it's what we all knew would happen...at least if we let ourselves think about it."

"Yeah?" Taylor was staring at Black with an odd expression on his face. "Well, guess who's the logical choice to take over 2nd Section…Sergeant Black?"

Black had a blank expression on his face for a few seconds before he erupted with laughter. "Thank you, sir." He snapped off a better than average salute, trying to suppress his smile as he did.

Taylor couldn't help but chuckle. "Sit down you asshole." He pointed to a small table and chairs in the corner of the room. "This strike force got itself shot to shit on Blackrock Ridge, and we need to do some reorganizing." He started walking toward the table. "I'm afraid we're both going to miss that card game, Sergeant Black."

Taylor sat quietly, looking across the table at Black with an "I told you so" expression on his face. "A battalion-scale operation," he said. The words hung in the air as he held up the pad displaying the orders. Combat on Erastus was mostly search and destroy, and a full strike force was considered a large deployment. "I knew something was going on. They must have found one of the Machine bases." As far as Taylor knew, there had never been an entire battalion committed to one battle on Erastus. But UNFE had never found a Machine factory on the planet either.

"I don't suppose I can call you a cocky asshole anymore now that you have those bars on your shoulders." Black sat in one of the hard plastic chairs wriggling around, trying to get comfortable. It had been hot the last few days, even by Erastus standards. It was twilight outside…and they were deep inside the base, but it was still damned uncomfortable.

"As long as you acknowledge my military genius, we'll be just fine, sergeant." Taylor smiled. "But, seriously, something like this is new ground for all of us. And we're not in great shape." The 213th had been reinforced to full strength, but that meant there were a lot of FNGs, true cherries who'd never been in a fight.

"We've got a lot of rookies for sure, Boss." Samuels' slow drawl was as distinctive in its own way as Black's inner city accent. "But we've got some real veterans too. I'll put 2nd Section's 1st and 2nd teams against any outfit on Gehenna." There was a touch of sadness in his voice. Chuck Samuels had been in the 2nd team since he'd stepped out of the Portal and into the blazing heat of Erastus, and for the last ten months he'd been its commander. But as of three hours earlier, he was Sergeant Samuels, leader of the 3rd Section. It was a big step up for him, and he knew Taylor needed someone he could count on to command the 3rd. But he was going to miss his team.

"Yeah, Bear, half of 2nd Section's fine." Black answered before Taylor. "Even 3rd and 4th teams are in decent shape. I wouldn't call them veteran formations by a long shot, but the guys are coming along OK." Black's eyes shifted to Taylor, catching the slight nod of agreement. "But your section's gonna be a handful. They got ripped to shreds at Blackrock." The 3rd Section had been on the forward line when the enemy ambush hit. They'd already had a high proportion of inexperienced troops, and they lost over 60% casualties in the fight. There weren't more than 3 or 4 real vets in the whole section.

"Look, there's no point bitching about things." Taylor made sure to beat Bear to a response. He'd seen Black and Samuels spar like this for hours. They didn't have time for that now, and Taylor didn't have the patience. "Blackie's right, Bear. I need you to do anything you can to whip your team into shape....starting tomorrow with maneuvers. You need to get them used to the heat, at the very least. We don't have much time."

"Can I get supplies for an exercise, or do you just want me to do some ferocious PT?" Samuels had a jovial personality, but he was dead serious now. Pleasant demeanor notwithstanding, everyone in the room knew Bear would mercilessly drive his troops in the field.

"Plan an exercise. I'll get you whatever you need."

"Seriously, Jake?" Blackie sounded surprised. "After all the ammo we blew through last week?"

"Not a problem." Taylor glanced down at the pad's screen. "I'm authorized to draw whatever I feel is necessary to have the strike force ready for action in one week." Jake glanced around the room at the surprised and concerned faces. None of them had ever seen such generous logistical support. "I told you guys this thing was trouble, didn't I." Limitless supplies from HQ could only mean one thing. They were about to march into hell itself. "But there's nothing we can do but make sure we're as ready as we can be."

He turned his head, looking toward a tall, skinny man leaning against the wall. "How about your people, Hank?"

"They're OK." Hank Daniels commanded 1st Section. He didn't sound too convinced, but he wasn't despondent either. "With your permission, I'd like to get them out for some maneuvers as well. I don't have as many newbs as Sergeant Samuels, but I have enough."

Taylor nodded. "I think that's a good idea." He looked over at Bear then back to Daniels. "You two plan a joint wargame, one section against the other." He let a small smile creep onto his lips. "Make it a two-day exercise. I'll see how far I can push this unlimited supplies thing."

Taylor had known Daniels for almost a year, but he was just beginning to work closely with him and form a real opinion. So far he liked the guy immensely. Daniels seemed like a conscientious team leader, and he had a good personality too.

Jake was a little worried about his overall force makeup, but he was very comfortable with his non-coms. They were crack veterans, and he trusted them to a man. He was still nervous about the upcoming mission, though, especially since he'd gotten almost no details. His orders were simple...be ready for a major operation by the entire battalion, commencing in approximately one week. That was pretty damned vague. And that could only mean trouble.

# Chapter 6

From the Journal of Jake Taylor:

We try to fight when one of the suns has set, when the temperature is closer to bearable. We call this time twilight, though it is hotter than noon in any Earthly jungle.

Sometimes the machines attack us, sometimes we attack them. Erastus was still a fairly new Portal world when I transited. I wasn't part of the original forlorn hope sent in to carve out a beachhead, but we were definitely still on the defensive when I got here. Back then the Machines attacked every day. I didn't think we could hold out for those first two years, but the reinforcements kept coming...new recruits, cherries like I was...feeding the slaughter.

When they discover a new Portal world, UN Central starts sending troops through. The first few times, before the Consolidation, the nation-states sent colonists and researchers...and the Machines slaughtered them all. The Machines protect the Portal worlds; they protect them by killing anything that sets foot on them.

We're not part of the official UN security forces. The offworld command is organized differently, each planet having its own dedicated military. UNFE. United Nations Force: Erastus. That's what we're called. They've changed the nomenclature at least half a dozen times since I got here, mostly dropping the colon then adding it back again.

I imagine there were some savage bureaucratic battles in New York and Geneva over that, but then no one ever accused UN Executive Branch of an inability to waste time and resources on useless red tape.

The wars against the Machines are relentless battles of attrition, so the first soldiers through just try to hang on, outnumbered and under constant attack. These vanguard units don't last long, maybe a few weeks. But UN Central keeps sending troops through; a steady flow of manpower until there is enough strength to hold a series of defensive bases. Then the stalemate begins; months, years...sometimes decades...before the deployed strength is enough to go on the offensive and take out the Machine bases. They'd found the first portal world before I was born; they'd secured five since that time, wiping out the Machines entirely. There were troops fighting on 27 more when I transited to Erastus. I used to wonder about those other worlds, what it was like on them, how their wars compared to ours. But the longer I was on Erastus the less it seemed to matter what went on anywhere else. This was my home now, and I knew I'd never leave it.

"Alright, mount up everybody." Blackie stood on the ledge of the antigrav, shouting so the troops could hear him over the sound of the engines. There were four of the big transports lined up next to each other, and the 2nd Section of the 213th Strike Force was lined up outside the rightmost one, waiting to board.

It was almost high noon, and both suns were baking the flat, sand-covered rocks of the landing area. Black's light, moisture-wicking fatigues were already soaking wet and stuck to his skin. He was wearing his body armor, like everyone else in the strike force. The long-chain polymers of the armor were self-healing, providing the ultimate personal protection in battle. The downside was weight and, on Erastus, heat. The breastplate and limb coverings tended to trap the heat inside, making it even more difficult to withstand the brutal temperatures.

"Begin boarding." Black's order was straightforward, and he spoke softly. The antigravs ran quietly, and his troops heard the command on their implanted com units, so there was no need to shout.

The troops of the section marched quickly to the waiting transport, climbing onboard and strapping in on the two long benches along the inside of the hull. The Mustang-class troop transports had been one of the first weapons systems to incorporate the anti-grav technology found on New-Earth. The first Portal world discovered had been given a painfully unoriginal name, but it had also provided humanity with a 100-year leap in technology. Powered by an onboard nuclear reactor, each of the big vessels carried 40 men, plus weapons and supplies.

The rest of the strike force was boarding the other transports, one section per, plus one ship for the support forces. The gunships that would escort them to the insertion point were deployed 500 meters to the north, just outside the strike force assembly area. The Dragonfires were awesome vessels, 60 meters long and bristling with weapons.

Black watched the last of his troops climb through the Mustang's hatch and, with a final look around the staging area, he pulled himself through and sat in the command seat. He quickly scanned the interior of the ship, checking, making sure all his troops had strapped themselves in.

The men were mostly quiet. Some of the veterans were talking, quietly laughing every now and then. A few of the other guys were speaking softly to themselves. Blackie knew they were praying. Religion was tightly controlled on Earth, but when you dumped a bunch of guys in a place like Erastus, a lot of them found God. Fast. Black himself had never drawn comfort from his beliefs, mostly because he didn't believe in anything. At least nothing besides his brothers in arms. But he was glad when he saw his rookies praying. Anything that distracted them, helped them manage the fear...that was good.

"Last call to get strapped in boys." The pilot's voice was loud on the speaker. "We're lifting in 30 seconds."

Black instinctively checked his harness, though he knew it was good. He'd strapped in a hundred times. He sucked in a deep breath, taking a few seconds to get ahold of his own fear. The rookies seemed to think the seasoned troops weren't afraid in battle. The ones who survived long enough to become veterans themselves would look back and realize what idiots they were. Everyone was scared... everyone. The experienced troops just knew how to control it...they realized that their chances of survival were far better if they could manage the fear. For all the mystique of crack troops, that was the primary difference...the triumph of logic over terror. The mind over instinct.

The ride would be smooth, at least. Half the rookies wouldn't even know they were moving until they looked outside. One of the techs tried to explain it to Black once. The antigrav generators radiated a force that altered the graviton particles beneath the ship, effectively canceling the force of gravity exerted by the planet. Black had nodded politely, but none of it meant anything to him. The technician could have been speaking ancient Greek. The thing flew. That's all Blackie cared about.

The four transports lifted in a neat formation, rising approximately 50 meters before they engaged their engines and blasted across the desert at 1200 kph. Black knew there was a similar scene taking place at each of the battalion's bases. Four small flotillas, with four transports and two gunships each would soon be converging on the target.

That objective was still a mystery, but rumors were rampant it was indeed a Machine production facility. If that was the case, Black knew they could expect one hell of a fight. The Tegeri weren't going to let 2nd Battalion just march in and take one of their key installations. Things are going to get bloody, Black thought grimly. Then he put it out of his mind and watched the featureless desert whip by.

"Let's go!" Bear Samuels was shouting at his mortar crews, frustrated with the time it was taking them to set up. He'd worked them as much as he could, but they were just inexperienced, and it showed in their performance. "I want fire on that valley, and I want it now." Unlike Blackie's accent, Samuel's southern drawl tended to vanish when he was excited and under stress.

"Almost ready, Sergeant." Corporal Jarrod had been onplanet around six months, which made him one of the closest things 3rd Section had to a veteran. He was a good man, but his two crewman were cherries who'd been on Erastus less than two weeks.

"Ready, Sarge." Isaac Stone was another corporal, an 18-month veteran from 2nd Section. Taylor had detached Blackie's and Hank Daniels' mortars and sent them to Samuels. Both of the borrowed crews were outperforming his own less seasoned team.

His section was advancing through a narrow, rocky valley. It was a rough position, with the flanks on both sides exposed to enemy positions on the heights. The overall mission objective was on the left, built into a jagged peak rising 500 meters above the desert floor. The valley itself was narrow, with a rugged series of small hills rising to the right. Although it still hadn't been confirmed officially, by now the entire battalion knew they were assaulting one of the enemy's Machine production sites.

It was the right flank that was worrying Samuels. There were enemy defensive positions up there, dug into those hills covering the approach to the base. His people had to take those out before the objective itself could be attacked. The rest of the strikeforce was stacked up behind his people, along with a section of the 1st and about half the battalion support elements. They were going to hit the base itself, but only after Samuels' people cleared the hills to the right.

Taylor had taken a gamble, sending his least experienced section in first, but he knew he needed his veterans for the main attack. He'd have never gone with 3rd Section if he didn't have Samuels to lead it. Bear was one of the best small-unit commanders Taylor had ever seen. The big man was new to handling a whole section, but Jake had complete confidence in his friend. They both knew what had to be done and, if anyone could do the job with a bunch of rookies, it was Bear Samuels.

"Ready, Sergeant." Jarrod's voice was a little wobbly, but it was loud and clear.

"Attention 3rd Section, prepare to advance behind mortar barrage. Team leaders sound off."

"Acknowledged." Corporal Clark Hemmerich was the first to respond, but the other three teams sounded off a few seconds later. The leaders had all been onplanet at least 9 months, though some of them commanded teams consisting entirely of new recruits.

"Mortars..." Bear was standing right behind the three deployed tubes. "...commence firing."

It couldn't have been more than a second before Samuels heard the first distinctive whoosh, followed closely by the other two. He pulled down his visor, flipping the switch to kick in the magnification. He could see the explosions in a small line along the rocky slope.

"Short, 30 meters." He snapped out the range adjust-ment. The three crew leaders were watching their impact points too, but Samuels beat them to it.

Visibility was shitty. Bear could make out maybe half a dozen Machines deployed on the hillside, but he knew there were a lot more of them up there. The terrain was great for defense. If he led his section straight up they'd be cut to pieces. There was a way up around the side, though. If he could get a jump on the enemy, distract them enough with the mortar fire, he might just manage to hit them on the flank. He liked his rookies' chances a lot better that way.

Bear smiled as he saw the second batch of mortar rounds impact along the enemy's first line. We drew blood that time, he thought, nodding with satisfaction.

"1st and 2nd Teams, move out." He had placed Hem-merich in overall command of the first two teams. The veteran corporal had been onplanet almost two years. He was the one other NCO in the section that Samuels con-sidered a true veteran.

"Yes, Sergeant." Hemmerich's response was crisp, just a touch of tension showing. This was a new kind of mis-sion for all of them, the biggest fight the 213th Strikeforce had ever faced.

"3rd and 4th Teams, prepare to advance." Samuels was taking the rest of the section in himself. They were moving up right behind Hemmerich's people. Once they got closer to the enemy position they would swing around, climbing higher up the hillside and hitting the enemy rear…right after the first two teams engaged the flank. With any luck, they'd have surprise on their side. If not, Samuels thought, it's going to be a long day.

"Widen that field of fire. That fucking thing swivels, you know." Clark Hemmerich was crouched down behind a large boulder, shouting across a ten meter gap to his HHV team. They'd gotten the thing up and firing quickly enough, but they were just shooting straight ahead. They had a line of fire on at least three enemy lines, but they were only shooting at one.

"Yes, Corporal."

Hemmerich grinned as he saw the stream of hyper-velocity projectiles begin to swing back and forth across the field. He shook his head, thinking, why do they have to be told that? They'd caught the Machines flat-footed, focused on the mortar barrage and expecting a frontal assault. Now his team was raking the enemy flank, firing into the Machine position at its most vulnerable point.

"Grange, Cruz, get your asses behind some cover before they get shot off!" The enemy still hadn't reacted to the surprise, and now his people were getting careless, not paying attention to their cover. It was exactly the kind of stupid shit that got soldiers killed. The Machines were slow to adjust, but when they did Hemmerich knew his line would be hosed down with fire, and anybody who wasn't keeping his head down would be a stain.

His orders were clear…put maximum fire on the enemy while Samuels took the rest of the section around the flank and hit the enemy rear. The Machines were confused, their flank wide open. He was tempted to charge now and try to exploit the chaos. But he didn't have the strength, not until Samuels and the rest of the section went in, at least. It was immaterial…his orders expressly forbid him to go in before the rear attack hit.

He tapped a small pad on his helmet, bringing the tactical display up on his visor. His troops were deployed across 120 meters, each team with six men on the front and two in reserve. The 2nd team's HHV was about 70 meters uphill from his position. It looked like a decent spot, but it was a little more exposed than he liked.

He peered around the boulder, trying to get an idea of the damage they were doing to the enemy. Normally, he'd have had a drone up, but Taylor had ordered him not to do anything during his approach that might alert the enemy they were coming. The Machines had detected the transports approaching the area, of course, but Taylor was betting that a complex assault plan would surprise them. He didn't think the Machines would expect an attack across the rugged terrain on their flank, which is exactly why Samuels' section was doing just that. Drones buzzing around before the attack might have been a tip off, though.

It looked like the enemy was taking heavy casualties, but it was hard to be sure. They still hadn't counterattacked – or even responded with more than token fire of their own. It was a gift, but one Hemmerich knew wouldn't last. The more he thought about it, the more he disliked that HHV position. The enemy was going to take them out as soon as they got their shit together.

"1st Team, maintain position and fire." He crouched low and crept out from behind the boulder, climbing slowly up the hill. He was going to find a better spot for that HHV.

"On three...3rd and 4th Teams, advance." Bear's people had made a wide march around the enemy flank. They'd gone at least a kilometer out of their way, but it looked like they'd made it without being spotted. He'd crept as close as he dared. The enemy rear was about half a klick down the rocky hillside.

"One." Samuels could hear distant explosions...his mortars still firing on the enemy front. It was hard to tell, but it sounded like all three were still active. He'd cut communications with the mortars...he'd shut down everything but low-power intra-team com. It was just too easy for the enemy to pick up a transmission and blow his secrecy.

"Two." Normally, Samuels would have his troops leap-frog forward, half providing covering fire while the rest advanced. But it looked like they had complete surprise going for them, so he'd ordered everyone to rush down the hillside and take advantage of it. A good old-fashioned charge, he thought. "No, not entirely," he whispered to himself. He wasn't looking to lead a bunch of rookies into close quarters combat with the Machines. They were going to rush down to point blank range and then stop and unload on the enemy position. He knew Hemmerich's people were hitting the flank the same way. With their flank and rear compromised and heavy fire coming in, the enemy would probably pull back. The Machines didn't break and rout in battle, not exactly. But they weren't utterly resilient automatons either. They cared about self-preservation... whether that was instinct, programming, doctrine...Samuels didn't know. But they would retreat if their position was untenable rather than fight hopelessly to the death. And that was all Samuels needed to clear the hillside.

"One. Move it!" He spun around the edge of the rock out into the open. This was a gamble. If the enemy realized what was happening and got some fire on his people, they'd be sitting ducks. If that happened, Bear knew he'd be one of the first to go...he was a damned big target out in the open.

He ran down the hillside, as quickly as he could without losing his footing. His vision was obscured...he had his visor down and the tactical display up. If he'd been leading his old team, he wouldn't have worried about the display, but he needed to keep an eye on the cherries. If they froze, or if half of them failed to advance, the attack could quickly turn into a disaster.

It looked like everyone was moving, at least so far. The line was a little more ragged than he'd have liked, but overall things looked OK. He shoved up the visor, finally getting a good look forward. He'd covered half the ground to the enemy already. There was a small gutter in the hillside, no more than a wrinkle in the ground, about 200 meters from the Machine position. That was the objective. If they could make it that far, they'd have decent cover, and they'd be firing from point blank range.

"They're shooting at us!"

Bear wasn't even sure who it was until he checked the com transponder. Private Esteban, one of the newbs from 3rd Team. "Let's stay calm, people. Keep moving." Bear was starting to notice some fire too, but it was sporadic, scattered. Probably a sentry or two who'd noticed the approaching force. He could feel himself stooping lower, instinctively trying to make himself a smaller target. The best thing he could do…that any of them could do…was to keep moving.

"I'm hit!" It was Private Slotsky from 4th Team. He wasn't fresh out of the Portal, but he was still pretty raw. There was pain in his tone, and panic.

"Keep moving, all of you!" Bear was almost to the objective. His rifle was in his hands, and his eyes were instinctively scanning for a good place to position himself. "Slotsky, how bad are you hit?"

"It's my leg, Sarge. Hurts like hell." Bear could hear the fear. Slotsky had never been wounded before, probably never had worse than a twisted ankle. "Stay calm, kid. Grab yourself some cover and get your medkit on it. We'll be back for you." The nanobots in the personal medical kit could stabilize most wounds long enough to get an injured soldier evac'd. Assuming there was any transport available, which there wouldn't be unless Bear and his men secured the area.

Samuels halted, crouching behind a small rock outcropping. It was only a meter and a half high, but it was good cover as long as he stayed prone. He slammed down his visor and gave the tactical display a quick glance. The rest of his troops were reaching their objectives. He switched off the projection and cranked up the visor magnification. He could hear the enemy fire now, still sporadic but definitely getting heavier.

"Everybody grab some decent cover and get some fire going." He peered around the edge of the rock, bringing his assault rifle up and firing half a dozen rounds on semi-automatic in the general direction of the enemy. "HHVs, I want you guys up and firing now! Make sure you've got decent cover." He'd been careful to ensure that each of the HHV teams had one veteran member. He had to transfer a man from 3rd Team to do it, but the HHVs were too important to entrust solely to rookies.

He pumped up the visor magnification to 300% and looked over toward the left. It looked like Hemmerich's people were really ripping the enemy flank to shreds. He could hear fire beginning from his own teams, scattered rifles at first, then one of the HHVs kicking in. The enemy position was bracketed by the fire of his two groups. The Machines' position was untenable...they had two choices. Launch a nearly suicidal charge against one of his forces or withdraw and reform. Either way, Samuels was going to take control of the hill and open the door for the rest of Jake's troops to assault the base.

Never win a battle with bullets when you can do it with boot leather. That was one of Jake Taylor's favorite maxims...and Samuels had learned it from him. It didn't mat-

ter that military boots hadn't been made of leather for gen-
erations...the point remained. And against an enemy like
the Machines, strong and well-armed but tactically sluggish, it was even more valid.

His whole force was in position now, pouring fire into
the enemy rear. The Machines were shifting forces, trying to put together a line to face the new threat. Samuel's
people were starting to take losses too, but they were light.
The enemy was disordered and their efforts to reorganize
under the heavy fire were slow and clumsy.

"Pour it on, boys." Samuels was firing on full auto now
as he shouted into his com. "Drive them off the hill."

# Chapter 7

From the Journal of Jake Taylor:

The Machines aren't actual robots. Not exactly. They are built, yes, but the technology is bio-mechanical. Imagine a reinforced supermetal skeleton, covered with a combination of mechanical and organic materials. Machines that learn, machines that heal. Relentless warriors that feel no fatigue, no pity, no mercy.

But the Machines are pawns in this war, even as my brothers and I are. They are the servants of the Tegeri, our real enemy. The Tegeri build the Machines and command them; they send them into battle against us. We don't know much about these shadowy puppet-masters, but we know what we need to know. They are our enemies.

But what of the Machines themselves? Are they evil? Or are they merely slaves with no choice, no self-determination? Do they deserve our hatred? Or our pity? Do they feel true emotions? Are they able to wish for something else, something better than a lifetime of war and death on a hellish world?

And how different are we, my fellow-soldiers and I? What choice do we have? We are sustained by our cause, protecting humanity from a ravaging alien horde. However many of us die, however callously we are used by the government, we know that we are protecting those we left behind. If we didn't have that, I doubt we could go on. I know I couldn't. Thinking of Beth, my family, safer because I am here fighting...it is all that sustains me.

But do the Machines also believe they are fighting for a cause? Do they see us as aggressors, invaders...streaming from the Portals onto the worlds they have protected for centuries? Are they as self-righteous in their purpose as we are in ours?

I wonder sometimes if the Machines can crave a life elsewhere, if they ever long for peace...or if they know nothing but the hell of war. And if they know nothing else, if they cannot understand love and family and happiness... do I pity or envy them?

"Keep laying down that fire. Don't give those bastards a chance to regroup." Taylor had his visor magnification on maximum, watching the engineers move toward the heavy metal hatch of the enemy base. The Machines had fallen back, abandoning their network of trenches in front of the entry, but now they were trying to organize a counterattack. Taylor's strikeforce had taken the enemy position... now they had only one job. Cover the engineers while they breeched the fortified hatch.

It had been a hard fight. Samuels' people had cleared the opposite hillside, outflanking and maneuvering the enemy out of their position. It had been masterfully done, and Taylor had been particularly impressed by Bear's execution. Taylor had expected a lot from him, but he'd gotten even more. Samuels had accomplished a virtual miracle with his pack of newbs.

The battle to seize the ground outside the base had been a different story. Taylor's men had paid for every bloody step. They'd had two attacks repulsed and, for a while, he thought they were going to come up short. Twice he'd called for fire support. But the narrow valley was a dangerous place for a Dragonfire gunship, and central command had refused both requests, instructing Taylor to continue his assault with the resources he had. He was used to the high command putting materiel over men, but he was surprised this time...he had thought this mission was important enough to override the usual bullshit protocol.

It was. Taylor didn't know it, but he'd twice been authorized Dragonfire support, only to have the orders countermanded by higher authority for undisclosed reasons. Jake Taylor was on his own, and his performance was being closely watched...though he had no idea any of this was going on.

Finally, he ordered Bear to post a small flank guard and attack down off the hillside with the rest of his men. The combined assault proved to be too much for the Machines defending the trenches. They pulled back, leaving 2/3 of their numbers behind, dead in their works.

Now the enemy was trying to integrate all the units that had withdrawn and organize a counterattack. Taylor's exhausted and shattered sections had to hold the ground they'd taken...and give the engineers a chance to break through the enemy fortifications. There were no reserves...they were on their own. The rest of the battalion had moved to cut off enemy reinforcements approaching from the north. If fresh Machine units got through, Taylor's people wouldn't have a chance. At 50% strength, fatigued, and low on ammo, they'd be swept away like dry leaves in the breeze.

"Jarrod, get those mortars repositioned. I want fire on those bastards. They don't get a chance to regroup. Understood?"

"Yes, Lieutenant." Voices coming through on the implanted com unit always sounded a little strange...hollow, tiny. But hearing himself called lieutenant was stranger still. "We're on the way, sir."

The enemy had taken out one of the mortars, along with its entire team. Corporal Stone and his people didn't have any warning. They'd been changing their position after every two shots, but the enemy still managed to target them and score a direct hit. Jarrod ran over to see if there were any survivors, but he couldn't find a piece of anybody bigger than a softball.

"Lieutenant Taylor…Captain Graves here." Graves was the lead engineer. His crew were UN regulars, not UNFE lifers. There was a lot of resentment between the conscripts condemned to Erastus and the short-term UN specialists with a ticket home, but Taylor had made it clear to his people he wasn't going to tolerate anything less than total support for the engineers.

"Yes, Captain." Taylor didn't share the resentment. He might hate the higher ups, the people who made the policies that sent him and his brethren to die on Erastus. But that animosity didn't extend to a team of engineers. He might envy their ticket home, but that wasn't the same thing. They didn't create the situation any more than he did. "What can I do for you?"

"We're going to blow the plasma charges in 3 minutes. I need all your people at least 500 meters from the hatch by then."

Taylor sighed. Three minutes wasn't much time. "Understood, Captain." There was no use arguing. Graves didn't have any latitude, and Taylor knew it. Getting into that base was worth more than his entire strikeforce to UN Command…worth more than all of Graves's men too. Any of his people who were too close in three minutes would be vaporized by a plasma charge. On UNFE's spreadsheet it would be just so many more casualties in the glorious victory.

"Attention all personnel." He was practically shouting into his com. "I want everyone a minimum of 600 meters…" He added an extra 100, just to be safe. "… from the hatch in two minutes." His voice was commanding, his tone urgent. He didn't intend to lose any rookies because they fucked around instead of obeying his orders immediately.

Taylor tapped the controls on his helmet, activating his tactical display. He took a quick glance, making sure everyone was obeying his withdraw order. Satisfied, he tapped his com to Black's line. "Blackie, I'll be going in with the engineers in a few. You'll be in charge out here while I'm in the base." With the rest of the battalion was positioned on the northern perimeter, Taylor was in command around the base itself. "If anything gets through the outer defenses, you need to keep the valley clear. Dig in on both sides, and put the mortars in the center so you can fire in either direction."

"Got it, Jake." Black's voice was sharp, but Taylor could hear the fatigue too. The 2nd Section had been in the forefront of the attack, and they'd borne the brunt of the losses. Taylor's old command was nearly shattered, but he knew they'd still do the job. He was trusting them with his life. He was leading Hank Daniels' 1st Section inside with the engineers, and if the enemy retook the valley while they were in the base, none of them would get out.

"Lieutenant Taylor, Captain Graves here. Detonation in 30 seconds." Taylor could see the engineers on his tactical display, running away from the base entrance, putting enough distance between themselves and the charges. "It'll take about five minutes for the area to cool down enough for us to go in." Cool down was definitely a relative term on Erastus. "Have your people ready and in position by then."

"Understood, Captain." Taylor felt a small flush, not

anger, really…more annoyance. He realized he didn't like getting anything that sounded like orders from the engineer. Not when they concerned one of his combat forces. But he bit back on it. "We'll be ready, sir."

"Launch light modules." It was dark in the passage, the kind of pitch blackness you could only dream about most places on Erastus. It was all well and good to wish for relief from the relentless sunlight, but Taylor and his men, their eyes adjusted to the brightness of two massive suns, were ill-equipped to maneuver in the dark.

There was a whoomp sound, then another. Then half a dozen more. The light modules could be attached to the assault rifles like grenades. They were polycarbonate globes generating light through a contained chemical reaction. They lasted around six hours, and each one could light up an area with a diameter of roughly six meters.

Taylor looked down the passage, now lit by the modules. It was about ten meters wide, and it stretched deep into the mountainside. The light globes were doing their job well. All of Taylor's people had flashlights, but a handheld light was more effective at giving the holder's position away to a hidden enemy than providing useful illumination. The modules were far more effective, and the grenade launchers could throw them several hundred meters.

"Alright, 1st Team take point." Taylor was going to follow just behind his advanced team, the engineers and the rest of the section falling in behind him. "Prepare to move out."

Hank Daniels had been at the end of the formation, organizing the teams bringing up the rear. Now he trotted forward to Taylor's position. "It's hard to believe we're actually inside an enemy base, isn't it, Jake?" He shouldn't have been calling his superior officer by his first name, but

Taylor wasn't a stickler for formality…and he certainly wasn't used to being an officer. Besides, Daniels was rapidly becoming a member of Jake's inner circle.

"It's pretty incredible." The response was perfunctory, without emotion. Taylor looked around him. The walls were smooth, the bare rock coated with some unidentified material. Taylor knew he was inside the lair of a species far ahead of his own, but all he could think about was the cost. Half his people had been killed and wounded taking this place…and from what he could piece together, the rest of the battalion had suffered almost as badly. He knew it was a big step forward for the war effort, but it was still too early to think of it in those terms. The losses were still too fresh.

"I know it was a hard fight, Jake." Daniels had a pretty good idea why Taylor was so somber. "But at least it wasn't a waste. We're a big step closer to ending the war on Erastus. That's something, at least. How many of our people have died on this miserable rock for nothing?"

Taylor took a deep breath. Daniels was right; he knew that. But it was still hard to see the big picture, to decide how many mangled and dead soldiers an objective was worth. "I know you're right, Spider." He paused. "But it's just hard for me to see it that way. That's all speculation… and these dead boys are real." Taylor knew he shouldn't be commiserating with a subordinate in the middle of an operation, but he had to get through all of this somehow. He tried to be the unmoving rock, always there for his men, never in need of support himself. That was a great image, but an illusion, an impossible standard.

Daniels had to suppress a smile when Taylor called him Spider. He'd picked up the handle when he was a sniper, and none other than Jake Taylor had given it to him. Taylor was a corporal and team leader when Daniels arrived on Gehenna. The rookie was a crack shot from the beginning, so Cadogan made him a sniper. But it wasn't his aim that was truly extraordinary…it was his patience. Daniels could stay in a hidden position, motionless for hours, just waiting for his shot. One day Taylor compared him to a spider sitting in its web waiting for prey, and that was that. The name stuck.

"Look at it this way, then." Daniels turned his head, glancing over at Taylor. "Maybe the war here will end sooner…and in ten years a whole batch of kids won't get blackmailed into throwing their lives away because of this."

Taylor didn't respond, but he thought about what Daniels said. It made sense, but it was still hard for him to accept that anything could justify the casualties and suffering his people had endured…and he figured that next group of kids would just get sent someplace else to die.

"OK, Lieutenant Taylor, we're all set." Captain Graves was walking up from behind. He had been in the rear, supervising his crew as they prepped their equipment. The engineer wore the same sand-colored fatigues as Taylor and his troops, but his were totally soaked through with sweat, making them look darker. Other than his obvious distress from the heat and the silver Engineering Corps insignia on his shoulder, he could have been any officer in UNFE. Except Graves was going back home someday.

"Very well, sir." He tapped the com pad on his helmet. "1st team, move out." Taylor turned his head and glanced at Graves, nodding. Then he followed his advancing troops down the dimly lit corridor.

"Machines moving down the west passage." Taylor could hear shooting in the background as Corporal Danton made his report. Taylor had sent Danton and his team to investigate the scanner contacts they'd been picking up.

Jake had been afraid it was an internal security force…a fear that now seemed well-founded.

The main force had worked its way deep into the complex, locating the main power core after a lengthy search. They'd encountered a few sentries, and they'd lost one man, but they managed to reach their objective without running into too much resistance. Graves and his men were setting the nuclear charge while Taylor's people guarded the approaches. Ideally, UN Command would want to hang on to a facility like this. The potential for researching the enemy's superior technology was considerable. But it was too risky to try and hold it. The base was deep in an enemy-dominated zone, and they would likely launch a counterattack to retake it. UNFE had only managed to mount an attack against the facility because of surprise. The enemy thought the location was secret, as it still would be had it not been for a random communications intercept and some educated guessing by UNFE Intelligence.

The only tactically sound choice was to destroy the place, thus beginning the long process of attriting the enemy's strength on the planet by destroying or capturing the production facilities. There had been 8-14 factories on the Portal worlds already conquered. If Erastus followed the pattern, the destruction of this facility would eliminate approximately 10% of the enemy's replacement capacity. The Tegeri didn't seem to bring reinforcements through the Portals…they produced the Machines on-planet. When the production facilities were all taken or destroyed, they seemed to give up the fight.

"Lieutenant, we've got a lot of Machines coming at us." Danton's tone was tense, harried. "They're advancing from two directions now." There was a short pause, then: "Sir, they seem to be very disorganized. Not like normal Machines at all."

"You need to hold them, Corporal." Jake's voice was firm. "At all costs. I'm sending you some backup now." He paused. "No one gets by you. Understood?"

"Yes, sir. Understood."

Taylor turned toward Daniels. "Hank, send another team to support Danton. He's got Machines coming in from two directions." Taylor was in overall command, of course, but he didn't want to step on Daniels' toes too badly. Danton had panicked and called Taylor directly... he really should have reported to Daniels. It was tough on a unit commander to have a superior officer along with no other units to command. It was easy to marginalize the junior commander. But Taylor had been in Daniels' shoes before, and he made sure to respect his subordinate.

"Yes, sir." Daniels flipped down his helmet and checked his tactical display. "I'll send Gomez' team." He flipped the com circuit. "Gomez, I'm sending you coordinates. Get your team over there immediately and support Corporal Danton."

"Yes, Sergeant." Gomez was one of the most junior team leaders in the 213th Strikeforce, but he was fast developing into one of the best. "We're heading there now."

"Gomez' people are on the way, sir." Daniels held Taylor's gaze for a few seconds...a silent acknowledgement. Neither one said anything, but they both knew what Taylor had done...and that Daniels understood and appreciated it.

"Lieutenant, we'll be finished in ten minutes...twelve tops." Graves' voice was loud, and the message startled Taylor. The engineer sounded distracted. He and his men were working as quickly as possible to set the nuclear mine so they could all get the hell out. Graves – and Taylor too – would have much preferred to nuke the factory with a missile, eliminating the need for the bloody ground attack or for any of them to be deep within the facility standing around a 3 megaton warhead. But the base was dug into a mountain, and it was far from certain any nuke in UNFE's arsenal would penetrate sufficiently to destroy it. And if they had tried and failed, the surprise so essential to the operation would have been lost. By the time they came in on the ground, the enemy would have massively reinforced. The assault would have quickly turned into a bloody disaster.

"Acknowledged, sir." Taylor signaled Daniels while he spoke to Graves, holding up both hands, all his fingers upright, indicating 10 minutes. "Be advised that we are engaging substantial enemy forces, Captain." A brief pause. "Any minutes you can shave off will make our withdrawal less problematic."

"We'll do what we can, Lieutenant. You don't want us rushing too much with this thing." Graves cut the line.

Taylor nodded. He wasn't going to waste his time thinking about what could go wrong with the mine. The nuke was Graves' problem. The Machines were his.

"Let's go, Gomez. Your people are moving like a bunch of old ladies." Taylor knew he wasn't being fair – the corporal's team was shot to pieces. Danton was dead, and Gomez was leading the survivors of both crews. They had more wounded than able-bodied personnel, and it was hard to withdraw under fire while carrying your comrades. But fair was bullshit, and Jake knew it. There was getting out of here and not getting out. Those were the two options. Fair had nothing to do with any of it.

"We're on the way, sir." Taylor could hear the pain in Gomez' voice. The corporal had reported he'd taken a minor wound in the leg, but Jake had a feeling it was a lot worse than that.

They'd killed a lot of Machines, but there were more coming. They were far less effective than typical Machines. Taylor figured they were fresh off the manufacturing line, and they had enough more than enough numbers to make up for reduced efficiency. There was no way to win a protracted fight and, besides, the nuclear warhead was going to blow in less than 15 minutes. The thing was booby-trapped to prevent the enemy from disarming it, but UN Command had ordered a short detonation countdown anyway. They didn't want to take any chances on the Machines deactivating the mine in spite of the defenses. If that put a lot of pressure on Taylor and Graves and their people to get the hell out, so be it. Destroying the facility was vastly more important to the high command than a section of infantry and an engineer crew.

Taylor and the main force were almost to the entrance. He didn't want to send anyone back, and risk more of his men not getting out. But he couldn't leave Gomez and his people behind. There was only one thing to do. "Hank, get everybody out and onto that transport."

"You're not thinking about…"

"Just do it." Taylor had already turned around. "And you lift off and get everybody out of here five minutes before detonation." He stared right at Daniels. "Not one second later. Do you understand me?"

Daniels stood silently, shifting his weight nervously back and forth. "Do you understand me, Sergeant Daniels?" Taylor's tone was imperious, almost angry. He didn't have time to argue.

"Yes, sir." Daniels answered grudgingly, his voice sullen.

Taylor spun around and jogged down the corridor. He unslung his assault rifle, holding it at the ready in front of him. The tactical display showed Gomez' group about 200 meters back. He also had blips showing enemy forces another 300 meters behind them. The data points on the Machines were courtesy of the nanobot detectors Gomez had dropped behind as his people ran for it.

He covered about 150 meters and rounded the corner. There they were, about 30 meters ahead. It was worse than he thought. There were only six of them, all the survivors from two 8-man teams. It looked like 2 were unhurt, and each of them was carrying a badly wounded comrade. Corporal Gomez was in the back, struggling forward slowly, his fatigues soaked in blood. He was waving ahead, yelling for the rest of the men to move faster and leave him behind.

"Let's go, you guys." Jake shouted down the corridor, gesturing wildly for the men to run toward him. He kept moving, passing them by, stopping next to Gomez.

"Lieutenant, you shouldn't be back here, sir. We might not make…"

"We're all going to make it, Corporal." Jake sounded sincere, but he was far from sure. He gave them about a 50/50 shot of getting to the transport before it lifted. Getting out too late was the same as not getting out at all…a front row seat to a 3 megaton blast.

Taylor grabbed Gomez and threw the wounded corporal over his shoulder. At least he's small, Taylor thought to himself. Jake was 2 meters tall, and he had at least 9 or 10 centimeters on the stricken non-com. He ignored Gomez' howls of pain and ran forward on the heels of the other troopers.

They rounded the corner just as the pursuing Machines began firing down the hall. "Turn left up ahead," Taylor shouted. They were almost there, but they were running out of time. They weren't going to make it.

He turned the corner and felt the pain in his back, the sudden weakness in his legs. He'd been hit. Ignore it, he thought…nothing you can do about it now. He gritted his teeth, trying to run harder, to disregard the pain.

He could see the light up ahead. It was late in the day, well into twilight, but even with only one sun in the sky, it was always bright on Erastus. "Move!" He screamed at the men in front. He knew they were tired and hurting, but they only had 30 seconds left. They ran down the last hallway and out into the bright sun of the valley. Taylor glanced at his chronometer and groaned. They were too late.

But he could hear the engines of the transport, and he looked up, seeing its hulking form just ahead. "Run!" His legs were on fire, and back was sheer agony. He could feel the slickness, his blood flowing down his back, his legs. Every step was torture, but he kept moving, running hard. Gomez had lost consciousness, and Jake was having a hard time keeping a grip on him.

He couldn't understand why the transport was still there. The countdown clock was at 4:15 to detonation…they should have taken off 45 seconds before. He could see the shape of the Mustang getting larger as he approached. Gomez' troops were reaching the open hatch of the hold, grabbing onto the outstretched hands of the men onboard.

Taylor still couldn't understand. He wasn't surprised that Daniels was ignoring his order to leave them behind, but the transport crew would have taken off on the dot, and no arguments would have stopped them.

Jake handed Gomez to the troops inside the hold and grabbed onto the handrails, pulling himself up. The strength wasn't there, and he started to slide. Then he felt the hands grabbing him, hauling him up and in. As they pulled him up, he got a view through the open door into the cockpit. He saw the two man crew…and Hank Daniels holding his gun on them both.

"OK…" Taylor shouted so loudly it wracked his stricken body with pain. "Let's get the hell out of here!"

# Chapter 8

From the Journal of Jake Taylor:

Have you ever watched anyone die? I don't mean a grandparent, old at the end of a long and happy life, lying in bed, surrounded by family. Have you ever seen a young person die violently, decades before nature intended?

Have you looked into the eyes of a boy, barely a man, and witnessed the terror, the pain, the confusion? Seen the look in his eyes as he begs you to help, to save him? Listened to him cry for life, even as death was taking him? Stared down at your clothes, now stained with the life blood of a dead friend?

I expected to die when I got to Erastus. My life wasn't mine anymore anyway...I'd signed it away to save my family. UN Central owned it. If they wanted to throw me into the burning sands of Gehenna to die, that was their decision.

But I didn't die. Battle after battle, I survived. I was wounded a few times, and thought I was done for more than once, but I'm still here. When I got to Erastus, the guys who'd been onplanet awhile took me under their wing. They taught me how to survive. They became good friends, all those guys. We fought together, lived together, watched each other's backs.

They're dead now. All of them. Burying your friends is one of the rewards of surviving on Erastus. There's a pain I can't describe in watching a friend die...19 years old, 20, his body mutilated beyond recognition. The bond between men who fight alongside each other, who bleed together and man trenches and share the same slop to eat...it can't be understood by someone who hasn't experienced it. Those men were more than friends, more than brothers. And I watched every one of them die.

But there's a different pain too, the agony of watching these stupid, unprepared kids stumble out of the Portal, knowing almost 2/3 of them will be killed or wounded in their first battle. UNFE training is fairly comprehensive, but it is woefully inadequate to prepare young men for the reality of this hell world.

The anguish is worse because I have lived so long. The good men who took me in didn't fail me. They taught me what I needed to know. They kept me alive until I could survive on my own. When I watch a cherry die, I know I have failed him, as I myself was not failed. I have failed a bewildered, terrified kid who needed me. And I have failed the dead men who saved me and asked nothing more than that I pay forward for what they did.

Why should I have survived so long when there are so many I cannot save? I thought fighting in hell was a terrible fate, but commanding there is worse. Watching men die, seeing the terrified looks in their cold, dead faces...it's more horrible than anything the Machines can do to me. If they kill me, I'll consider it a mercy. But if I have to look at one more dead kid, face transfixed in fear, in agony, I think I will lose my mind.

Taylor sat quietly, watching the desert whip by as the Mustang raced along at 1,200 kph. He was strapped in, sitting alone in the cavernous hold of the otherwise empty transport. His back hurt like crazy, but Doc had cleared him for the flight. The round that struck him went right through his back and out the front without so much as nicking a vital organ. It took Doc about 30 minutes to patch everything up and fuse the wound closed. Jake would be sore for a couple weeks, and off combat duty, but he was more or less fine for normal activities.

UNFE HQ was 3,500 klicks from Firebase Delta. Taylor knew the destruction of the enemy base was a major victory, but he'd never seen a transport dispatched such a distance to pick up one lieutenant…especially not one escorted by a Dragonfire gunship, like this one was.

It had occurred to Jake they might give him a medal or some type of award. They loved giving out decorations… something for the cherries to look up to, another reason for them to throw their lives away heroically.

Taking out the first Machine production facility on the planet was certainly a major win, and a crucial turning point in the war on Erastus. The first phase was over… from now on, it would no longer be a continuing fight just to hang on. The war had morphed into an ongoing effort to chip away at enemy strength until their defenses collapsed. It was too early to say the momentum had shifted entirely, but it was definitely a move in that direction.

Taylor understood the implications, and he appreciated the tactical significance. But all he could think about was how many of his boys didn't come back from the glorious victory. The thought of smiling while some asshole from UN Central did a drive by on Erastus to pin a piece of silver on his chest was more than he could stomach.

The Jake Taylor who had just arrived through the Portal might have valued a shiny new medal. But the war weary lieutenant was repulsed by the idea of accepting a reward that was bought with the blood of his men. He had no choice, but there was no part of him left that wanted any of it. He wished he could go back to base to be with his shattered unit as the men mourned their dead. That was where he belonged.

"We should be on the ground at HQ in about 20 minutes, Lieutenant Taylor." The pilot's tone was half-disinterested, half respectful. Antigrav jocks didn't usually pay much attention to ground pounders. But Taylor was one of the heroes of the Battle of Shadow Valley, as they were calling it, and he rated a transport all to himself. That was worth a little respect. And the story of him running back into the facility to rescue his men – then getting wounded himself - was taking on the status of a legend. It irked the hell out of him, but there was nothing he could do to stop it.

The air crews weren't lifers like Jake and his people. That didn't mean they weren't real combat soldiers, though. Their loss rate didn't equal the infantry's, but no one would call their duties safe. But if they survived a tour of duty on Erastus, they'd go back to Earth. Jake and his brothers could only imagine a hope like that.

Taylor picked up the small mic and flipped it on. "Thank you, Lieutenant." He leaned back and mopped his forehead with a small cloth. The units on Erastus didn't have dress uniforms or anything like that. There was just no need for them. But Jake was wearing his full duty uniform, not just light combat fatigues. He was getting some air from the small vents in the Mustang's hold, but it was still damned hot, especially wearing the uniform's high-collared jacket.

He'd been surprised when he arrived on Erastus to find that virtually nothing was air-conditioned. Not the barracks, not the transports. Nothing. Even the infirmary was only moderately climate-controlled…better by a considerable margin than anywhere else, but still pretty hot.

He was confused at first, but he came to understand. Adapting to the heat of Erastus was the most important thing a soldier could do to survive. Those who failed to do so, who became weak and fatigued on the battlefield...they were the first to die. The men of Erastus, especially the life-service infantrymen, had to make the inferno into their natural habitat. And popping in and out of comfortably air-conditioned areas was not at all conducive to effective acclimation.

I wonder what headquarters is like, Jake thought idly. It had been five years since he'd felt truly cool air, and he wondered if HQ might have some to offer. He found himself hoping so, but when he thought about it a bit more, he decided it might be better not to be reminded of things that were lost to him.

Jake watched the terrain passing below the transport. Firebase Delta was situated in the deep desert, an area so devoid of moisture, the time between rains was measured in years. The last measured precipitation had been before Taylor even arrived onplanet.

He'd served in the jungles of Erastus too, a steaming hot equatorial belt, brutally humid and filled with venomous predators. It was the only area of Erastus with a significant number of lifeforms. The rest of planet was virtually lifeless, like the desert, or was home to a limited range of plant life, like the grass-covered polar plains he was now passing over.

UN Command Headquarters was built near the center of the northern polar region, the closest thing Erastus had to a temperate area. The Portal from Earth was located very close to the planet's north pole, and HQ had been built near the transit point. There were other advantages as well...the slightly more moderate temperatures were easier on the specialist troops and UN brass based at headquarters.

"We'll be landing in just a minute, Lieutenant Taylor." Taylor could feel the antigrav turning slowly. He could see the flat paved area ahead. Most of HQ was subterranean; only the landing pads were above ground.

The Mustang flew over one of the flat areas, and it gently descended in place as the antigrav generators slowly cut power, gradually restoring the effects of gravity. It was a soft landing…Taylor had to look outside to confirm they'd actually hit ground. He unstrapped himself and slowly stood up, wincing a bit as he did. It was time to see what the high command really wanted from him.

Taylor walked into the room, removing his hat as he did. He was distracted by an unfamiliar feeling as a wave of cool air rushed over him. He fought the urge to close his eyes and stand there savoring the blissful sensation. The crispness brought back a flood of memories, things he'd thought long-forgotten. For an instant, he was back in New Hampshire in autumn.

He'd expected to meet with a middling-high level officer, a major, or even a colonel. Instead, he'd been advised that an assistant UN under-secretary named Kazan was waiting to see him. To almost anyone on Earth, such a creature was unimaginably lofty, a senior Admin and a powerful and respected member of the government. To a grunt on Erastus such a meeting was without precedent.

"Greetings, Lieutenant Taylor. It is a great pleasure to finally meet you." Gregor Kazan was extremely polite, but Taylor was immediately uncomfortable around him. His tone sounded sincere, at least on the surface. But there was something unsettling about him, something that made Jake suspicious.

"I feel we have known each other for quite some time." Kazan walked toward Jake, extending his hand.

Taylor reached out and took Kazan's proffered hand, a confused look on his face. "Welcome to Erastus, sir."

It was all Taylor could think to say. Then: "Known each other? Have we met before?"

Kazan pointed to a small table with two chairs. "Please, Lieutenant, sit." He turned and walked toward the table himself. "You have had a hard time of it these last few days, I'm afraid. Kazan stood and watched as Taylor walked over and pulled out a chair, slowly lowering himself into it. "And to answer your question, no, we have not met. But I have known of you for some time."

Kazan sat down, harder and less gracefully than Taylor had. He noticed Jake taking a deep breath. His eyes darted to the air vent and back. "Yes, Lieutenant, I am sure my air conditioning is quite a change for you. I'm afraid I would be quite unable to function without it." He smiled. It was intended to make Taylor comfortable, but there was something odd about Kazan's thin lips. The official had been nothing but flawlessly polite, but Jake just wanted to get out of there, air conditioning or no. Something about Kazan made him uncomfortable.

"It is a terrible shame that you and your soldiers must exist in such hostile conditions." He said the words, but Jake was pretty sure the creepy little prick didn't give a shit what happened to the men in the field. "But it wouldn't be a service to you to allow you to face the Machines unprepared, would it?"

Taylor wanted to scream out, to tell Kazan that UN Central sent unprepared men to Erastus every day, and that most of them still weren't ready when they fought their first battles. Which was why most of them died. But he held his tongue and said only, "No, sir. It wouldn't."

Kazan sat quietly, looking across the table. Taylor wanted to ask why he'd been brought to HQ, but he decided to wait and see what Kazan had to say. It turned out he only had to wait a few seconds more.

"I am sure you are wondering why you are here, Lieutenant." Kazan still had the narrow smile on his face. The longer he kept it there, the phonier it looked.

"Yes, sir." Taylor spoke softly, matter-of-factly. "I am somewhat curious." More than somewhat, he thought… but he was determined to play it cool. His father had told him not to trust anyone from the government. He'd ignored the old man at the time, writing it off to one of his anti-establishment rants. But now his father's words were there again, playing at the back of his mind, sounding a lot more rational than they had five years earlier.

"Well, to deal with the simplest matter first, you are to receive a Silver Starcluster, and I will be presenting the award." Kazan watched, clearly expecting more of a reaction than Taylor gave him.

Jake sat still, staring back at his companion with emotionless eyes. Medals, causes, speeches…they are all worthless…they are as corrupt as the puppet masters who use them to control men. His father's words again, fighting their way from memory to the forefront of his consciousness.

"Thank you, sir. That is quite an honor." Taylor said what was expected of him, at least minimally. He didn't manage to put much feeling behind it. Jake wasn't as accomplished a fraud as Kazan.

Kazan noticed the lack of enthusiasm. "I am certain this is all a lot for you to absorb, coming so quickly after fighting such a terrible battle."

The door buzzer sounded. "Enter." Kazan didn't sound surprised by the intrusion.

A steward walked swiftly into the room, carrying a tray with a pitcher and two glasses. "Just set it down on the table, Joff." The neatly attired servant swiftly obeyed Kazan's command.

"Will there be anything else, sir?"

Kazan glanced at the pitcher full of ice water, then at Taylor, who couldn't keep his eyes off it. "No, Joff. That will be all."

"Some water, Lieutenant?"

Taylor was trying to maintain his detachment, but it had been five years since he'd had a drink of water that wasn't piss warm. "Yes, sir. I would appreciate that."

Taylor watched Kazan reach out and grab the pitcher. It was clear, but fogged over with condensation. Kazan poured slowly, and Jake's eyes watched the water and the ice cubes – Ice! – flow into the glass.

"I don't wish to overwhelm you, Lieutenant, but there is something else I wanted to discuss with you." He reached over and placed the glass in front of Taylor.

Jake eyed the water greedily, but he forced himself to wait. "Yes, sir. What else can I do for you?" He paused another few seconds, his hand shaking the entire time, wanting to reach out for the icy cold water.

Kazan watched. This soldier has good control, he thought…perhaps we chose well. "Lieutenant, UN Central Command has developed a new program, one designed to improve survivability for our soldiers fighting on difficult worlds." He paused, then added, "Like Erastus."

Taylor was listening, trying – and mostly failing - to look cool and uninterested as he raised the glass to his lips and felt the icy water slide down his throat. He drank half, forcing himself to put the glass down before he drained it. "A new program?" Taylor found himself interested. This was an unexpected topic.

"Yes, Lieutenant." Kazan suppressed a satisfied smile. He had Taylor's attention now. "I'm afraid it is quite complex and more than we can discuss in true detail at this time." He looked across the table with a broad smile that made Taylor's stomach flip. "But the good news is that your strikeforce has been chosen to be the first to participate in the program. Your people are receiving their orders now. They will be here in two days."

Taylor say quietly for a few seconds, before speaking. He wasn't sure what to think about any of this, but he also knew he didn't have any choices here…no more than he'd had back on the farm when he'd given his life to UN Central. "Will Sergeant Daniels be with them?"

Kazan had an annoyed look on his face. "I'm afraid Sergeant Daniels is under arrest, Lieutenant. Threatening a superior officer at gunpoint is a very serious offense."

Taylor knew it was serious. It was a capital offense. "I understand the gravity of the situation, but I believe that prosecution is misplaced in this case. Sergeant Daniels was only acting to save…"

"It is immaterial to our discussions, Lieutenant Taylor. I'm afraid it is out of my hands." Kazan's tone made it clear he considered the matter settled.

Taylor stared at the UN bigwig, his eyes boring like lasers. "I am prepared to cooperate with your new program, sir, but I must first insist that Sergeant Daniels be pardoned."

Kazan glared back at him, clearly outraged at the audacity of someone he considered well beneath him. "You have no authority to refuse any orders, Lieutenant. Regardless of the sergeant's fate." His voice dripped with contempt. Taylor knew it had been there all along, but his defiance had stripped away the veneer of civility and respect.

Taylor sat rigidly upright in his chair. He was uncomfortable facing off against a high UN official. The last five years of his life had been all about following orders, and before that, he'd had the usual fear of government officials. He didn't know exactly where Kazan fit into the

UN hierarchy, but he was sure it was pretty high up. But Hank Daniels was a good soldier and a friend. His actions that day saved not only Jake, but six other soldiers. He deserved better than to be shot in some dark cellar somewhere after a perfunctory trial.

"I'm sorry, Mr. Kazan." Taylor had faced death a hundred times since he'd arrived on Erastus. He wasn't going to back down now. "I will not cooperate in any way unless I have an assurance that Sergeant Daniels will be released and that no charges will be filed."

Kazan looked on the verge of an apoplectic fit. It was obvious he enjoyed wielding his power, and equally apparent that people rarely stood up to him. But Jake didn't care...he didn't care if he was dragged out of the office and shot right now. He wasn't going to abandon Daniels.

Kazan was silent for a long while. He stared at Taylor the entire time, as if trying to take the measure of the man. Finally, he spoke softly, slowly, his barely restrained anger obvious in his voice. "Very well, Lieutenant Taylor. I will grant your request." He had a sour look on his face, like a child being compelled to finish a plate of some hated vegetable. "But you will do everything exactly as you are told from now on without precondition or argument. Do you understand what I am saying to you?" His tone was deadly serious.

"Yes, sir." Taylor was surprised his stand had worked. This must be important, he thought...whatever it is they want me to do. "I understand."

"Good." Kazan glared at Taylor, not even trying to hide his disdain. "Because if you so much as hesitate an instant before following another order, I promise that you will be dragged into some hidden hole somewhere and shot without so much as the formality of a court martial." He paused, still glowering at his silent guest. "And the same for Sergeant Daniels. Do you understand me, Lieutenant?"

Taylor just nodded, wondering what he had gotten himself into.

# PART TWO
# SUPERSOLDIER

# Chapter 9

From the Journal of Jake Taylor:

I've begun to wonder how different we are from the Machines. They are constructed; I was born. They are part flesh, part machine. With my implants and exos, I am also part machine.

What did they do to me when they installed my mods? They took my eyes, and replaced them with ones that work better. What did they do with mine? The ones I was born with. The ones just like my mother's and, I was told, my grandmother's. The blue ones speckled gray that Beth used to look into when she touched my face. Did they end up in some garbage can, discarded like so much trash?

My ears are half circuitry now, and my muscles are interlaced with synthetic fibers that triple my natural strength. I heal rapidly, and my blood carries more oxygen. I can run farther and faster than before, and jump and climb too.

Then there are the exos. There are metal fittings on my shoulders now - and my legs and spine - where the exos attach to me. Part armor, part weapon, the exos make me the deadliest warrior mankind has ever produced. Fully equipped and prepped for battle I could beat 20 armed hardcores from any urban free zone.

Then there is the neural intelligence system. A constant voice in my head, the NIS is a sophisticated artificial intelligence, my own internal computer connected to my neural pathways. It feels like part of my own mind, somehow both new and old at the same time. I control it effortlessly with my thoughts, as it collates and stores information vastly more efficiently than my natural brain. I remember everything now...everything I see, everything I hear.

I am the ultimate warrior, the embodiment of Death, standing between my people and the doom of an alien enemy bent on destruction. But am I human anymore? Or just another manufactured soldier, like those I fight, built to wage a never-ending war?

"They're breaking off, Major!" Sergeant Simpson was pointing wildly as he shouted. "They're running." Simpson had proven to be a valuable aide, but he was a bit too excitable. Taylor knew it was a lack of experience, even though the sergeant had been two years onplanet. To Jake Taylor, almost everyone on Erastus was a rookie.

Taylor stood still, not even bothering to look. His NIS had recorded every aspect of the battle his eyes had witnessed and his ears had heard. Jake could remember every rock, every fold in the ground, every com message verbatim...for that matter, every smell too. He knew what was happening on the battlefield. He'd seen it enough times. The Machines were nothing if not predictable. He'd compromised their position and they were withdrawing. Like always.

They weren't defeated...not yet. The Machines were resilient. They followed their standardized tactics with an almost frightening regularity. They weren't afraid; they weren't running. Their basic tactical training told them to pull back from a compromised position and regroup, and that is what they were doing.

"They're not running, Simpson." Taylor's voice was

calm, almost disinterested. "They're pulling back to regroup on the higher ground to the south." Which is just where I want them, he thought.

Rigid adherence to basic tactical doctrine could be effective when facing an average commander. The Machines didn't make many mistakes, and their maneuvers were always flawlessly executed. But against a leader like Jake Taylor, predictability was suicidal.

Taylor directed a thought to his NIS, activating the com. After five years he was finally getting used to the fact that his thoughts could manage more equipment than what he'd been born with. "Lieutenant Simone, move your strikeforce to intercept the enemy and block their retreat." He paused, just for an instant, then added, "The same coordinates we discussed previously." A little reminder never hurt. He turned back toward Simpson. "The main force will pursue at once."

"Yes, sir." The aide stood rigidly erect and snapped off a salute before turning and running off to execute the order.

Taylor sighed softly. The formality around him had increased considerably in the last five years, as his rank continued to rise. He hated all the saluting and military pomp. He was a soldier now in every fiber of his being, almost nothing left of the naïve country boy who wanted nothing more than to live on the farm and write. But he still craved simplicity and straightforwardness...that part of him had survived.

When he was a sergeant he'd longed for the days on the farm back home. Now, he just wished he was still leading his section, with no responsibility beyond watching his 40 or so men and following the lieutenant's orders. He didn't want to command, didn't seek any glory. He did what he was ordered to do...and what he knew would help those kids still coming through that hated Portal. But every salute and every "sir" grated on him.

Jake had been a Five Year Man when was selected as the first participant in the Supersoldier program. Now he had been on Erastus for a decade. He'd been called a Ten Year Man a couple times, though the phrase was rarely used, probably because there were so few soldiers who qualified. Almost no one lasted that long in hell.

He wasn't sure what was worse, the stupid awestruck look in the eyes of the rookies or the obviously insincere respect he got from the UN Command staff. Jake was a field officer and one of the heroes of the war on Erastus, but he was still a lifer, and he had more in common with the rank and file footsoldiers than the politically-connected UN staffers and senior commanders.

"Jake...Simone's people are in place. I reinforced him with an extra ten HHVs." Jake enjoyed the causal familiarity of Blackie's voice. There was war and chains of command and military hierarchy, but Tony Black wasn't part of that to Jake. He was like a brother...more than a brother. "We're gonna catch these bastards in one hell of a kill zone, Dog."

There was a bloodthirstiness in Black's voice, one most of the men shared. They hated the Machines, rejoiced at their destruction. Taylor had felt that way once too, but the intense loathing was gone, replaced with fatigue, with uncomfortable apathy. Jake killed Machines because it was his job...and because destroying them saved his own men. But the bloodlust was gone.

"Thanks, Blackie. I think we've got them in a box." Taylor turned slowly and stared out over the battlefield. His cybernetic eyes focused rapidly, magnifying the image when his gaze fell on the withdrawing Machine formations. He felt an odd feeling, as he always did when his enhanced eyes locked on an image. It wasn't a shock, exactly…more of a tingling sensation. He'd found it quite unpleasant at first, but now he was so used to it he hardly noticed.

"And Blackie?"

"Yeah, Jake?"

Taylor took a quick breath. "I want some more cover on the flanks. We're going to have them bracketed, but they can still try to slip out to the side, especially the east. That's their last open line of retreat." He paused, reviewing the order of battle in his head. He'd always been pretty good at remembering the important details of his commands, but with the NIS just under his temporal lobe, he could recite the height, weight, and marksmanship ratings of every man in the battalion. It was unquestionably a useful ability, but one that made him uncomfortable. Men weren't supposed to remember every last detail they heard or saw.

"Send Hank Daniels over there. That'll still leave most of Bear's people in reserve."

"It's done." Black hesitated. "I gave half of Spider's HHV crews to Simone, Jake. Should I steal some from Bear to replace them?"

Taylor thought for a few seconds, but he decided he didn't want to take anything else from Bear's reserves. Daniels would be fine, even light on HHVs. "No." He paused again. "And Blackie, make sure Spider knows this isn't a hold at all costs situation. If the Machines come his way, I want him to inflict as much damage as he can, but his priority is to minimize his own losses. I'm expecting the enemy to go in his direction, and I'm ready to deal with the ones that get through his line."

"No problem. I'll get the point across."

"Make sure you do, Blackie. Because we both know Hank will fight to the last man otherwise." Taylor's voice was firm, commanding. He wasn't about to get any more of his boys killed than was absolutely necessary. UN Central didn't care how many men he lost as long as he won the battle, but Taylor sure as hell did. Daniels was a close friend and an excellent officer, but his aggressiveness sometimes got the better of him.

"I'll handle him, Jake. Don't worry. There was a brief pause then, "Black out."

Jake switched the com. "Captain MacArthur?"

"Yes, Major. How can I help you?" The squadron commander's response was crisp and proper, but Jake could detect the same undercurrent of superiority as always. He was continually amazed how those with return tickets to Earth considered themselves superior to lifers like his men and him. He wondered if MacArthur knew how effortlessly his augmented muscles could drive his hand through the pilot's breastbone and rip out his heart.

"Get your birds up in the air in ten minutes, Captain." Taylor's voice was, imperious, commanding. More than one can play that game, he thought. He didn't like to get into staredowns with arrogant fools, but sometimes he couldn't help himself. "The enemy will be retreating to the east. I want you over there to pick off the survivors. It's wide open ground. You should be able to just about wipe them out."

"I don't know, Major. We can't know where they will head. Maybe we should stay in a more centralized position."

There it was again…the arrogance. Jake felt a flash of heat behind his neck…one noticeable even in the relentless inferno of Erastus. He was angry, sick of putting up with bullshit from assholes like MacArthur. "You will follow my commands to the letter, Captain…or I will find you when this operation is over, and I will shoot you myself. Do we understand each other…Captain?"

"Yes sir, Major." MacArthur's reply was sullen. "We will lift in 9 minutes 30, as ordered."

Taylor knew the snotty shithead was pissed, and he couldn't help but smile. He cut the line without another word. You know a war's been going on too long, he thought, when you want to kill people on your own side more than the enemy.

"OK, boys. Here they come." Hank Daniels was lying on his stomach, his enhanced eyes focused on the approaching enemy. "Remember, we're going to drop as many of them as we can, but the ones we don't get...we let them break through. Do not...I repeat, do not...engage in close combat. Our priority is to minimize our own casualties. If the enemy approaches your position, you are to withdraw." Daniels tried to issue the order coldly and unemotionally, but he ended up sounding like he'd just tasted something bad. He trusted Taylor's judgment implicitly, and Blackie had made Jake's orders exceedingly clear. But it still ran against his grain to let any of the enemy go when he had a chance to wipe them out. To Hank Daniels, every battle was a fight to the death. He'd been torn from his life and family and sent to an alien hell...all because of the enemy. The Machines and their Tegeri masters were good for one thing in Daniels' mind, and only one. Killing.

His assault rifle was slung, unused, over his back. Instead, he held a heavy Gauss gun, the long, thick barrel stretching over a meter in front of him. He shifted his body so he wasn't lying on the heavy cable that connected the magnetic coilgun to the power supply on his exoskeletal attachments. The weapon was far too heavy for a normal soldier to manage, but Daniel's enhanced muscles and powerful exos allowed him to handle it with ease.

"Mortar crews..." Daniels had his strikeforce's own

mortar, plus a second one Black had stolen from Bear Samuels' group to reinforce him. "...commence firing."

Barely a second or two passed before Daniels' cybernetic ears picked up the whistling sound of two shells heading for the enemy line. The mortars were using enhanced plasma rounds, and each shot packed a heavy punch.

The first two rounds landed short, erupting with blinding flashes about 100 meters ahead of the approaching enemy. The second shots were right on target, and a dozen of the Machines were caught in the kill zones and engulfed by the expanding, superhot plasmas.

The Machines were moving east in a tight formation, driven that way by the pincers closing around them from every other direction. Now they scattered, trying to minimize their vulnerability to the mortar fire. But the whole force was trapped in a narrow defile, with minimal room to extend their formation.

"Gauss guns and HHVs...prepare to open fire." Daniels had ten of the magnetic autoguns, all in the hands of crack shots. Normally, the strikeforce commander wouldn't handle one of the heavy weapons, but Daniels had come up as a sniper, and there wasn't a better shot in the battalion. And he wanted every hit he could get before he let the survivors through.

"Fire!" The word was barely out of his mouth when his finger depressed the trigger. The Gauss gun was firing on full auto, but Daniels' didn't need it...his shots were all spot on. His targets didn't just drop, they practically ceased to exist as 5 or 10 hyper-velocity projectiles tore them apart.

Up and down the line his people were raking the approaching enemy, inflicting enormous casualties. Normally, he'd have kept some of his assets in reserve, but he wanted to take every shot he could get before he was forced to withdraw. He'd follow his orders, but Jake's command didn't prevent him from doing everything he could to drop as many of the enemy as possible before he bugged out. The Machines were firing back, but it was light and sporadic. They'd already been in a fight, and they were disordered and low on ammunition.

"Keep firing until I give the order to withdraw." Daniels would never disobey Taylor, but he was going to push it to the limit.

He'd put down at least 20 of the Machines already, and he kept firing as quickly as he could pick out targets. He was really liking the Gauss gun. The weapon wasn't a new one, but it hadn't been a battlefield success until recently. It packed too much recoil for a man to effectively handle, and it needed a heavy power supply that was hard to move in the field. Both problems were neatly solved when the Supersoldier program started implanting artificial muscle fibers and installing exos on troopers. A soldier with mods could easily manage the Gauss gun's kick, making it an extremely effective, yet highly portable weapon. And the powered exoskeleton had no trouble at all mounting the coilgun's power unit.

"HHV crews, focus your fire on the flanks. Let's force these fuckers to bunch up in the center." With the added firepower of the Gauss guns, Daniels could divert his HHVs to drive the enemy where he wanted them. The Machines were getting close, but he still had time. He could take out a few…

"Hank, it's Jake." Taylor's voice was loud and a little distorted on Daniels' implanted com unit. He sounded a little odd…almost amused.

"Jake…I was gonna pull back in…"

"Pull back now, Hank." Taylor was trying to suppress a laugh. "I know you don't like leaving the web, Spider, but I've got this covered. MacArthur's birds are ready to hit them as soon as your people are clear." He paused. "Ya killed enough, buddy. Just get the hell out of there so the Dragonfires can hose them down. Then we can all go home." What passed for home, at least.

Daniels smiled. He hated the idea of not taking out as many of the enemy as possible...but if someone else was going to kill them, he figured he could share the honor. "Got it, Jake." He took one last shot, targeting a cluster of three Machines and taking them all down. "We're on the way."

MacArthur looked down at the field. The Machines were fleeing in disarray...and there were a lot fewer of them that he'd expected. He hated to admit it, but that obnoxious prick Taylor knew his shit. There was nothing left for his people to do but mop up.

"Raptor 05 and Raptor 06, assume covering position." His squadron had driven off the enemy air support before the ground forces went in, and the scope was clear of any contacts. But Machine stealth technology was strong, and MacArthur wasn't about to risk getting caught with his pants down. He knew he'd be expected to explain the loss of any Dragonfires and, if he was going to take casualties, he wanted something better to say than, "I got ambushed by enemy gunships because I was careless."

"Raptors 01, 02, 03, 04, commence attack run." He angled his ship, pulling back on the antigrav output, descending sharply. "These fuckers are disorganized and out in the open. Let's take 'em down."

The Dragonfire gunboats were bristling with weapons. Each boat had six U-270 "Chainsaw" guns designed to intercept incoming missiles and ordnance. MacArthur's squadron had engaged the enemy air support earlier, and they'd won total superiority over the battlefield. With the Machines disordered and in wholesale retreat, they were getting only spotty antiaircraft fire from the ground, and the Chainsaws intercepted it all almost effortlessly.

The four ships came across the field at perpendicular to the enemy line of retreat. Each Dragonfire mounted ten heavy autoguns, and they strafed the field as they flew across. The massive hypervelocity rounds almost disintegrated anything they touched, tearing Machine bodies to shreds.

"Reposition for second attack run." MacArthur's voice was loud, feral. He hated the enemy with a raging passion. His grandparents had been scientists, and volunteers on one of the early colonial expeditions. They'd been slaughtered by the Machines, just like every other human being on New Earth. MacArthur hadn't even been born, but hatred for the Tegeri and their creations ran hot in his family.

The massive gunships angled up slightly, coming around 90 degrees to hit the enemy along their line of retreat. Flying an antigrav was a lot easier than a plane or copter... at least once you got used to it. Altitude was controlled almost totally by the power fed into the antigravity generators, and the overall piloting had a much more two dimensional feel to it.

"Arm EFAs." The enhanced fuel-air explosives were an area effect weapon, designed to cover a large section of ground with an intensely hot fireball. The EFA's were like Napalm on steroids, and they were extremely effective at clearing out sections of a battlefield.

MacArthur stared straight ahead as his gunboat headed for the approaching enemy. The Machines didn't panic, at least not the same way humans did. But they could evaluate threats and respond appropriately. They were running now...scattering and trying to flee anywhere they could. It might not be a rout, at least technically, but it damned sure looked like one.

"Sergeant..." MacArthur didn't turn to face his gunnery chief, didn't even move a muscle as he gave the order...he just stared at the enemy survivors 100 meters below helplessly trying to flee the death he was bringing them. "...commence EFA drop."

As soon as the last of the ordnance dropped, MacArthur increased the antigrav power, arcing the gunboat up and away from the inferno it had just unleased. The billowing flames reached 100 meters into the sky, and the explosions obliterated everything in an 80 meter wide swath across the plain below. MacArthur checked the scanner. All four of his attacking boats had completed their runs. It was impossible to see anything on the ground but the flames. A wicked smile crossed his lips. He couldn't imagine how anything could have survived down there.

"MacArthur to Battalion Command. Attack run complete...destruction total. Raptor Squadron, returning to base." MacArthur took one last look back at the stricken field. He didn't like Jake Taylor...he didn't like him at all. But the man knew how to wage war.

# Chapter 10

From the Journal of Jake Taylor:

When I was home, I never gave much thought to the things my father complained about. I tried to keep him quiet, just as my mother did. We were both scared he'd end up at a reeducation facility. I heard it all, of course, over and over, but I never really thought much about what he was saying. He was always talking about obscure things...things I'd never heard anywhere else, topics it was hard to learn anything about.

It's easy to dismiss what you are told, to tune out the rantings you hear over and over. Almost everything my father said was contradicted by what I learned in school or saw on television. To believe what he was saying, I had to disregard virtually everything else I was taught. I had to ignore my teachers, the news...everything. It's easy to discount an extreme opinion, even when it's from someone close to you. Of course, just because a statement is extreme doesn't mean it's wrong. But that's not how it seems when you're listening to it, especially when you're 18 or 19, and you think you know everything. When you think you have your whole life ahead of you.

My years on Erastus have given me lots of time to think. War consists of short bursts of intense effort and terror separated by long periods of boredom and inactivity. My father's rants don't seem so unfounded anymore.

I know UN Central can't be blamed for the Tegeri and the Machines. Indeed, a united mankind has been far more able to fight off the alien menace than a fractured and squabbling world could ever have managed. But now I think about the monitoring, the assembly restrictions, the endless list of rules and regulations, the seemingly random enforcement of sometimes draconian laws. Now I wonder why all that was necessary. I started to think about the things I was taught in school, and the more I thought, the more questions I had. I understood the need for mankind to stand together and face the Tegeri, but I started to realize that didn't explain everything. It didn't even come close. Now I question how I ever thought it did.

Pre-Consolidation history is a heavily proscribed topic, and back then I generally believed the official texts, just like everyone else. Everyone but the old-timers like my father. The government can rewrite the history books and tell as many lies as it wants...but it can't erase the memories of living people. Or perhaps it can...perhaps that is what the reeducation camps are for.

I wish I could see my father again, talk to him, truly listen this time. He had so much to teach me, so much life experience...and I threw away the chance to learn. He'd lived through incredible times, but no one would listen to what he had to say. I was young and stupid, and I thought everything I'd been taught at school and heard on the media was true. I regret it. I regret it all.

"I must congratulate you on the continued success of the Supersoldier program on Erastus." Anan Keita stood next to Kazan, wearing a finely-crafted black suit. His expression was solemn, even mournful, as befitted the funeral of a member of the UN Secretariat. It was a mask, however, the kind he'd worn so often in his tenure at UN Central...a career that saw him rise from a low-level operative to the verge of a Seat on the Secretariat. Raj Patel had been Secretary of Military Affairs since the Consolidation, and that meant he'd been in Keita's way for at least the last decade. Keita had waited with growing frustration as the sick old fool took his sweet time about dying.

"Thank you, sir." Kazan often called Keita 'Mr. Secretary,' but the obsequious exaggeration seemed misplaced at the previous Secretary's funeral. "Progress on Erastus has outstripped our most optimistic projections." Kazan caught himself speaking too loudly and lowered his voice. "As you know, the original tactical plan set forth a 40-year timetable for total pacification. We are currently in year 12, and I have just completed the newest modeling."

Keita was looking forward, pretending to listen to the protracted eulogies and glancing only occasionally toward Kazan. He was getting impatient with his subordinate's pointless chatter, but his eyes opened wider when Kazan mentioned the projections. He was extremely anxious for the revised tactical estimates, and he hadn't expected them for at least another few days. "What is your current timeframe for completing the conquest of the planet?" He spoke softly, but he couldn't hide his interest.

"Five years, sir." Kazan was still whispering, but the excitement was obvious in his voice.

Keita had been looking straight ahead as he listened, but now he turned his head and stared at his subordinate. "Five years? Are you certain?" He was a master at containing and disguising his emotions, but he couldn't hide all his excitement. This was incredible news…and it couldn't have come at a better time. Keita was the logical choice to succeed Patel to the Secretary's office, but in politics you could never be sure. This would clinch it. No one could challenge him. His political enemies would have to retreat. Keita had been acting-Secretary for five years, and under his supervision, the Supersoldier program had been a stunning success. The implications of a rollout beyond Erastus were staggering. Keita had a fleeting thought – might he ride this triumph not only to the top of the Military Secretariat, but ultimately to the Secretary General's chair itself?

Kazan couldn't keep the smile off his face. "Yes, sir. We ran it through the central planning computer three times with identical results. I have the findings and all the supporting documentation. No one will be able to contest the projection."

Keita saw the obnoxious smile on Kazan's face. The news was good for both of them. Kazan wanted the under-secretary's seat that Keita would be leaving. The little worm would sell his grandmother for that promotion, Keita thought. He felt derision for his grasping underling, even as his own lust for the Secretary's chair was no less consuming. But he knew there was no way to deny Kazan the step up. And he had to admit the creepy little bastard had earned it. He'd done a superb job on selecting the pilot specimens for the program…and they had done the rest. Keita had always been amused by the soldiers…at the superhuman efforts a pat on the head and a flag to follow could generate from ordinary men. They are simple, he thought, but useful tools nonetheless.

"I have a Secretariat meeting tomorrow, and I want to be prepared. They will undoubtedly wish to explore expansion options for the program." Keita was speaking softly, trying not to draw attention to himself. It wouldn't serve his purposes to offend anyone, certainly not before he was formally confirmed. No one had really liked Patel, and he seriously doubted anyone cared that the old fuck had finally died. But he had been a Secretary, and the bureaucracy required respect for the position, not the man.

"I will have the data ready for you first thing in the morning, sir." Kazan spoke quietly as well, his eyes focused forward, watching as the 7th or 8th dignitary began speaking about the life of Raj Patel. Kazan couldn't wait to get away and go back to his office. He and his staff would be up all night as it was, but he didn't mind. Supersoldier had been his project, and he was going to see it through. And ride it as far as it could take him.

"So you see, gentlemen, not only has the rate of pacification increased almost 350%, but this has been accomplished with a corresponding 55% reduction in casualties." Keita stood at the head of the polished teak table, addressing the assembled Secretariat of the UN, the 14 men who ruled the world...currently 13 men and one empty chair. Keita was still acting-Secretary, at least officially. He'd been nominated to succeed Patel, but the wheels of bureaucracy moved slowly. He knew he had six votes locked up, so he only needed one of the others...and the news he was delivering today had a good chance of delivering him a unanimous appointment.

"Your report is very impressive, Under-Secretary." Anton Samovich was Secretary of Internal Security and generally considered the number two man on the council, after the Secretary General. "It is not my intention to catch you unprepared, but do you feel you can offer some insight on how quickly the program can be rolled out to the other Portal worlds?"

Keita suppressed a smile. He'd wondered for some time if Samovich was a potential ally. The wily old Secretary was unpredictable and hard to read, but he was a formidable force to have on your side. Now he had his answer. Samovich knew very well Keita would have the data he requested. He was providing a chance for Keita to elaborate on his success.

"Certainly, Secretary Samovich." Keita spoke deliberatively, making sure to keep any trace of arrogance out of his voice…anything that might offend anyone. Now wasn't the time to be careless, and he was well aware of the size and the volatile nature of some of the egos in the room. If Samovich was in his corner, he had a great shot at a unanimous confirmation vote. He'd take the chair any way he could get it, but if he squeaked in, he'd have a target on his back from day one. With all 13 votes, he'd have a lot more freedom to pursue his agenda. "We have examined the situation from two perspectives, depending on the aggressiveness the Secretariat wishes to employ." He glanced around the room, adding the body language to back up his faked, but convincing, respectful deference to the Secretaries.

Samovich nodded. "I believe we should examine both options. I am certain we can consider the pros and cons for each approach."

Keita waited until he was sure Samovich was done. "We can certainly implement the Supersoldier program on a single additional world fairly quickly." He moved his eyes up and down the table, looking at each of the Secretaries in turn. "Constructing a new production and implanta-tion facility will take a minimum of six months, including transport time through the Portal." Half a year was a tight schedule, but Keita was sure he could make it work if he had to. "While construction is underway, we can select our initial candidates from the forces currently engaged."

"And if we wish to extend the program simultaneously to all currently disputed Portal worlds?" It was a new voice. Chang Li was Secretary of Finance, and probably the third most powerful member of the Secretariat, after Samovich and the Secretary General. And a world-class prick, Keita thought. He tried to maintain good relations with all the council members, but if he had an enemy lurking out there,

Keita knew it would be Chang.

Keita paused, carefully considering his response. "Simultaneous introduction on all disputed worlds would be an enormous project, Secretary Chang, and the costs involved would be astronomical. Probably exceeding any…"

"But it funding were made available, Mr. Keita, how long would your people require to implement." Chang again, interrupting.

"In that case, I would estimate a minimum of five years to reach full implementation." Keita had no idea…he was pulling guesses out of his ass. He'd never considered a project on the scale Chang was suggesting. It was unfeasible at best, impossible at worst. It would require an investment exceeding gross world product, and there weren't enough specialists available with the required skills. It was a stupid hypothetical being floated by an arrogant ass for reasons Keita couldn't quite divine…at least not yet. "Just training a sufficient number of personnel would be an enormous project. And the investment required would be truly enormous, far beyond the scope of any project yet undertaken."

"I don't think we need to consider such a massive expansion anyway." It was Samovich. He glared at Chang as he spoke. There was something going on between the two, some kind of dispute. That much was clear. "I believe we are in agreement that the ongoing struggle with the Tegeri serves a valid social purpose, one that it is in our best interests to continue for the foreseeable future." Samovich's department was responsible for maintaining order in a world that just 30 years before had been divided into almost 200 separate, often warring nations. Much of the propaganda continually pumped out by his ministries was based on the alien threat. If sustaining that useful crisis cost an annual toll of dead soldiers, so be it. "Accelerating our progress is a useful goal, however total victory is not desirable."

"We are not all in agreement on that." Chang again, challenging Samovich directly. "There are other ways to control the masses. And the potential to exploit the full technology of the Portal worlds unhampered is extraordinary."

"Enough." The Secretary General's voice was deep and commanding. He was getting older, and perhaps it was a little weaker, hoarser than it had once been. But one word was enough to silence the room. Raul Esteban was the most powerful man in the world, Secretary General of the UN, chief executive of UN Central. His demeanor was always flawlessly measured and professional, but his ruthlessness and brutality were well known, at least among the inner circle.

"We are not going to have that debate at this time. Mr. Keita is here to brief us on the status of the Supersoldier program, a project he appears to have handled quite well."

Keita had been listening respectfully, but he had to catch himself when Esteban mentioned him. I have the Secretary General, he thought excitedly. Esteban's support made his elevation to Secretary a dead certainty.

"I suggest we focus on the matter of reasonable expansion for now." When Raul Esteban used the word 'suggest,' everyone present took it as a command. "We should not take any more of Mr. Keita's time than we require. I am sure he has much to do, since he will likely be assuming the Military Affairs portfolio formally in the near future."

The room was silent for a few seconds. "Thank you, Your Excellency." Keita managed to speak in a calm and relaxed tone, though every bit of it was false. The Secretary General had as much as promised him the elevation. He was about to become a member of the Secretariat. Get control of yourself, Keita, he thought nervously…don't screw up now.

"Your Excellency, esteemed Secretaries…if you will indulge me, I will try to provide some meaningful insight into the details of expanding the program at various rates." He glanced at Esteban, who nodded ever so slightly. "If you gentlemen will refer to page 11 in the reports I have provided, we can begin."

# Chapter 11

From the Journal of Jake Taylor:

I had friends back home. Not a lot of them, but a few good ones. My enlistment turned them into one more group of people sharing a tearful goodbye. I still think of those guys from time to time, remembering things we did together...how close we were. In my mind, they're still my friends, though I know that's just something I tell myself. Is an old buddy still a friend when you haven't seen or talked to him for years? Or even exchanged a letter? Would I really know any of them if I saw them again? Would they know me?

I want to think it wouldn't matter, that we'd all go back to where we left off...but I know that's a fool's dream. I'm dead to them...I died a long time ago. The Jake Taylor who remains - jaded soldier and half machine – would be a stranger. Oh, they would embrace me and act as if nothing had happened. But the closeness, the brotherhood we used to share? I know that is gone forever. Better that they never see me. Let them remember me as I was...as one of them.

I have new friends now. They're all soldiers...condemned men like me. We share a fate, and we stand together in battle. As tight as I was with my friends back home, I've never experienced anything like the closeness I feel toward these men. I can't imagine how I would survive the blood and pain and death without them.

They all look at me like a rock, some kind of invincible robot...the man who'd survived Erastus for a decade. But I'm not any of that; I'm just a man...and a worn out, sad, exhausted one at that. Sometimes I wish I could tell them how much I hurt inside, how bone tired and soul sick I really am. I wish I could make sure they understand how important their support and companionship is for me, how it is the only thing that keeps me going. But I can't. They need me as that invincible monolith; I have to stay strong... to perpetuate the stupid legend, the Ten Year Man. I have to do it for them...and for the rest of the troops. They draw their strength from me, and I have to maintain the illusion. I have no real strength left to give them.

The burden of command is like nothing I've ever experienced. Back home, the closest I came to being responsible for anyone else was watching my little brother. Now, my decisions determine whether men live or die. Sometimes they die no matter what I do...though I never know for sure. Would they have survived if I'd made a different choice, if I'd read the situation better?

My closest friends here...they're an odd group. Me, the New England farmboy. Blackie, the inner city gang banger. Bear Samuels, the gentle giant from Alabama. Karl Young, Hank Daniels...every one of these guys is closer than a brother to me, yet beyond the endless war we fight, we have little in common with each other.

Now we share something else, something new...one more thing that makes us a unique fraternity. We're all cyborgs now. They get annoyed with me when I use that word. Men try to hold on to their humanity any way they can. But what else can you call us? I can run as fast as a horse, jump 6 meters straight up. I can read a computer screen from 100 meters. My hearing, my strength... everything is enhanced. There's even a computer in my brain, one I control with thoughts (or does it control me?). I can't play a sport with another human being, or a game, not one where my opponent has any chance of winning. I thought it was a lonely, detached feeling being sent to Erastus, away from everything I knew. Now I even wonder if I am a man anymore.

I can't argue that the changes have made it easier to survive. My friends have all made it through the last five years since we got the mods...because we got them. All except Tom Warner...and he took at least 50 Machines down with him before they got him.

I miss Longbow, but I am grateful the rest of the group managed to survive. We've all been wounded...and every one of us would have been dead by now without the mods. Our systems are different now. When we get hit, our bodies are flooded with nanobots that immediately begin repairing the damage. I can actually watch a small cut heal if I stare at it carefully, seeing it close up before my eyes. And even major wounds are mended before they can become life-threatening. If I'm not killed outright by a wound, I will almost certainly survive it.

It is a gift, but also a curse. I'm not sure men were meant to live so long in a place like this. We all have survival instincts, but I wonder if they don't lead us astray sometimes. Perhaps we shouldn't try so hard to escape death. Perhaps, for us, death is a reprieve...a gift.

"Alright, Jake. Out with it." Taylor hadn't noticed Blackie walking into the room behind him. "You've been moping around for weeks." He walked over and sat next to Jake. "So what's getting to you, pal? 'Cause you're the strongest one around here, and if you lose it, we're all fucked."

Jake didn't answer right away. He just sat quietly, not moving at all. Black knew Taylor better than anyone, understood his body language, his subtle expressions. He didn't look at Jake, didn't say anything. He just sat there for a minute or two, waiting until Taylor was ready to talk.

"Don't worry about me, Blackie." Taylor's voice was distant, distracted. "It's nothing, brother. Just thinking."

"Fuck you, my friend. Just thinking? Who the hell do you think you're talking to?" Black's voice was gentle but also firm. He wasn't going to let Jake wiggle his way out of a long talk, superior officer or not. "So, are you going to tell me, or are we both going to sit here and stare at the wall?"

Taylor sighed, and then a brief smile crossed his lips. Black was the closest friend he'd ever had. Sometimes, he'd have sworn the little shit could read his mind. "Honestly, Blackie. It's nothing in particular. Just thinking. About home. About the war."

Black sighed. "I know, Jake. This place gets us all down. But you have to remember the code. This is home for us. There's no point thinking about everything that is gone. Laying around here, mooning about mom's apple pie or taking Mary Jane Funbags out into the barn for a romp isn't gonna help. It'll eat away at you from the inside, Dog." Black reached out and put his hand on Taylor's shoulder. "I know all that is harder on you. Home for me was a shithole…different than this one, but no better…not really." Black's normally coarse tone had become gentle, sympathetic. "You had more to lose."

Taylor smiled. "You're a good friend, Blackie. The best I ever had." He paused for a few seconds. "But that's not what I'm thinking about. I said my goodbyes to home long ago." That wasn't entirely true, he supposed, but close enough. "I'm just wondering about what we're fighting for…why we do it."

Black had an amused look on his face. "You mean besides the fact that they'll shoot us for desertion if we don't?"

Taylor let out a short laugh. "Do you really care,

Blackie? Do I? How long has it been since you really cared about living? What do we live for anyway? Another day in hell? Another battle…out on the burning sands or on some blasted plateau?"

Black let out a deep breath. "To protect Earth." He paused. "To save everyone back home from the Machines. Better we fight them here than in New Hampshire…or Philly or New York."

"Yes, I know. I've heard it all before. Hell, I've said it all at least a thousand times." He hesitated, looking down at the floor. "Why didn't they just nuke the Portals?"

"What?" Black had a confused expression on his face. "What are you talking about?"

Jake was still staring at the ground. "If the Machines are such a threat to mankind, why didn't they just destroy the Portals on Earth…lock the Machines out." Black was just staring at Taylor. "I know it would have been a huge scientific loss, but we have men fighting and dying on almost 40 planets now, and people starving at home because of the massive cost of it all. Is it worth it?"

Taylor looked at Black, saw the confusion, the surprise. This was something they'd never discussed before. "So when they say we're fighting for Earth, that's bullshit. Isn't it? We're fighting so they can exploit the science and technology on the Portal worlds. I'm not saying that's not a good thing, but fighting to save the race sounds a lot better, doesn't it?"

Black didn't have an answer. For any of it. He'd never considered what Jake was talking about. His perspective on things tended to be grittier, less philosophical than Taylor's. "Whatever, Jake. You may be right about all that. But we fight for those boys coming through that Portal. Because whatever you and I think, they're still gonna keep coming." He blurted it out loudly. "Those stupid, clueless kids who couldn't manage to stick their hand down their pants without help." He stared at Taylor, a hint of desperation in his face…a need for Taylor to agree, to understand…to acknowledge at least one reason their sacrifices weren't in vain. "Do you know how many of them you've saved in ten years, Jake?"

"Have I? Have I saved any of them? Or just pushed their deaths back a few months, or a year? Have any of them gone home, Blackie? How can you save someone from death when they're already in hell?"

Black just looked at Taylor. He didn't know what to say…or what to think. Everything Jake said was true. It was stuff they all knew but never let themselves think about. But Taylor's defenses had crumbled. He was thinking the unthinkable, about the things that could destroy him, rip from him the fragile false hope the veterans of Erastus created for themselves. Black was really beginning to worry about his friend.

The two sat quietly for a few minutes, each deep in his own thoughts. Finally, Black broke the silence. "Jake, I can't give you the answers you want…I'm not sure anybody can." He sucked in a lungful of air and exhaled it slowly. "But you're my friend. You make this place more bearable for me…for all the guys. And you're right…we're all lost men, condemned." His voice was thick with emotion. "But I don't want to die, Jake. Not yet. I can't explain why I want to live. It's not hope. Maybe it's just pure animal self-preservation instinct. But if you make one day something I can live through…I am grateful for that. If you save my life so I can live another month, year, whatever… I'm grateful for that too. Even if I live that extra time on this shithole of a planet with no hope of anything better."

Taylor moved his eyes slowly upward toward Black's. "Thanks, Blackie. I'd have never made it this far without you and the guys either." His voice was wistful but sincere as well. He let out a hard sigh. "Don't worry about me, old friend. I'm just having a bad day."

Black stared back at Taylor, a suspicious look on his face. "Are you sure, Jake? It feels like there's something else bothering you." He paused, staring inquisitively at his companion. "I'm here for you. You know that."

Taylor smiled, reaching out and lightly slapping Black on the shoulder. "I'm alright. Just feeling like a whiny little bitch today." He held the smile for a few seconds. "Don't worry about me. Like I said, I'm just having a bad day."

"You sure you don't want me to stay? I was going to go over this month's logistics report, but that can wait."

"No, I'm OK." Taylor looked over at Black. "Really. I just need some quiet."

Black stood slowly. "OK, Dog." He turned and started toward the door, still clearly worried. "Call me if you want to talk. Or just hang."

"I will."

Black nodded and opened the door.

"Hey Blackie."

Black stooped and turned around. "Yeah, Jake?"

"Did you ever know someone who went to a reeducation facility?" Taylor looked intently at his friend, the fragile smile gone.

"Sure, I guess." Black was staring back at Jake. "A few."

Taylor spoke softly, almost without emotion. "Did you ever know one who came back?"

The room was silent.

# Chapter 12

From the Journal of Jake Taylor:

Strategy and tactics.  Two words that are often used – incorrectly – as synonyms.  In reality, they are two very distinct things, managed by entirely different personnel within a military organization.

The science of tactics is grittier, closer to the ground. Tactics is about how to achieve specific objectives.  Generally more focused than strategy, it can still vary enormously in scope.  Five men deciding how to take a hill is tactics.  An army of 10,000 planning a major battle...that is tactics too.

I knew nothing about tactics when I walked through the Portal; in fact, I knew almost nothing military at all.  But when they put me in the line, I just seemed to understand somehow.  It was normal to me, right from the beginning, like it was all just common sense that anyone could see. Then I began to realize that things that were obvious to me were complex and difficult for many of my comrades. I could tell good ground from bad...my instincts on when to attack, when to pull back...they seemed to be right most of the time.

Tactics is like art...you can train someone, teach them all the fundamentals, but you can only make them good, never great.  There's something inside that makes a natural tactician.  If you don't have it, you can learn, but you'll never become more than unimaginatively competent. The Machines are like that. They know everything we do, but they just don't have that spark to maximize it. They know how to maneuver; they don't do stupid things...but they're limited, predictable. Given anywhere close to comparable numbers and resources, I can beat them every time.

Strategy is different. I use tactics to win an individual engagement. The high command uses strategy to decide when and where I should fight that battle. Strategy is the science of managing part or all of an entire conflict...or even a series of wars taking place over many years. For example, UNFE HQ has a strategy for pacifying Erastus. The commanding officers direct troops all over the planet, with the ultimate goal of searching out and capturing the Machine production centers. When the last one is taken or destroyed, the war on Erastus will be over.

Like with tactics, there are multiple levels of strategy, each dealing with successively larger problems. At the top, UN Central directs the overall strategy of mankind's war with the Tegeri. They allocate resources to the various planetary theaters, and they direct the development of new weapons and systems. Like the Supersoldier program. UN Central's strategic planning determines which planetary battle zones get more supplies. They decided to launch Supersoldier on Erastus. They could have done it on Frigida or Corealus or Oceanus, but for some reason, they picked us. That was a strategic decision.

The gift I possess for tactical operations never extended to strategy, or at least I was never placed in a situation where strategy was in my control. Large-scale logistics, planetary allocations of resources...I always felt such things were beyond my understanding. For years I didn't question any strategic directives. I just did my best to execute the orders given to me. I considered anything outside my immediate area of operations to be a waste of time. But recently I've begun to think about the bigger picture, and I don't like what I see. Things don't add up. There's more to UN Central's strategies than it appears at first glance…I've become certain of that. I'm starting to think we've all been lied to far more than we ever imagined.

Taylor stared at the enemy positions on his visor. He squinted, trying to get a good look at the flickering projection. He hit the controls and darkened the visor, trying to keep out the light so he could get a better view of the images. Both suns were up, and it was bright out, even for Erastus.

The drone feed could provide direct neural input to his NIS, but that was one of the mods that didn't work quite the way it was supposed to. He'd be able to see the images in his mind, but there were side effects, ones he didn't want to deal with in battle. He had 2 reinforced battalions to handle, and a battle to fight on difficult terrain. Now wasn't the time to risk dizziness, nausea, and disorientation. The visor projection would be just fine.

The terrain was worse even than he'd expected. The walls of the gorge rose almost 500 meters on both sides of the dry riverbed running along the bottom. The waterway that had cut its way hundreds of meters through the rocky ground had been dry for at least 50 million years according to the geologists. But its handiwork remained…a deep gash in the ground, running for over 20 kilometers. The whole stretch was difficult to traverse, with sheer cliffs in some spots dropping 350 meters or more.

It was called Devil's Claw Canyon. He thought, as he often did, about how this place got its name. Stupid, he thought…how do these spots end up getting such silly monikers? He didn't come up with a good answer; he never did. Men liked to name things…that was the most he ever deduced. The canyon didn't look anything like a claw… not from the ground, certainly, and not on the drone feeds from the air either. He could only assume some grunt had imagined it looked like something the devil might have scraped into the ground with his claw. That wasn't a very good explanation either, but it was the best he could come up with. The devil and other hellish images were always popular for naming conventions on Erastus. That never surprised Taylor...the place was as close to a vision of hell as his mind had ever conjured.

In ten years, Taylor had never been sent anywhere on Erastus that didn't already have a name. He wondered how many more years he'd have to fight before he got to give someplace its title. Probably never. Maybe it was the prerogative of those first waves coming through a Portal into the teeth of an entrenched enemy. If so, he thought, it's the least those poor bastards deserve. Taylor knew it was rough when UN Central first invaded a new Portal world. He didn't know just how bad, but he'd heard a few rumors he wished he could forget. Though UNFE denied it, Jake had been told more than once that the life expectancy for newbs during the first month of the war on Erastus had been 31 hours.

He shook himself out of his daydream and focused again on the data feed from the drones. It wouldn't last much longer...they'd put up a dozen of the sophisticated aircraft, but there were only two left. As soon as the enemy targeted that last pair, he'd be blind again. He could launch another spread, but his supply was limited, and he wasn't planning to burn them all this early.

His objective was the bottom of the canyon. It was the only route within 3,000 klicks that offered terrain passable for a large force...and it led directly toward the largest Machine factory yet discovered on the planet. The ground closer to the enemy base was rugged, too broken for transports to land. The only practical avenue of attack was a march right through the canyon.

But the riverbed was perfect ambush country too, and the enemy was dug in all along both sides of the canyon. Taylor and his people had to clear them out completely and take undisputed control of the heights, or any force moving through would be hit from both flanks and destroyed.

"They're really dug in there, Blackie." Taylor's voice was grim. A lot of his boys were going to die in the next few hours.

He stood quietly for a minute, maybe two, then he let out a loud sigh. "Alright, Blackie…sitting around here's not going to accomplish anything. Let's kick off this dance. Send in the Dragonfires." Taylor's people were only getting one pass from the gunships. The canyon was a deathtrap for antigravs making low-level attacks…and the battlefield was too constricted for effective higher altitude support. Long-range fire would hit as many friendlies as enemies once the battle was underway.

Black switched on his com. "Raptor, Condor squadrons…commence attack run. Blackhawk squadron, assume covering position." That was 12 gunships inbound, weapons blazing…and six more protecting them from enemy air units.

"Frantic's strike forces will move out under cover of the bombardment." Lieutenant "Frantic" Young was leading two reinforced strikeforces set to move up the north side of the canyon. The ground was less steep there, and his people were going to climb up and hit the enemy flank. Taylor paused, waiting while Black relayed that order as well.

"When do we grab the heights?" Black turned and looked right at Taylor. The 213th was dropping onto the edge of the canyon. Taylor and Black had a special affection for their old unit, though there weren't many guys left there from the old days.

Taylor hesitated. He was worried about the drop. The personal antigravs were a new system, never before tested in combat. If everything went according to plan, the strikeforce would jump from hovering transports, dropping slowly – and safely – to the ground as the antigrav harnesses slowed their descent. Tested or not, the drop was the only way he could get men up there quickly, so the 213th was going in no matter what.

"As soon as Frantic's boys are in place." He paused. "Then we drop onto the heights." He looked out over the field…in the direction of the main enemy position. "Then it's a fight to the death."

The Dragonfires streaked along the top of the canyon, moving at 800 mps. "Prepare for attack run." Captain MacArthur was edgy, more so than usual. This was a rough gauntlet for his gunships to run. They were going in low, flying below the edge of the canyon when they attacked. Their firepower at such close range would be enormous, but they'd be tightly packed, with no room to maneuver. They'd be easy targets to AA fire from the ground.

"Arm all weapons." They were only making one run, and MacArthur was going to make it count. Taylor's troops were coming in right after the air assault, and they needed his people to do as much damage as possible. He didn't envy the ground pounders this one. This was some of the worst terrain he'd ever seen.

MacArthur still didn't like Taylor, but he was finding it difficult not to at least respect the hardassed cyborg-soldier. Besides, he wouldn't put it past Taylor to track him down and settle things if his birds didn't give 100%. He'd almost certainly blame MacArthur for any extra casualties he suffered because the gunships did a half-assed job. And

MacArthur didn't want any piece of that kind of grief.

He stared at the command console. All 12 ships confirmed readiness. The drones had fed him the enemy positions, and the coordinates had been downloaded into the attack computers. Target visibility was terrible. It was almost impossible to pick out the Machine forces hidden among the rocks, so he was going to let the AIs handle the targeting.

"Squadrons, follow my mark." He grabbed the controls, easing off on the antigrav, dropping into the canyon. "Here we go." He was muttering softly, mostly to himself. He pulled back on the throttle, dropping to 400 mps. "Commence firing."

The autoguns opened up, raking the steep hillsides below with hyper-velocity fire. It wasn't like the last fight...that had been shooting fish in a barrel. But the enemy troops were saturated with fire nevertheless...even with their cover, they had to be taking heavy losses. It was hard to assess the damage, but MacArthur knew his people were hurting the enemy.

An alarm sounded in the cockpit. Incoming fire. MacArthur could see the missiles tracking on the scanning display. He banked the Dragonfire hard, angling its path away from the approaching ordnance. "We've got interdictive fire coming in," he shouted into the com. The missile zipped past, and MacArthur turned his ship back, moving toward his original course. "Keep your eyes open. And target launch sites for return fire."

He turned to his own gunner. "Take out those launchers, Sergeant." He angled the ship again, swerving to avoid another pair of incoming rockets. "Now."

"Yes, sir." Sergeant Toomey was a solid gunner...one of the best in the force. He was already targeting the enemy rocket batteries when MacArthur issued the order, and it wasn't more than a few seconds before the ship lurched hard....half a dozen sprint missiles launching, homing in on the ground batteries.

MacArthur turned his body 90 degrees, flipping the switches that armed the EFAs. He wanted Toomey focused on taking out missile sites, not dealing with the fuel air bombs. "All units, prepare to drop EFA's on my mark." He flipped the last switch, slaving all the drop controls to a single button. "Three...two...one...mark." He flipped the last control, and the ship pitched side to side as it dropped the full weight of its EFA complement.

The gunship raced along and slowly rose as MacArthur gunned the engines and started feeding power to the antigrav. He'd made it through. He looked at the scanner. There was nothing on the screen but a series of large white blooms, the massive heat signature of the inferno below. It was a straight line...all his people had dropped right on target, blanketing the entire enemy position with fiery death.

He fed more power to the antigrav, arcing his ship up and away from the gorge. One after another followed... eight...nine...ten. Ten. And then nothing.

"Raptor 05, report." There was nothing but staticky silence on the com. "Condor 03, report." Still nothing. "Raptor 5, Condor 3...report immediately." MacArthur was yelling, but there was still no answer.

Finally, a voice responded. "Raptor 01, this is Condor 04. I saw Condor 03 go down, sir." His voice was tentative, cracking. They crashed right into the firestorm, Captain."

MacArthur was silent for a few seconds. "Acknowledged, Condor 04." He was staring straight ahead, his right hand on the stick, his left balled hard into a fist. He'd never lost two birds in one battle. The Dragonfires were state of the art both offensively and defensively, and they outclassed anything the Machines had to throw at them. But the battles on Erastus were getting more intense. Taylor and the rest of the Supersoldiers had won a series of big victories, and the enemy was getting more and more desperate.

MacArthur took a deep breath. "Raptor and Condor squadrons, assume pre-programmed covering positions." His people had done their part to hit the Machine ground forces. Now they had to make sure no enemy air got through to Taylor's people.

"Alright, boys…on my mark…" Lieutenant Riley Bergen was leaning out of the transport, looking down 200 meters to the jagged edge of the canyon below. "…three, two, one…mark."

Bergen jumped through the open hatch of the transport. His body expected a gut-wrenching drop but, instead, he drifted slowly down. The antigrav was working. He turned and tried to look up, to confirm his people were dropping behind him. He caught a glimpse of a few of them, but he couldn't bend his head back far enough to get a good look.

His stomach jumped…the antigrav would keep him from smashing into the ground, but it was giving him a touch of motion sickness. It was an odd way to fall… unnatural. He looked down. The ground was still a good 150 meters below. His LZ was right along the rim of the canyon, but he was drifting south. Any farther and he'd come down in the gorge itself, and his antigrav didn't have enough power to get him safely to the bottom. He pressed one of the small buttons on the harness, firing one of the small airjets…maneuvering himself back from the canyon edge. They hadn't had a lot of time to practice the drop, and he hoped the limited training his people had on the maneuvering jets would be enough.

The enemy wasn't positioned to oppose their drop. Taylor's entire force was approaching from the bottom of the canyon. All except for the 213th, which was doing the antigrav drop up on top. It was a surprise move, one Taylor had devised to insert forces where the enemy wasn't prepared to face them.

Riley gritted his teeth for landing. He was coming in a lot slower than he would have in freefall, but it was still hard enough to be unpleasant. His feet slapped down on the gravelly sand, and he felt the enhanced muscles in his legs tense, his knees bending to absorb the shock.

He slapped the release button, ejecting the antigrav harness from his exos. His head snapped around, getting a bearing on his troops coming down. Most of them looked good, but he could see a few that were struggling…drifting out over the gorge. He tensed when he saw the stragglers, but there was nothing he could do. He didn't have time to worry about it anyway…he had to get the unit organized. He reached around, pulling his assault rifle off his back. "Section leaders, form your units." He could see that 2 of his 3 section chiefs were already down, climbing out of their harnesses.

He walked slowly to the edge of the canyon and looked over. The terrain was as brutal as Taylor promised him it would be. There were large stretches where it was sheer cliff, but there were three or four functional paths down. They were narrow, often with deep drops on one or both sides, but they were passable. It didn't look like there were any Machines this far up. The enemy wasn't expecting an attack from this direction.

The air was pungent with smoke. The Dragonfires had incinerated the enemy positions below with their fuel air bombs. There was no way to do a reliable damage assessment in terrain like this, but Riley could tell that the bombardment had been effective.

He saw one of his men slip down below the top of the canyon, missing the LZ. There was no place near him to try and land, and the antigrav power wouldn't last much longer. Riley was watching a KIA...he knew it, but there was no way he could stop it. He stared, paralyzed, trying to think of something...anything he could do. Then he caught another one in the corner of his eye. Then a third.

He knew intellectually that three fatalities on a drop like this was a pretty good result, but those were his men he was watching. He was watching them die, and there wasn't a damned thing he could do about it.

He spun around and looked behind him. Most of his troops were down now, and the section and team leaders were trying to get them organized. The personal antigravs had worked as advertised...more or less, but the strikeforce was scattered and disorganized.

Riley had been told that soldiers from some of the nation states had conducted similar operations before the Consolidation, using only cloth chutes to slow their descent. He couldn't imagine keeping any semblance of order during a drop like that. Such tactics hadn't been practiced by any armed forces for almost half a century, and even if they had been, the atmosphere on Erastus was too sparse for it to work anyway.

"Section leaders, confirm readiness to advance." He had to hold back a bitter laugh, glancing at the tactical display on his visor. There wasn't a team in the 213th that was really ready. But there wasn't time to waste. Organized or not, they were moving out in two minutes.

"First Section...ready." The answer was wobbly. Sergeant James' section was less of a mess than it had been a few minutes before, but Riley knew James needed another ten minutes minimum. But it was time they didn't have to spare. The enemy had almost certainly detected the drop. If the 213th didn't hit them before they could reposition, the whole operation would be wasted.

The leaders of 2nd and 3rd Sections sounded off in turn, each bullshitting Riley, telling him they were ready, though neither one was any better a liar than James.

"All sections, advance." Riley started walking toward James' position. He was going to follow 1st Section with the support elements. "You've all got your assigned paths on your tac displays. Make sure you stay on them." The terrain was worse than rugged, but the recon drones had spotted the best routes down the cliff. It was still going to be a hard time, but it would be much worse if the troops strayed from their assigned positions.

Riley watched as James' men started on the winding trail, following along as the last of the 1st Section headed down. It was a narrow path, barely wide enough for two men abreast and descending at a 30% slope, at least. It was hard to get a good footing on the loose gravelly surface, though Riley's enhanced legs increased his stability. The rookies, he thought, the ones who hadn't gotten their mods yet…they were going to have a hell of a time getting down the path.

"Lieutenant, are we sure this is the right way?" It was James, sounding nervous. "I thought those drones were supposed to find us the best ways down."

Riley sighed softly. "This is the best way, Sergeant." They might manage to surprise the enemy, he thought, but they weren't getting it for free. "What did you expect, a stroll on the beach?" He felt bad mocking the veteran sergeant, but the last thing he could do was lend credence to any doubts. His people were going down this cliff.

Whether they did it in an orderly fashion or approaching terminal velocity was going to depend largely on keeping their cool.

Riley shot a thought to his com, cutting the line. There was nothing more to talk about. He stumbled a little himself, sliding down about a meter on the loose stones before he caught himself. The path was getting worse…and from the sound of James' voice, he assumed that was going to continue as they moved forward. There had been a fairly steep drop to one side when they started, but now the right was a sheer cliff of at least 100 meters, and the path itself was narrowing further.

Riley could see that the tail of 1st Section had stopped completely. He reopened the com line. "Sergeant James, why has the column stopped?"

"Sorry, sir." James was distracted, clearly in the middle of something. "The path keeps getting smaller, sir. I had to put the men in single file."

"Very well, Sergeant." Fuck, Riley thought…this is really the best route? That's what he'd told James, and it was exactly what Taylor had said to him. But he was finding it hard to believe now. "Carry on. Let's keep moving."

"Yes, sir."

Riley stood, looking out over the terrain below, trying to spot enemy positions. A minute passed, then two. Finally, he could see the men ahead begin to move. Looking carefully, he stared down slowly, waving for the troops behind him to follow.

The path angled sharply, and suddenly it became a knife edge, steep drop-offs on both sides. Riley stared straight ahead, his eyes downcast, focused on the ground in front of him. He could feel his heart pounding in his ears. He didn't like heights…didn't like them one bit. It crossed his mind how silly it was to be so disturbed by a pointless pho-

bia when he was on his way into battle. He was far likelier
to get shot by a Machine than to lose his footing and fall.
But it didn't matter…all he could think about was getting
down off the heights.

"Lieutenant, we're approaching the enemy line." James
again, sounding excited. "They're on the move, trying
to reposition. It looks like we caught them flatfooted.
Request permission to attack."

Riley smiled. Young's people must be engaged on the
flank, he thought. "Permission granted, Sergeant. Attack."
He switched the com to the strikeforce command line. "All
sections…attack."


"Keep moving…all of you." Young's voice was loud
and urgent. They didn't call him Frantic for nothing. His
people had been attacking nonstop for over an hour, but
he wasn't about the give the enemy a chance to regroup.
Or even breathe. "Forward! Now!"

He glanced out from behind a jagged rock outcropping,
spying another position about 60 meters forward. He'd be
in the open, at least for a few seconds, but the Machines
were disordered and pulling back. It was worth the risk.

He leaned forward, keeping his head low as his surgi-
cally enhanced leg muscles powered him forward. The
ground was steep and rugged. He wasn't sure he would
have been able to keep his footing before the mods, but
his upgraded legs were more than up to the task. He knew
stronger legs would make him faster, but he'd been surprised at how much the added power helped his balance.

He spotted a Machine as he was running, and he swung
his rifle around, firing a dozen shots in 3 round bursts. He
hit his target with at least half the projectiles, tearing off
most of its upper body. The alien cyborg didn't look all
that different than one of his own soldiers going down.

The Machines were not enormously unlike humans. Their bodies were partially mechanical, and they had fewer bodily fluids and soft tissue…that tended to make them neater corpses. Their systems were more compartmentalized, and they were generally better equipped to survive wounds. Until the Supersoldier program began implanting millions of healing nanobots into human soldiers, at least.

Young smiled. It was a tough shot, and he'd nailed it. His new eyes were a help in aiming, but he suspected it was the NIS that truly made the difference, compensating for the motion as he ran. He felt the rush of excitement, as he always did after a kill, and he let out a feral howl.

Young had been on Erastus less than two weeks when the guys started calling him Frantic. He'd always been excitable, but during the stress of combat he became truly wild. As a rookie it had been a problem…he was slow to listen to the veterans' advice, and his uncontrolled aggression had almost gotten him killed on a number of occasions. Only luck had saved him…that and his enormous fighting ability.

Eventually, experience settle him down somewhat. He was still aggressive, almost savage in combat, but his rational mind was in control now. To everyone's surprise, Frantic had become an extraordinary NCO and, unexpectedly, his loss rate was well below average. He still took personal risks that made Taylor cringe, but Young had become one of the top sergeants in the strikeforce…and a member of Jake's small group of close friends.

He slammed hard into the rock outcropping at the new position. He was still getting used to the momentum from his enhanced legs. He lost his breath for an instant, but otherwise he wasn't hurt. He shook his head, and forced his focus back to the battle.

He checked his tactical display. Riley's boys were almost

into the fight. The Machines were being attacked from two sides. He knew the enemy wouldn't panic like a human force might, but he wasn't sure what to expect. Normally, they'd realize their position was compromised and pull back to regroup. But this time they were defending a vital location, and they almost certainly had hold at all costs orders. The canyon led almost directly to a production facility, and if they lost the high ground, they'd lose the whole position. UNFE could pour more forces through and attack the factory at will. And the Tegeri couldn't afford to lose another base.

He heard a series of distant explosions, and his head snapped around. That's 1st Battalion, he thought, hitting the south side of the canyon. Most of that side was sheer cliff, and there were fewer enemy positions to assault.

"All teams…move it!" Young was firing his assault rifle at a cluster of Machines crouched behind a pile of boulders 100 meters ahead. He got one, hitting it just under the left eye and tearing the top of its head off. The others ducked down and started returning his fire. He pulled back around the outcropping, swearing under his breath. They had him pinned. If he dashed out to move forward, they'd nail him in half a second.

He was covered with sweat. The mods made him a vastly superior fighter, but the exos were just one more thing trapping the heat, making combat on Erastus even more unbearable. He twitched a few times…he was a little claustrophobic by nature, and the exoskeletal attachments made him feel trapped, confined. He could usually put it out of his mind, but he was most vulnerable when he was frustrated. Like now.

He moved his hand behind him, fingering one of the grenades clipped to his exos. Maybe, he thought…just maybe I can drop this right behind them. It would be a tough throw, but it was the only way he could think of to deal with the Machines who had him trapped. His tactical display told the same story. All along the line, his boys were getting pinned.

He pulled hard, snapping the spherical grenade from the harness. A normal man would never be able to throw half a kilogram of steel and explosive far enough, but Karl Young was no longer normal. The muscles in his arms and shoulders were interlaced with artificial fibers, increasing his natural strength by a factor of three, and the exo attached to his arm gave him even more power. The problem wasn't distance…it was accuracy. He had the strength, but 100 meters was a hell of a range for precision aiming.

He flipped the small lever, activating the weapon. He stepped back from the rock and swung his body quickly to the left. He gave himself a second to aim, a dangerous luxury when he was exposed to enemy fire. He threw the grenade, imagining its flight path to the target.

He kicked right with his legs, using the momentum of the throw to propel him back behind his cover. A rookie might have paused, watching to see if the throw landed on target. That rookie would have died, riddled with fire, before the grenade even reached its target. There were a hundred small factors, things inexperienced guys didn't even think of. But they were the difference between life and death on the battlefield.

He heard the loud boom. It was a heavy grenade, with a significant blast. He peered cautiously around the rock, trying to get a view toward the enemy position. He brought his assault rifle up and hosed the area down, emptying a clip at full auto. Nothing. No motion, no return fire.

There was no way to know for sure. He stared out at the ground ahead, picking out his next objective. There was a small gully up ahead, maybe 2 meters deep. Good cover.  He slammed a new clip into his rifle and took a deep breath.  Then he spun around, running full speed, diving for the protection of the small trench ahead.

Private Sanjay Chandra glanced up at the two suns in the sky.  The heat was unbearable.  His uniform was soaked with his sweat, as wet as if he'd dived into a river.  A river, he thought bitterly…a river is an elusive dream in this hell.  Chandra was crouched behind a small rise in the ground, as bullets flew all around.  He was terrified, paralyzed.  And the heat was so bad, he felt like he was going to pass out any minute.

Chandra was a rookie, as raw as they came.  He'd come through the Portal and taken the transport to Firebase Delta.  He barely had time to dump his gear and take a crap before the assembly alarm went off.  An hour later he was strapped into another ship - a combat transport this time – and en route to this hellish gorge.

He was hyperventilating, trying in vain to cool himself.  The air was hot…so hot.  When they told him he was going to Erastus, he figured he'd be well prepared to handle it.  He grew up in the streets of New Delhi, and he thought he was used to the heat.  But there was heat and then there was…this.  It wasn't Earthly heat on Erastus… the coolest temperatures on the planet matched the worst equatorial heatwaves in terrestrial history.

He was moving through the valley, struggling to keep up with the rest of the team.  Corporal Tse had yelled at him twice for lagging behind.  But the heat…it was just too much.  He tried to move faster, but he almost fainted, and he had to slow down.

He looked at the cliffs on both sides.  The Machines had been dug in on those rocky slopes, at least that's what the corporal told everybody.  "Be glad you grunts didn't have to go up those cliffs," he had said. "And be fucking grateful to your brothers who did the job, because they lost half their number doing it."

Chandra couldn't even imagine fighting on terrain like that. And a strikeforce losing half its strength? How do men do that, he wondered...how do they stand and fight even after taking such losses? His strikeforce was moving through the dry riverbed to assault the remaining enemy line. The Machines were in bad shape, outflanked on both sides, taking fire from the steep high ground...the very positions they had held a few hours before. Chandra and his comrades were tasked with delivering the final blow, opening up the riverbed, allowing fresh forces to move on a major enemy base.

They had it a lot easier than the men who'd gone in already, but Chandra was still scared to death, struggling to keep himself from shaking.

"Attention, 109th Strikeforce." The voice on his com was firm, commanding. How, Chandra wondered, could anyone sound so calm, so controlled, minutes before going into combat? It was Lieutenant Daniels, who was commanding both Chandra's unit and the 84th, which was in reserve right behind the 109th.

Chandra had caught a glimpse of Daniels from a distance as the strikeforce was boarding the transports, but this was the first time he'd heard the lieutenant's voice. Daniels was a lofty figure to a newb like Chandra. Commander of over 250 men, Supersoldier, a member of Jake Taylor's inner circle. The young soldier was in awe, even forgetting his fear for a few seconds.

"Prepare to assault enemy positions." Daniels still sounded under control, maddeningly so.

Why isn't he scared, Chandra thought...how can he be so calm? He held up his own hand, focusing hard but still unable to stop it from shaking. His head snapped around quickly, prompted by a loud crack. There was just the one sound, and for a few seconds the air was silent and still. Then the Machine line opened up.

Chandra froze, his rifle still strapped across his back. He was looking forward, but his legs wouldn't move, no matter how hard he tried. It took all he had not to turn and run as quickly as his legs could carry him. But he stayed in place. He saw another man, about 50 meters down the line, thrown back, crumpling to the ground. Part of him wanted to run over, to help his comrade. Another part said, move forward...attack. But all he could do was stand in place.

"Chandra! Get your worthless ass moving." It was the corporal, and his sharp rebuke snapped Chandra out of his paralysis.

"Yes, Corporal Tse." He moved forward, taking slow, jerky steps. He looked ahead, toward the enemy line. He couldn't see much...a little movement here and there, but that's all. The Machines were hunkered down behind cover. Most of his teammates were too. There were large boulders scattered all across the riverbed, and the troopers had taken position behind them.

Chandra stumbled forward, his legs limp, like noodles. He tried to remember his training, but it was hard to focus. He reached around, pulling his rifle from his back. His eyes darted back and forth, looking for a good place to crouch down. He saw a boulder none of the others were using. It was a little over a meter high and perhaps two wide. He'd have to stay low, but it was good protection.

He moved toward it, his heart pounding in his ears, rivulets of sweat streaming down his face. His eyes stung from the sweat, blurring his view. He kept moving, staring at the rock, trying to ignore the sounds of bullets ripping by.

He felt like he'd never get there, that he'd been running forever. But then, suddenly, he was behind the rock, prone.

The rifle felt hot in his hands. The dense plastic material didn't conduct heat very well, but the weapon had been on his back for over an hour, with both suns beating down on it. He glanced cautiously around the edge of the boulder. His heart leapt. There was a Machine! He was peering out from behind his own cover about 80 meters ahead, taking aim at something – someone, Chandra realized – down the line.

He spun around, snapping up the rifle and pulling the trigger. It was all a blur. The gun was set on semi-automatic, and the first burst of three shots went high, zipping over the target's head. The Machine reacted, starting to pull back and angling his weapon in Chandra's direction.

Chandra felt the adrenalin flooding his system. His arms felt stronger, his mind more alert. He stared down the barrel of his rifle, pulling the trigger three times in rapid succession, sending a flurry of projectiles toward his enemy.

The Machine was pushed backward, the left side of his chest and midsection almost gone. The remnants of the shattered alien warrior fell to the ground. It couldn't have taken more than a second or two, though the whole thing played out in slow motion to Chandra.

He could feel the energy inside. I hit him, he thought, his excitement building. He'd killed one of the enemy... and maybe saved one of his comrades in the process. His blood was up, and the fear was momentarily forgotten, pushed aside by his elation.

He gritted his teeth and scanned the enemy line. He spotted two Machines crouched over a heavy autogun. They were mostly under cover, but not completely. A perfect shot could take either one of them down. His eyes locked on his targets, and he brought his rifle up to fire.

Suddenly he was moving back, his body twisting. He saw the spray of blood from his shoulder before he felt the wound. His legs went weak…he was falling. As he did, he spun around…just before second projectile slammed into his back. Then a third. They were heavy hypersonic rounds, and they tore right through his body armor.

Suddenly, he was looking up at the sky. Both suns were still there, the second close to setting. He couldn't remember how he'd ended up on the ground…then it came to back to him. He realized he must have blacked out after the projectiles hit him.

He felt strange, like he was floating. Then there was the pain. His back was on fire, waves of agony wracking his body. There was wetness under him. He pulled his hand up and stared. It was covered with blood. His blood. He began to panic, screaming. The tears started to stream from his eyes. "Help," he shouted, as loud as his stricken body could manage. The pain in his chest flared up as he tried to yell, but he repeated his cry nevertheless. It was in vain. There was no response. He was alone.

He was starved for air, and he tried to take a deep breath, but the pain was unbearable. There was a gurgling sound from his throat, his chest, and every shallow breath he managed was a torment.

"Please," he muttered piteously to whatever powers might exist in the universe. "I don't want to die."

He was still staring at the sky, staying still to minimize the pain. His mind began to drift, random thoughts moving in and out of his dwindling consciousness. It is beautiful in its own way, he thought, seeing the Erastian sky differently than he had before. Men looked up and saw the two suns, the source of the terrible heat that made every moment on the planet a misery. But now Chandra saw it differently. Two majestic suns, and the long, sparse clouds that ran for kilometers across the horizon. There is beauty, he thought, a brief smile crossing his stricken lips...even in hell.

# Chapter 13

From the Journal of Jake Taylor:

Do you ever wonder about the odd assortment of things you remember? Most days of your life vanish into the inaccessible depths of the mind, but a few seemingly random events remain in the forefront. Years later, decades later... you still remember them like they happened yesterday.

One day when I was young...seven, eight, I don't recall that part exactly...we were driving into Concord. It was sometime around my birthday, and we were heading for one of the restaurants in town. It was always a treat to eat out someplace. It wasn't often we had the extra money for things like that.

I was in the back of the truck, probably fighting with my brother. Suddenly, my father pulled over to the side of the road. There was an accident ahead of us. A motorcycle had been swiped by a tractor, and it wiped out hard.

My father told us to stay in the car, and then he got out and went to the back of the truck. He always kept a blanket and a first aid kit in the storage locker, and he got them out and ran over. I could see the rider through the window of the truck. He was lying on his back, and the street around him had puddles of blood on it. I wondered for a second if he was dead, but then I saw him move.

It was the first time I'd seen blood like that. Not a few drops from a cut, but pools of it. I knew immediately he was badly hurt, and I couldn't move my eyes away. I watched my father cover him with the blanket, even as I heard the approaching sirens of the sheriff and the rescue squad.

When the medics arrived, my father walked back to the car, and we continued toward town. I remember wondering how we would get our blanket back. I don't recall what we did in Concord that day, or what restaurant we went to. But I remember the image of that man lying in the street, covered by our old gray blanket...feeling bad for him and worrying about how we'd get the blanket back.

I think about that day often, even now. I wonder if that man lived or not. I feel sadness, thinking about his suffering, about the fact that he might have died. I always imagine that he got up that day, just like any other. Maybe he was excited, as I was when we left the house. It could have been a special occasion. He could have been going to meet friends. Instead he ended up hurt and bleeding... and maybe dying...on the cold pavement.

I can't explain the reaction I had...that I still have...the melancholy, the sadness I feel for that man. Even now, after ten years of war and thousands of casualties...after all the suffering and death...I still remember the biker lying on that back road in New Hampshire.

Empathy. Such an odd emotion. Sometimes it is predictable. Clearly, the suffering of a friend or a loved one triggers it more profoundly than that of a stranger. And yet it seems to have a mind of its own, manifesting in unexpected situations. As in the memories and feelings I still have over something that happened 20 years ago...to a person I never knew. An event that I witnessed from a distance for no more than 3 or 4 minutes.

What makes some things affect us so much more profoundly than others? Why do we remember some events, yet forget so many others of equal import? I've seen thousands of young men die in this place, some I knew, others who were just names on a roster sheet. Why do some

**burn themselves into your consciousness, while others are quickly forgotten? Why does one stranger's death or suffering affect you more profoundly than another's?**

The battle was over. They were calling it a brilliant victory, but all Taylor could see was the terrible cost. With all his tactical ability and ten years of combat experience on Erastus, he couldn't claim ignorance....couldn't even fool himself. He knew the losses he would suffer before the attack even began. And he sent his men in anyway.

Taylor's savage attack had cleared the entire canyon, opening up the route for 5th and 6th Battalions to advance on the Machine production facility beyond. He wouldn't command that attack...he'd be back at base, training the flood of FNGs his units would need to build back to full strength. But his people had already won the victory. The canyon had been the real line of defense. The base itself was isolated, situated 4,500 klicks from the nearest supporting enemy forces. It would inevitably fall now.

Jake looked out at the debris of battle as he walked along the ancient riverbed his men had died to conquer. It was late twilight, and only the dimmer of the two suns was in the sky. This was as close as Erastus came to night, but it was still as bright as late afternoon on Earth.

The canyon was quiet. His troops had advanced through, forming a defensive position on the far end of the gorge. He knew the enemy didn't have the strength to counter-attack, but he wasn't taking chances. Exhausted or not, his people were going to stand guard until 5th Battalion got there and relieved them.

There were a few medical teams rounding up the last of the casualties. The ones who had the Supersoldier mods would almost certainly survive if they hadn't been killed outright. The others had a good chance too, as long as they'd remembered to activate their medkits. Taylor knew from experience that about 15% of his wounded would forget. And most of them would die.

Taylor stepped on something and twisted his ankle slightly. He looked down. There was an assault rifle under his foot. It had been partly covered with the dusty sand of the valley, and he hadn't seen it until his boot rolled off it.

"Help me." The voice was soft, barely audible. "Please."

Taylor snapped his head around. He wouldn't have heard the strained whisper if it hadn't been for his mechanically-enhanced ears. It had come from the right, and he turned and walked that way.

There was a large boulder, and Jake spotted a pair of legs on the ground. He trotted over, around the giant rock. It was a man…one of his privates….lying on his back, barely moving. He was a mess. His shoulder was ripped open, a large portion of the muscle exposed. There were two holes in his armor too, right through the chest plate. Taylor couldn't tell if the rounds had gone in the front and out the back or the reverse, but either way, he knew the man was badly hurt.

Taylor looked down at the soldier's belt and harness, trying to see if he'd applied his medkit. The wounds were bad, but if he'd gotten the nanobots into his system right away, he'd have a chance. Jake's eyes darted across the trooper's form, but Taylor felt the hope drain away as he focused on the small rubber pouch, still in its place, unused.

"H…e…l…p…" The soldier moved, his arm sliding slowly a few centimeters along the ground. His voice was weaker than it had been a moment before. There was a heaviness there too, a gurgling sound behind the words.

Taylor flashed a thought at his com, opening a line to the med teams. "Medical…this is Major Taylor. I need a team at my location ASAP." He was about the cut the line, but then he added, "I found a wounded soldier." No point letting them misunderstand and think he was injured. The way they all looked at him half the time…if they thought he was down they'd all panic.

He looked at the stricken figure lying at his feet for a few seconds then he knelt down beside the wounded man. "Private…this is Major Taylor." He reached out, taking the man's hand in his. "Can you tell me your name?" He pulled the medkit from the soldier's belt, and took out the injector. He thrust it in the soldier's leg, but even as he was doing it, he realized it was too late.

Jake could feel the man try to move. His hand was cold, but now it squeezed gently on Taylor's. "M…a…j…o…r?" He tried to turn his head to look toward Taylor.

"Stay still, son." Taylor's voice was soft, gentle. "Don't try to move." He was looking at the stricken soldier's wounds as he spoke. He sighed softly as he did, wanting to turn away, to run from this mangled kid. He can't be more than seventeen years old, Taylor thought grimly…and he's going to die right here, scared and in pain.

"What's your name, son?" Taylor whispered softly, his mouth next to the kid's ear. Jake's tactical display would normally have shown him the man's complete file, but the stricken soldier's transponder wasn't working. That explained why he hadn't been found by the medics. Most of the wounded in this sector had been evac'd, but Chandra had fallen behind a rock outcropping on the edge of the field…and without his transponder, no one had seen him.

"Private…" He had a coughing spasm, and Taylor could see the spray of blood coming from his mouth. "…Private Chandra, sir." He was still breathing heavily, but the coughing mostly subsided.

Chandra, Jake thought…I don't remember a Chandra.

He closed his eyes tightly, feeling a wave of guilt. This boy could march out here on my orders and fight...and get hideously wounded...but I can't remember his name. Taylor commanded a lot of troops now, but his expectations of himself hadn't changed with the scope of his responsibilities.

"What's your first name?"

Chandra had another coughing spasm, not quite as bad as the previous one. "Sanjay, sir." He coughed again, spitting up a blob of partially congealed blood. "My name is Sanjay, sir." Chandra was silent for a few seconds. Then he finally managed to turn his head toward Taylor. "Please help me, sir. I don't want to die."

Taylor opened his mouth, but he couldn't force the words out. Finally, he leaned down and whispered, "You're not going to die, Sanjay." He almost choked on the lie. "I already called the medics."

He wasn't sure if Chandra believed him or not. Taylor was a 10-year veteran of Erastus...he'd killed hundreds of Machines, and he'd watched thousands of men die. But he couldn't bring himself to be honest with this broken kid lying in front of him. What would honesty serve now, he thought...what could it do but scared this poor boy even more?

"I want to go home." Chandra spoke the words softly, wistfully. He was crying, tears streaming down his dirt and blood spattered face.

"I know, Sanjay." Taylor was trying to sound as soothing as he could. The detritus of battle was all around, but right now all he could think about was comforting this shattered, terrified kid. "I wish I was home too." He pulled a rock out from under Chandra, trying to make him more comfortable. "Where are you from?" Just keep talking to him, Jake thought...don't let him die alone.

"New Delhi, sir." He coughed again, though only for a few seconds this time.

Taylor sat in the hot sand, holding Chandra's hand. He was trying to think of things to say...anything to keep the dying soldier distracted. He knew it wouldn't be long. It was a miracle the kid was still alive. So many men have died in this war, he thought, alone and unsuccored...does comforting one really make a difference?

Chandra's body tensed and wracked with another coughing spasm. He fell back, moaning in pain. "I'm scared, sir."

"I know, Sanjay." Jake was trying to keep the emotion in his own voice under control, but it was hard to answer. He felt grief...and anger. He railed inside against his own helplessness. Veteran...Supersoldier. None of it meant a fucking thing. There was nothing he could do, nothing he could say. Nothing but sit and watch Sanjay Chandra die, terrified and in pain, in the bitter sands of an alien world.

"Don't be afraid. We'll have you out of here soon." Taylor hated himself even as he said it. "Just be calm. Close your eyes and stay still." He could hear Chandra's breathing become rough, unsteady. It won't be long, now, he thought. He watched the young soldier struggling for his last breaths, and the grief welled up inside him. He wanted to cry for this boy, but he couldn't. His mechanical eyes didn't produce tears. One more thing they had taken from him.

Chandra's chest heaved with one more deep rattling breath, and then he was still, silent. Sanjay Chandra was dead.

Taylor sat silently for a few moments, turning away, unable to bring himself to look at the dead soldier lying next to him. He knew nothing about Chandra...nothing at all, really. But he realized he'd never forget him. The image of this dead soldier would stay with him the rest of his life.

"Sir, are you OK?" The medical team trotted around the outcropping, looking down at Taylor and Chandra.

Jake felt a wave of anger. Why, he thought, why are you worried about me? But he pushed it back. It wasn't the medics' fault.

"I'm fine, Sergeant." He started to get up. The medic closest to him moved to help, but Taylor waved him off. "He's dead." Taylor was looking down at the still form of the boy he'd been talking to a few minutes before. "Transponder was damaged…and he forgot to administer his medkit." Rookies, Taylor thought sadly.

He turned and walked away slowly, without another word.

# Chapter 14

From the Journal of Jake Taylor:

I met a girl here. I met her a long time ago. I don't know why I never wrote about her before. Maybe it was too soon after I'd lost Beth. Or maybe I wanted to keep one thing just for myself, not even to share with this journal. I don't know for sure.

Her name is Hope. I remember laughing when she told me. It's a pretty name, but I can't think of one less appropriate on Erastus. It's no great romance story, ours... there is no such thing here. The only women on the planet are sex workers assigned to provide support services to the thousands of men in the combat units. There are no female soldiers serving in UNFE...not in any UN military force...nor are any UN administrators I've ever encountered women. I haven't even seen a woman outside the brigade brothel in ten years.

The brothels are an integral part of every military force structure serving on a Portal world. We fight a war with no leaves, no trips home, no towns to visit for R&R. Not even a box of cookies sent from mom. Desertion isn't a problem...there's nowhere to go anyway, so why run? But mental breakdowns are common. You can force a lazy man to work, even compel a coward to fight. But when a man doesn't care anymore...really doesn't care...then he is uncontrollable. Punishment doesn't work, threats don't work. When a man loses it on Erastus, UN Central's investment in training and transport goes up in smoke. The brothels provide a release, a stress reliever. The keep men on the brink from falling into the abyss.

UN Command calls the whole thing Sexual Support Services, or SSS. The program exists for a number of reasons, and the brigade facilities are an integral component of the military discipline system. Periodic visits to the SSS compounds are a privilege, one that can be withdrawn for soldiers or units that don't perform as expected. For a lifetime soldier with no prospect of going home, a few hours with a woman is the only escape from a life of constant duty and bloodshed. It is part of the delicate morale system that kept men with no hope in the field and fighting.

I've sometimes wondered what the women had done to be consigned to such fates. Were they criminals? Political prisoners? Or just women blackmailed or conscripted, as I was? As far as I can tell, they serve life terms, just as we do. I'm not sure how that works over the long term. No one worries about what to do with a 70 year old soldier, because none of us live that long. Sooner or later, the god of battle comes for all of us. But the women of SSS don't have the attrition rate we do. Certainly, some succumb at a young age, victims of a hostile environment or virulent alien pathogens. But most can expect to live something approaching a normal lifespan. What will happen to them when they are too old to continue their function effectively? I don't know – the war on Erastus hasn't been going on long enough for that situation to arise. But I don't like the things that come to mind. Another dark secret, the kind of thing most people would rather not know about.

My father served alongside women in the old US Navy. Indeed, a woman had been the U.S. president when he enlisted. He mentioned it incidentally when he was telling me about his time in uniform. It was something I've never much considered, not until recently. I didn't really know anything about military service, not before I ended up a soldier myself. And when I found myself on Gehenna fighting the Machines, I just adapted to the military establishment I'd become a part of.

Now it's been ten years, and I've started to think more about it... about a lot of things I'd given cursory attention before. I know that some of the old military establishments had been gender-integrated but, again, that was pre-Consolidation history, and it wasn't safe to go poking around too much. Most serious information on the old nation-states was on the quarantined list, and it was next to impossible to get anything reliable. UN Central didn't want people waxing poetic about their ethnic and nationalistic histories...not while there was still living memory of the time before the Consolidation. I thought I understood that thinking once, and even approved. Eliminating anything that threatened the peaceful unity of mankind seemed worthwhile, even if it came at the cost of intellectual freedom. Now, I see other perspectives. Darker ones.

I used to wonder why UN Central didn't recruit women, how the female gender had taken such a massive step back in equality and opportunity. Then I realized. The Consolidation had necessitated combining different cultures, each with their own gender, racial, and religious traditions. In the end, terrified by the prospect of the Machines invading, all of the nations of Earth voluntarily surrendered their sovereignty to the UN. The earliest nations to push for world unity had the greatest impact on the coalescing multinational culture...and most of those states were from the developing world, places where gender inequalities were often deeply ingrained in the way of life.

Back home things were different. My mother, Beth...all the women I knew...they weren't treated as second-class citizens in any way I'd ever noticed. But New Hampshire had been part of the old U.S., and from what I knew of pre-Consolidation American culture, the genders had been more or less equal in terms of rights and societal obligations. UN Central didn't interfere too much with local customs. They didn't make a big deal out of it...nothing that could turn into a rallying cry. They didn't talk about it at all; they just went ahead and did what they wanted. Now that I thought about it, I'd never noticed a woman in any significant government position. The Inquisitor who'd come to our farm demanding the taxes...the recruiting agent who offered a waiver of the debt in exchange for my enlistment. Our local UN Admin...and every other one in the surrounding areas. All men.

I remembered my father's rants, his constant complaints about UN Central and how much we had all lost since he was younger. Now I wondered about those women he'd served with, about what they felt they had lost. They had served their country, bled for it – some had died for it - and their reward was to see their daughters and grand-daughters barred from the same freedoms and opportunities they had enjoyed. I saw my father's anger first hand, but now I wondered about those women. I couldn't imagine how they lived with the bitterness. It was a different hell than mine, but perhaps one as painful in its own way.

Taylor was sitting on the edge of the bed, leaning forward, holding his head in his hands. He hadn't said a word in over an hour. He used to look forward to his allotments at the SSS facility, especially after he met Hope. She was pretty enough, especially by Erastus standards...but it was more than that. She had a tenderness, an empathy...a gentleness that was utterly at odds with every other aspect of his life. He was drawn to her; she made him feel whole again, at least for a little while. He felt a longing to help her too, to give to her the same comfort she provided him. Indeed, much of the solace he got from her came from knowing that he was there for her as much as she was for him. It made him feel normal, just for a few minutes. It might not be a real relationship they shared, but it was close enough that they could both pretend.

He enjoyed the sex, of course, but he also looked forward to just seeing her, sitting and talking. Jake was fortunate enough to have a close knit group of friends he could talk to when he needed an ear, but there was something different about spending time with a woman.

Troopers weren't supposed to see the same women all the time…UNFE Command didn't want relationships developing, just scheduled recreation. But as Taylor's rank rose, so did his influence…and he was able to insure that he only saw Hope.

Now he sat with his back toward her. It had been five years since his mods had been installed, but he was still self-conscious about it. He'd avoided using his SSS allotments for months after the surgeries were complete. He made one excuse after another but, finally, he was ordered outright to go. SSS services weren't optional in UNFE. They were a crucial part of the morale and mental health program designed to keep the army in the field at top fighting efficiency.

When he finally saw her for the first time after the surgery, she acted like everything was normal, even though it was the first time in almost a year that she'd seen him. She tried not to stare, but it was hard to ignore the metallic fittings protruding from his shoulders and his hips. He was still getting used to his increased strength, and when she finally coaxed him into bed, she came out of the encounter bruised from head to toe, a long, bloody scratch on her leg from the rough metal of one of his exo interfaces.

When he saw what he had done to her, he was horrified. It was months before he touched her again. He kept every appointment as ordered. But he wouldn't go near her, wouldn't risk hurting her again. It was at least another year before their encounters reached something like normalcy.

"Jake, are you OK? You've been so quiet." Her voice was soft, gentle. Life had dealt her a fate as bitter as his, but she never seemed angry or resentful because of it.

Jake had kept himself from sliding down that slope for a long time too, but now his grip was failing. The anger, the bitterness…they were starting to win, starting to take control. Maybe if they hadn't made him into a cyborg, he thought…perhaps then he could have maintained a few shreds of the faith that kept men – and women – going on Erastus. But they weren't happy just taking his home and family and the only life he'd known…now they had come back for his humanity. Now, Jake believed, he truly was good only for war.

He was silent for a few more seconds before he turned to face her. "Oh…sorry." He tried to hold back a sigh. "No, nothing's wrong. I'm just thinking." He forced a smile for her, though he couldn't imagine it was very convincing.

"You don't expect me to believe that, do you?" She reached out and gently ran her hand down his back. He flinched at her first touch, but then he settled down. "You're so tense. Are you sure you don't want to talk about it?"

He did want to talk…at least he didn't want to shut her out. But he didn't know what to say…how to put it into words. Even if he managed to explain…he didn't want to burden her, or bring her down with him. He'd been troubled lately, more than usual. And it was getting worse.

She slid across the bed, putting her arms around him from behind, pulling him closer. She rested her face on his shoulder, expertly avoiding the metal fittings protruding from his skin.

He closed his eyes, just for a few seconds. The feeling of her soft skin against his relaxed him, but only for an instant. He was too distracted, too consumed by thought for anything more.

"Jake, what is it?" She kissed him softly on the neck.

He felt an urge to pull away from her, but he resisted. That would only be hurtful to her...and that was the last thing he wanted. He didn't intend to talk about it, to unload on her...but then it just started to come out.

"I saw a kid die." He paused. "It was during the battle we just fought." He laughed derisively. "I don't suppose that should be a big deal. I've lost count of how many rookies I've seen butchered in ten years on this shithole planet."

He turned toward her, keeping his head at an angle, trying to hide his mechanical eyes from her misty green ones. She took his face in her hand and turned, forcing him to look at her. It was his eyes, she had long ago realized...that was what he was most self-conscious about.

"Was there something special about this one?" She didn't like the sound of that when she heard herself say it, and she immediately restated it. "I mean anything beyond the ordinary about the incident?" Her voice was warm, sympathetic.

Taylor was silent for a few seconds. He subconsciously tried to turn his eyes away again, but her hand gripped his face, stroking his cheek gently and turning him back to face her.

"No, not really."

There was exhaustion in his voice, and disillusionment. He'd been like this before, but this was the worst she'd ever seen him. She laid her face against his shoulder and listened quietly.

"But it feels different. He was just like a thousand kids I've watched die. They all hurt." He paused again. "But this isn't the same. I think maybe every man has his limit.

Watching every one of these boys die takes away a part of your soul. Maybe mine is just empty."

She knew he didn't really want to discuss things...he just wanted to let it out. There was nothing she could say that was going to make him feel better anyway, so she just listened, running her hand gently across his bare back. He always liked that...it relaxed him.

"Every man has his limit," he repeated. "I should have died a long time ago, Hope." His voice sounded distracted, far away...as if he was lost in old memories. "It would have been a mercy."

"Don't say that, Jake." Her voice was soft...and a little sad. She didn't like seeing him suffer so...watching him punish himself. "You know better than anyone how many boys you've saved. If you'd had died yourself, none of them would have survived either."

"Maybe." He sounded unconvinced. "But most of them died anyway...just a month later, or a year later." Another pause. "And maybe they were the lucky ones. I've only prolonged the suffering for the men I saved."

He looked down, staring at the stark whiteness of the bedcovering. "I'm going to quit, Hope." His voice was deadpan, utterly serious. "I'm going to tell them to take this stupid war and shove it up their asses."

She felt the tension in the pit of her stomach. If Taylor refused his duty they would take him away. If he continued to resist, they would shoot him. She was afraid of what might happen...and terrified of losing him. She had no more illusions about their relationship than he did, but she knew she needed him. She had lost a life and a family just as he had. Now she was consigned to spend the rest of her life as a sex worker on the most miserable hell man had ever found. Her visits with Jake were the only thing she cared about. They sustained her. Thinking of the next time she'd see him carried her through her days. It made her want to live. She didn't think of it as love...she didn't even know if such a thing was possible someplace like Erastus. But he was a kindred spirit of sorts and, for two lost souls, that was enough.

"Jake, you can't." There was a touch of desperation in her voice, a need to convince him, to pull him back from the brink. "I understand how you feel, but they'll shoot you."

He almost smiled. "Would that be so bad? Quick, almost painless."

"Yes, it would be bad." She was speaking louder, almost yelling. "You're not thinking clearly right now. And what about me? What about your friends? Your men? Think about all of us before you do something stupid and reckless." She was forcing back a sob as she spoke. "We need you."

He was quiet for a few seconds, looking up at her, reaching his hand out and taking hers. "You're right." His tone was soft, almost apologetic. "I'm just frustrated."

She didn't say anything, but she wasn't convinced. It was a lot more than frustration; that was obvious. She knew Jake needed her help, but she didn't know what to do, how to reach him. She smiled at him, but inside she was scared to death.

She watched him get dressed, and she kissed him goodbye before he left. She heard the click of the door closing behind him. Then the tears came.

# Chapter 15

From the Journal of Jake Taylor:

I have too much time to think. When you are young, your mind wants to believe in things. Belief is a powerful force. It can sustain a person through grueling trials and agonizing torment. It can also cloud judgment, lead even an intelligent person to accept and passionately defend the worst sort of nonsense. Some of the most amazing things in history were driven by belief...and some of the most horrific calamities as well. I'd like to say I think belief is a good force more often than a bad one. I'd like to say that, but I can't.

I believed when I was younger. I looked past the things that seemed needlessly hurtful, tried to understand why things were done to me, to my loved ones. I accepted the rules and regulations...and the heavy taxes and levies that barely left us what we needed to get by...and sometimes not enough. I didn't question anything I was told, not seriously at least. There were people with less, people UN Central was struggling to help. The war against the Tegeri was raging too, and that struggle was funded by Earth's citizens. I believed, as I was told, that it was unpatriotic to question any of it.

Even when I was taken from my family and sent to Erastus I still believed. I was bitter and heartbroken certainly, but I told myself I was fighting to defend hearth and home...my family and friends and billions more like them. I was doing the ultimate duty as a citizen.

The restrictions, the regulations, the monitor installed in our home...I believed it was all necessary. UN Central had eliminated war on Earth; it had thwarted terrorism. All the terrible things mankind endured throughout history. Why would anyone question their motives?

I wonder now how I was so stupid, so blind. For ten years I've seen the arrogance of the UN personnel sent here on limited tours. I've seen the contempt they feel for those of us consigned here...the ones without influence or patronage. They see us as pieces of equipment they use and discard...nothing more. Any organization that produces such people is rotten...unworthy of belief, of faith.

They enlist us for life, denying us return trips to Earth, even if we survive five or ten years in this hell. They blame the cost, say the energy to transport us back would be too expensive. I believed that once, but now I feel like a fool for it. The few miserable wrecks of men who survive a five year enlistment...how much could it cost to send them home? When I think about it, I am amazed at how little it takes to get people to believe, to throw away their judgment, their intelligence, and blindly follow their masters' orders.

It has nothing to do with energy. They've transported hundreds of times my body weight in food and ammunition just to sustain me over the last ten years. Yet I am consigned to die on this miserable rock because it is prohibitively expensive to send me home? How could I have been such a fool to believe nonsense like that? How could all of us have been?

The truth is, they don't want us back on Earth. Trained killers who've lived for years outside the normal Earth routine of constant surveillance. That's why they don't let us go home. I figured out part of that a while back, but now I realize the whole truth. They are afraid of my brethren and me, even as they need us to fight their wars. It is from stuff such as us that revolutions are made.

I know I shouldn't be writing these things. Blackie would tell me to stop, that it wasn't safe. I know that's true, but I don't care. I just don't care. Let them come... let them take me away. Let them come and destroy the perfect little soldier they spent so much to build. But they better bring a lot of force with them when they come. Because I am the killing machine they created, and I won't go down without a fight.

"I said I'm done." Taylor sat calmly in the soft leather chair. He was a little surprised to be in a fancy office and not in shackles in some prison cell, but he didn't let it show. "I've given you enough...more than any of you deserve." Taylor had told his story twice already, first to his immediate superior and then to General Hammon, commander of UNFE. Now he was in the office of the man who'd recruited him into the Supersoldier program.

Gregor Kazan was angry, but he was hiding that as well as Taylor was concealing his surprise. He felt it was beneath him to argue and negotiate with a soldier...even a war hero carrying the rank of major. But he didn't need this shit right now. He would be confirmed as Undersecretary in another two months, and the success of the Supersoldier project was the primary reason. Bringing up the first participant of the program on desertion charges would be disastrous. It would delay the vote, at least... and very possibly cost him the promotion. And he wasn't about to let that happen. Whatever he had to do.

"Major Taylor, I understand that your experiences in battle have been - how shall I put it? - troubling." He looked over at Taylor, his manufactured expression one of sympathy, of understanding.

Jake knew it was fake, every bit of it...but he couldn't help but admire the skill it must have taken Kazan to look so sincere when he was so full of shit. If nothing else, a career in government teaches you to lie like a pro, he thought. "I am not troubled, Mr. Kazan." He stared at the UN functionary with an emotionless expression on his face. "I am simply done."

Kazan felt the rage surging through his body, but he clamped down on it. He'd only been on Erastus to make a display of how closely he was watching the program... a little theater preceding the confirmation vote. Now, he realized how fortuitous it was for him to be here when Taylor decided to have his meltdown.

"Major, you know better than anyone that the army does not function in that way. Your service, as much as it is appreciated, is not optional. You voluntarily enlisted and, in doing so, you agreed to abide by the regulations and responsibilities of the service."

"Voluntarily?" Taylor spat the word. "You think my enlistment was voluntary?" He glared across the desk.

"Indeed I do, Major Taylor." Kazan returned the stare. "My records indicate that the Revenue Department forgave a massive underpayment of taxes in return for your agreeing to serve." His eyes narrowed, boring into Jake's. "I believe that was very fair. Perhaps it wouldn't have been necessary if your family had met its obligations."

"We almost starved that year, Mr. Kazan." Taylor was determined to suppress his anger, but he was starting to lose his hold on it. "How do you imagine we could have paid the taxes?"

Kazan took a breath and shifted in his seat. "Do you suppose the government's obligations disappear because of your family's financial mismanagement? Does the war cease? Do the soldiers on the front no longer require food and weapons?" His voice was becoming sharper... not angry, at least not yet...but the tension was showing.

"I do not propose to rehash the facts surrounding your enlistment, Major, nor debate UN policies. You agreed to the terms of service, and your government requires you to comply." He paused, eyes still fixed on Taylor. "Now return to your unit, Major. Because of your war record, I will see to it that this unfortunate incident is forgotten."

"No." Taylor just sat where he was, not uttering another word.

"Major Taylor, I don't think you understand me. If you reject my offer, you will be arrested, court-martialed for desertion and, in all likelihood, executed." Kazan's anger was showing now, and his shock as well. "Do you understand?"

My God, Taylor thought...the miserable little prick actually thinks he's being generous. "I understand, Mr. Kazan." Taylor paused, just for emphasis. "I simply don't care."

Kazan could feel his hands curling into fists. Taylor was calling his bluff. He thought for a minute, wondering if there was a way he could endure Taylor's downfall without risking his appointment. He'd love nothing more than to see the arrogant piece of shit dragged from his office in chains. But there was no way. The first participant of the program? A hero of Taylor's stature? It would cast doubt on the entire project...and on his supervision. It would be a devastating blow.

"Major Taylor, whatever opinions you may have developed toward UN Central or UNFE, surely you understand the importance of the war effort." Kazan was trying another approach. "We must defend Earth against the alien threat."

Taylor hesitated. Kazan had hit a weakness. Whatever sins UN Central may have committed, he still felt a responsibility to the civilians back on Earth. "Yes, Mr. Kazan. I agree. However, I have served ten years. I have done my duty. Far more than others have." He didn't say anything further, but he glared right at Kazan.

"Major, you may feel that what you have done is enough, but that is not your decision." Kazan's voice was getting colder. "Now, I am going to tell you this one last time. Return to duty immediately, and we will forget this conversation."

Taylor almost smiled. What a lying piece of shit, he thought...does this imbecile really think I believe anything he is saying? Taylor knew Kazan wouldn't forget...he wouldn't forget anything. He'd wait, pick some time when it was less politically damaging. But Taylor knew one day Kazan would come for him. The die was cast. He had crossed his own Rubicon.

"Tell me, Mr. Kazan..." Taylor's tone became darker, more threatening. "...why are we enlisted for life? And please don't tell me it's the energy needed to transport us back. Because that is the biggest pile of bullshit I've ever heard."

Kazan was almost apoplectic with rage, but he still managed to hold most of it in check. "Major Taylor, I can assure you that everything you have been told about UN policy is the absolute truth."

Taylor snorted derisively. "Spare me, Mr. Kazan. I am not the stupid, inexperienced fool you drafted and sent here to die." Jake's tone was icy, like death itself. "Do you think I really don't know why you don't want any veterans returning home?"

Kazan sat looking back, a stunned expression on his face. Taylor was taunting him, challenging him to call for the guards and have him arrested. The crazy fool really didn't care what happened to him.

"I fought for ten years to defend Earth...it's the only

good reason I was ever given to be here." Taylor's sat perfectly still as he spoke. "But now I wonder if a species that voluntarily surrendered its freedom to the likes of you out of nothing but base fear is even worth defending."

Kazan slammed his hand on his desk. "That is enough, Major Taylor." He stood up, his chair falling over backwards behind him. "You will go back because you are told to do so, you arrogant, insignificant nothing!" Kazan had lost all control over his rage.

"You will go back because I need you there. Because those miserable recruits stumbling like cattle through that Portal will die that much more quickly without you there." He stared at Taylor, hatred burning in his eyes. "I don't care how many we have to send through...how many thousands die. Do you? There are always more ignorant farm boys to send through." He moved closer, his face 30 centimeters from Jake's. "How do you feel about that? Do you care about the thousand...the ten thousand...others that will be sent here, ones who might have remained home to live out their miserable lives?"

Taylor was silent. Kazan had hit a tender spot. Jake had come to believe the newbs he saved were doomed anyway, but the thought of more young men being forced into service to replace them was something he hadn't considered.

"You like the thought of that?" Kazan's voice dripped with bitterness and condescension. "How about those friends of yours?"

Taylor's gaze had shifted from Kazan, but now it snapped back.

"Captains Black and Samuels...Lieutenants Young and Daniels...if you defy me again, they will lead their forces into the most hopeless battles men have ever fought. You will sit in a cell, and before you are shot, you will know that every one of them is dead, their bodies left to rot and blow away in the desert."

Taylor's shoulders fell. Kazan's words were slicing into him like daggers, draining his resolve.

"And that girl you like so much…" Kazan's voice dripped with venom. "…I will find the most sadistic gang of twisted sodomites in Earth's worst freezones, and I will have them conscripted and sent here. And I will give her to them, let them use her to vent their anger. I'll make sure she knows why before I do." Kazan was relishing the words as he spoke them. "She'll think she was fucked by a felled tree by the time they're done…by the time they have used her in every sick and degrading way you can imagine. And a hundred you can't. And then she will die too, cursing your name."

Taylor sat silently, hunched over, his spirit broken. The fight was gone, the determination drained entirely from his body, from his soul. He had lost, and he knew it. "I'll go back." He spoke softly, almost a whisper.

"What was that, Major?" Kazan was gloating, the arrogance in his voice unmistakable. "I couldn't quite hear you."

"I said I'll go back." Taylor forced it out, loud and clear.

Kazan nodded. "Then get going." He gestured toward the door. "But first, don't you think you should thank me, Major? For making you see the light." Kazan was determined to humiliate Taylor.

Taylor was struggling, trying to keep from lunging at Kazan. He could kill the miserable little bureaucrat in less than a second; he was sure of that. But Kazan would have his vengeance from the grave…every punishment he'd promised, every horror he threatened to heap on Hope and Blackie and the others…Jake knew all that would happen if he killed the miserable piece of dogshit.

"Thank you." Taylor spat it out.

"You are welcome, Major." Every word was a mockery, sapping what little remained of Jake's spirit. "I trust that you will be a good little soldier from now on?"

Taylor just nodded. Then he got up and wordlessly walked to the door.

"Wait, Major." Kazan's voice was imperious.

Taylor turned and looked back. "Yes?" His voice was pure exhaustion.

"Here." Kazan tossed a small box to Taylor.

Jake glanced down. There were two small silver eagles in the container. What is this, he thought...some kind of sick fucking joke? He stared at Kazan, a confused look on his face.

"It's a schedule promotion, Ma...Colonel Taylor. And we don't want anyone thinking anything is out of the ordinary, do we?"

Taylor didn't say a word. He put the box in his pocket and walked out the door.

# Chapter 16

From the Journal of Jake Taylor:

Darkness and despair. They are my world, my reality. The closer we get to victory, the more leaden my spirit becomes. There is a feeling of hope in the air among the men...but it is false. The troops can feel victory; they can perceive the weakening of the Machines. But that triumph will not be ours, the men who fought and bled for it. It will be UN Central's. For us, banished forever from home, there is nothing.

People will trust in something simply because they cannot face the reality that there is so little worth believing in. It's a defense, your mind's attempt to protect itself from surrender, from madness. I look back on things I accepted, that I believed, and I feel like a fool. Being honest with yourself, seeing things for what they truly are... it is exhausting. I feel a gloominess I cannot adequately describe. I am lost...there is nothing, nothing at all to work for, to strive for, to fight for. Nothing I do, nothing any of my men do, will make any difference.

I see how people think, how they convince themselves of so many things, utterly ignoring the facts to do so. Part of me wants to grab them, shake them...make them see things for what they really are. The hopelessness...the corruption and evil that permeate every aspect of life. But what would that serve? I let them deceive themselves...it is little more than a mercy. I see the truth, but they, poor deceived fools, are far better off than I.

Even my own mind is conflicted. I've learned to manage my fear in battle, but it's still there. Every time. It has been years since I really cared if I came back from a fight, but it doesn't matter. It's instinctive. No matter what my intellect dictates, how much I long for the peace of death, to lay down my burdens...my subconscious wants to survive. It pushes me, makes me use all I have within me to stay alive. And that is really starting to piss me off.

"I'm worried about him, aren't you?" Tony Black spoke softly, though he and his cohorts were alone in the mess hall.

"Jake's the toughest guy I've ever met, Blackie." The small plastic chair looked almost like a toy under Samuels' huge frame. "I can't believe he's losing it. He's just tired. How could he not be?"

Hank Daniels let out a long sigh. "I don't know, Bear." He looked at the big man then at Blackie. "Have you ever thought about how much pressure he has on him? 24/7?" He paused. "We all lean on him too. We're his friends, but tell me there's one person in this room who doesn't look to Jake when he's got a problem."

There was no response. They were all quiet for a minute. Daniels had put into words what they were all thinking. He was their leader, their friend. There wasn't a man in the room who didn't love Jake Taylor like a brother. But now they wondered, second guessed. Taylor had always been there...for all of them. Now, they questioned themselves...had they been blind to his pain...or at least the extent of it? Had they failed to be there for him?

"I've known Jake for eight years. Nobody's saying he's losing it." Blackie looked around the room. "But he's more stressed now than I've ever seen him. He's always been strong for us, Goddamn it, it's time for us to be strong for him." Black's tone was firm, definitive. "We're moving out at 0700 hours tomorrow. I want everyone at 150%. No slipups, no mistakes. We execute perfectly. We don't give him a reason to worry about anything." He looked around the room again, pausing to lock eyes with each of them in turn. "Understood?"

"Blackie's right." Daniels was nodding as he spoke. "Jake needs us to back him up now. We need to be at our best tomorrow. Even more than usual." He looked up at Blackie. "Are we all agreed?"

Daniels was being technically insubordinate. Blackie was the highest ranked after Taylor, and anything he told them to do was, by definition, an order. But Black knew Daniels was on the same page...and what he wanted from everyone wasn't something a command could compel. He was after everything they had deep inside...their inner strength. He wanted them to give their all, even more than they always did.

He took a step forward toward the others and extended his hand. Daniels did it next, followed by Samuels and then Young. They grasped hands in the center of the circle.

"For Jake." Black said it first, and they all repeated his words. "For Jake."

"The men are ready, Colonel." Major Black stood next to Taylor, his body upright, almost at attention. They were about to launch the biggest battle since the war on Erastus began. Black was usually pretty relaxed, but something about the scope of the operation was making him feel more formal than usual. He was nearly as cynical as Taylor most of the time, but now he felt like they were really moving toward victory.

Taylor looked back, a sour look passing over his face as

it usually did when someone called him colonel. "Excellent." His tone was deadpan, devoid of emotion. "That's the third time you've updated me in the last fifteen minutes. What's up with you?"

Blackie looked back at Taylor. "Nothing's up. It's just one hell of a big force we've got here, Jake."

Taylor looked back suspiciously for a few seconds then smiled. "That it is, my friend." He let out a long breath. "We will advance as soon as the Dragonfires complete their second attack run." The gunships had already made one pass, and they were coming around for another. There was a wind coming in from over the enemy positions, blowing the pungent residue of the fuel air bombs over Taylor's troops.

The objective was a crucial one, the main enemy base and Machine production center on the planet. The location of the facility was the enemy's most closely guarded secret on Erastus, but a simple communications intercept had disclosed its location.

Taylor was suspicious. The enemy was never careless, and this error had been downright reckless. His instincts smelled a trap. But no one listened to his warnings. The high command saw a chance to slice years off the duration of the war, and they were determined to seize the opportunity. Their greed for a victory overruled caution. Taylor was ordered to take command of the operation over his boisterous objections. He knew what it would mean to refuse, what a betrayal it would be to his friends...and to Hope. He had not forgotten Kazan's threat, and he knew they would pay the price for his defiance. Taylor didn't care what they did to him...threats against him didn't give them any leverage. But the small circle of people he truly cared for...they were his Achilles heel.

He may not have been able to cancel the attack, but

he was damned sure going to run things the way he saw fit. He'd chosen an LZ 10 kilometers from the target and marched the rest of the way, with clouds of scouts out in all directions.

He heard the sound of the Dragonfires raking the enemy positions with autogun fire. The first pass had been devastating, but Taylor had ordered the second attack anyway. He didn't know what the enemy was up to, but he was sure it was something. He was damned sure going to do everything he could to protect his forces…against whatever was waiting for them.

"Colonel Taylor, Major MacArthur here." Taylor and MacArthur still didn't really get along, but they'd learned to respect each other after a fashion. "The second attack run is complete. Returning to base to rearm."

"Very well, Major." Taylor's enhanced eyes were scanning the raging hell of the enemy position. "It looks like you really smacked them hard." MacArthur was an arrogant shit, but Taylor figured he could be a big enough man to praise a job well done."

"Thank you, Colonel." The gunship commander couldn't keep all the surprise out of his voice. "MacArthur out."

Taylor sighed. He was still troubled, worried about what surprises the enemy had in store for his people. But if he couldn't get out of attacking, now was the time to get started. He turned and looked at Black. "Blackie, it's time for you to get up there. You may commence your attack when ready."

Taylor paced back and forth in the command post. He hated being back from the action when his men were in the battle line, but he was responsible for 3 full battalions, and he couldn't do his job pinned down in some foxhole.

He hated every minute of it. He longed to turn over the burden of command to someone else, and go back and run his section. But he knew his responsibilities...there were 3,500 men fighting out there, and every one of them was depending on him.

"Jake..." It was Blackie, reporting in. "...they're pulling back. MacArthur's birds must have really kicked the crap out of them, because they aren't putting up much of a fight."

It was good news, but it made his stomach lurch. He was expecting some sort of a trap, and this only made him more suspicious. "Blackie..." Taylor's voice was firm, but the tension was obvious too. "...keep your eyes open, OK? I mean really open." He paused. "I have a bad feeling about this."

"They're wide open, Jake. And the rest of the guys too. We're all looking for any kind of trap or surprise." Black's tone was reassuring. He was worried about the stress he heard in Taylor's voice, and he wanted to do everything he could to help his friend shoulder the burden he carried.

"Thanks, Blackie." Taylor sounded a little relieved. He knew Black's little show of being calm was bullshit, but it still made him feel better. A little. "Keep me posted."

"Colonel Taylor!" It was Lieutenant Brandon, manning the scanner. "Enemy air inbound. Defensive squadrons are moving to intercept, but they're going to be outnumbered." He paused and looked over at Taylor. "Heavily outnumbered."

Fuck, Taylor thought...most of MacArthur's birds were on their way back to base to refuel and rearm. "I knew something was going on." He muttered under his breath.

Taylor reopened the line to Black. "Blackie, we've got an enemy air attack coming in. A big one. All units deploy anti-air assets immediately."

"Got it, Jake." He could hear yelling in the background. Black's people had detected the incoming enemy birds themselves, and they were already preparing. "We'll be ready."

Taylor cut the line. Black had his hands full, and he didn't need more distraction. He walked across the room and stared at the monitor over Brandon's shoulder. The entire screen was covered with small red triangles...wave after wave of enemy antigravs heading right for his army.

The sound was almost deafening. The enemy gunships were plastering the area around the command post, dropping hundreds of incendiary bombs, surrounding the HQ with an impenetrable circle of flame.

Taylor was hunkered down in a foxhole, just outside the portable command shelter. He'd ordered everyone out and into defensive positions as soon as the enemy air wings vectored toward headquarters. He was sure it was the trap he'd been expecting...the enemy wanted to take out HQ and the communications nexus before hitting the rest of the force with a counterattack. It was a good plan...far more innovative than the Machines usually managed. If they could badly damage 3 battalions, they could indefinitely delay the offensive against their base, and even reverse the momentum of the struggle.

But the command post was still standing, and not a man of Taylor's staff had been hit. They were cut off from the rest of the force, trapped by the inferno the enemy antigravs had unleashed. But they were unhurt.

Taylor's mind was racing. What, he thought...what am I missing? The enemy air units had paid heavily to break through the defensive squadrons MacArthur had left behind. His best guess was that the enemy massed most of their planetary airpower to stage this operation...and lost almost half of it in the process. Why were they failing to exploit their surprise?

He heard the loud whooshing sound of an anti-air rocket launching. HQ had two AA batteries, and Taylor had his best men on them. They'd brought down four of the enemy birds so far, and both launchers were still in operation. There wasn't room to reposition after firing, and Jake had expected them both to be knocked out quickly. But the enemy didn't seem to be targeting them... or anything else inside the outer perimeter.

"Transports incoming!" It was Lieutenant Brandon shouting from his foxhole. He'd grabbed one of the portable scanner stations and took it with him when Taylor ordered the command post abandoned. The thing was small enough for one man to move, and it had enough battery power for at least 8 hours of constant operation.

Taylor turned slowly, looking over toward Brandon's position. Strange, he thought...why would they land troops in here when they can take us out from the air?

"I've got 6 transports inbound to this position, sir." Brandon sounded as confused as Taylor.

"All personnel, prepare to repulse airborne assault." He pulled his own assault rifle off his back, double-checking the magazine as he did."

He directed a quick thought to the implanted com unit, opening the command line to Black. "Blackie, it looks like they're going to try to land some troops to take out the command post." He paused, scanning the area ahead of him carefully, looking for the first glimpse of the incoming antigravs. "What the hell's going on out there?"

"I'm trying to get two strikeforces back to you, Jake." Black sounded almost frantic. "But we can't get through that bombardment corridor. They keep pouring more ordnance into that zone."

"Fuck us…you worry about the rest of the men. Are they hitting you guys hard?"

"Not at all." Black sounded as surprised saying it as Taylor was hearing it. "They're pulling back all along the front, and the air units are concentrating everything on your perimeter." He paused. "I don't get it."

Taylor sighed. "Me either." He hesitated, staring out, looking for the approaching enemy. There was something…a tiny speck, growing, coming closer. Then another…and another.

"They're coming in now, Blackie." Taylor brought up the assault rifle, his eyes unmoving, focused on the approaching aircraft. "You keep your eyes open out there. You understand me?"

"Yes, sir." Black rarely called Jake "sir," but he did this time. "You can count on me."

"I know, brother. Just be careful and come the fuck back from this mess." Taylor cut the line. He didn't have time for a protracted discussion, and neither did Black. His second in command knew his shit. Now Taylor had to trust him to do his job.

The transports were clearly visible now, coming in fast. Taylor watched, eyeballing the spot he figured they'd put down…but they kept coming, flying 60 meters above the ground.

"What the fuck?" Taylor whispered to himself as the transports continued, zipping straight overhead. He looked up, watching them fly by. They were dropping something…small spherical devices. Taylor activated the unitwide com as he lurched up with his rifle and began firing. "They're dropping something! Some type of…"

A blinding light filled the sky. Taylor's body convulsed wildly, falling to the ground. It felt like a little like an electrical shock, but somehow different too…more. He couldn't move his body voluntarily, or stop his limbs from twitching uncontrollably. He was disoriented, confused, unable to speak or even focus his thoughts. Then everything went black.

# Chapter 17

From the Journal of Jake Taylor:

The Cause.  History is full of war, of death, of sacrifice... of unimaginable brutality.  All in the name of the Cause. The mighty Cause.

It is not the idea of fighting for a cause that saddens me so.  It is the ease with which people devote themselves to it.  Men have flocked into the streets, marched, argued, fought, killed...for causes they didn't even understand.  They do it because they follow along, to be part of the group...or because they don't want to be left out. Because they are told to, or because they crave to be part of something.  They follow the Cause for many reasons, with great passion and staggering ignorance.  Disturbingly rare among them, are people who fight because they truly understand the reasons for their struggle.  Most are simply followers, nipping at the heels of their leaders, like dogs begging for scraps.

Throughout history, men have fought for uncounted reasons.  For land, for money, for hegemony over their neighbors. They have fought for religion, to avenge insults, to impose belief systems...or to resist such being forced upon them.  Wars have been waged to preserve or eliminate slavery, to escape the yoke of political masters...or to impose such rule upon others.  Men have fought against those they branded inferiors...and struggled against those who called themselves their betters.

The drum has beaten the call to war throughout history, rallying men and women to fight for the Cause...to accept the inevitable pain and suffering of war. To sacrifice sons and daughters to the slaughter. To see cities burn and millions die in confusion, agony, and despair. All for the Cause.

Since the dawn of recorded history, the flags have waved and the crowds have cheered. The soldiers have marched...they have marched to fight for the Cause.

What did most of them get back from those who called them to war? Famine, disease, shortages, despair. Burned cities and broken dreams. A flag-draped coffin in place of a live son or daughter. Words, endless, professionally-written platitudes, offered by the masters in justification of the slaughter.

How often was the Cause truly just, worth the pain and death and horror of war? How many of those billions, who took to the streets for 5,000 years and cheered and sang and rallied for the Cause...how many of them really understood? What percentage took the time to consider the facts, the situation...to question what they were told and ultimately decide for themselves if the Cause was true and righteous? How many mindlessly believed the words of their masters, giving their all to a cause they didn't even comprehend? A Cause that wasn't worthy of their sacrifice?

What if the Cause is false, corrupt...a fraud created simply to urge men to fight? What if it serves nothing more than the base purposes of the leaders, buying them power with the blood of the people? What does the reasonable man, the just man, do if he discovers the Cause is false? Is there any retribution, any action, any violence unjustified in punishing those responsible? Could any horror that the oppressed and manipulated victims visit upon their former masters be unjustified. Does righteous vengeance become the new Cause?

Taylor was staring straight up. He was in a room, though that was about all he could tell. He could see the light in the ceiling, but it was hazy, distant. Everything else was a confused blur. He tried to think, to remember where he was, how he'd gotten there.

His head ached…his whole body throbbed with soreness. He felt like he'd been turned inside out and then back again. He tried to lift his head, but the room started spinning. He caught himself, choked back the vomit he felt starting to rising.

"Colonel Taylor, I want to welcome you." The voice was coming from the side, somewhere he couldn't see. It was English, but there was something odd about it, something he couldn't place. It was an accent he'd never heard, but there was more than just that. "Please do not try to rise yet. I am afraid we were forced to use a neural stun beam in order to facilitate bringing you here." There was a short pause. "I am afraid the effects can be rather disorienting…especially on your species."

I'm a prisoner, Jake thought. The Machines…no, the Tegeri…have captured me. He was scared, overwhelmed. His grim lack of concern for himself was gone, replaced by a gaping fear of the unknown. I am laid bare, defenseless before my enemy, he thought. It was one thing to accept the inevitability of death, and quite another to stare into the face of the unknown, to deal with utter helplessness.

"What…are…you…going…to…do…with…me?" It was hard to speak, but Jake forced out the words, slowly, hoarsely.

"Nothing, Colonel Taylor. Or at least I intend no harm to you. I merely wish to converse with you."

He speaks my language; he knows my name, Jake thought…did I speak when I was unconscious? What did I tell him?

"Allow me to introduce myself, Colonel." The voice was moving, coming closer. "I am T'arza. At least that is my appellation closest to what you would call a name." He was moving around, positioning himself in front of Taylor. "May I call you Jake?"

"Call me whatever you want." Taylor's voice was becoming stronger, clearer. "I'm your prisoner."

He could feel the movement, his captor coming closer. It wasn't a Machine moving toward him, he could tell that much. But it wasn't human either. Taylor had never been this close to one of the Tegeri. He felt the urge to lunge, to attack his enemy. Here was one of the leaders, the masterminds who'd ordered the attacks on the human colonies… the ones who started 40 years of bloody war. He was a meter away from one of the worst, most depraved monsters a man had ever faced…and he had no strength, no chance to avenge the thousands of dead.

"You are certainly not my prisoner, Jake. At least not in a conventional sense." The being moved into Jake's view. He – it? – was taller than a man, with paler skin and longer, thinner appendages. It was humanoid, certainly, different from a man only in superficial aspects.

"It is true that you are confined here, however that is a temporary situation. I only wish to communicate with you for a time…to provide you with information. Then you will be released." T'arza paused, observing Taylor's reactions. "And I assure you that I have no intention of harming you."

"Am I supposed to believe that?" Taylor's voice was angry, his suspicion obvious. He pulled himself up, facing his captor. His stomach did a flop, but he was able to control the nausea. "You clearly know who I am. You targeted me for some reason." Taylor's mind was still fuzzy, but he was beginning to put things together. "The intercept…"

Taylor's expression betrayed his incredulity. "You staged the entire thing...lured us into this attack." The shock was clear in his voice. "Just to capture me?" Taylor could feel the room beginning to spin. He groaned and fell back.

"The effects of the neural stun weapon are temporary, but as you have experienced, they can be quite debilitating until they pass. I have administered a drug to counter-act the worst symptoms. However, I am unfamiliar with the specifics of human pharmacology, and I have there-fore been conservative regarding dosage. Please refrain from any abrupt movements until your disequilibrium has passed. I do not wish to see you injure yourself."

T'arza watched as Taylor tried again to rise, ignoring his request. "I assure you, Jake. No harm will come to you here." T'arza paused. "My compliments to your deduc-tive capabilities. To answer your previous question, yes, we intentionally allowed your people to intercept the location of this facility." Another pause. "Your forces are tempo-rarily disordered, and they have pulled back. But we do not have the strength to defeat them here. We have essentially given up our primary planetary base of operations – and all hope of ultimately holding Erastus - to arrange this meet-ing." T'arza hesitated yet again, not wanting to overload Taylor. "I trust this lends credence to the importance of what I have to say to you."

Taylor opened his mouth, but he couldn't find any words. Everything T'arza said made perfect sense. Yet Jake couldn't quite accept it all.

The Tegeri saw he had Taylor's attention. "My peo-ple did not build the Portals. We call those who did the First Ones, though we know little more about them than you do." T'arza paused briefly. "We evolved on our own world, as humanity did upon Earth. One day, we discov-ered a Portal."

Taylor was silent, listening to T'arza's words. He still regarded the alien with anger and fear, though his companion's conduct and demeanor were so calm, so rational...the intensity of those emotions began to fade.

"It is obvious, even by cursory visual inspection, that our races share some genetic link. Perhaps those who created the Portals also sowed the seeds of both of our peoples. Or, possibly, there is some other connection between our races, long in the distant past. We cannot know. But in a universe of almost infinite diversity, we are far more alike than not. Shockingly so. Would you not agree?"

Taylor looked at T'arza, but he didn't respond. After a few seconds he nodded silently, grudgingly. It was a minute gesture, barely perceptible, though it did not go unnoticed.

"There are crucial differences, however. By whatever accidents of time and evolution, my race achieved a state of technological advancement several millennia before yours. Perhaps this was by design of those who came before, or maybe it was nothing more than some infinitesimal difference in our environments. Or simply random variation. Several thousand years is but an instant in the context of the evolution of our species. I do not know the answer. Clearly, my people are more advanced than yours in many ways...yet equally obviously, we are slowing losing the war. Indeed, we have much in common with each other, yet we differ in some ways too."

T'arza looked down at Taylor as he spoke. The alien had two eyes, not unlike human ones, but deeper, more three dimensional on close view. "My brethren – the Tegeri, as you call us - are fiercely independent, so much so that we do not fully understand the ways in which humans can form large monolithic groups. Like armies. We cannot defeat you at war, because you are far more suited to sacrificing your individualism and accepting orders without question. Indeed, my people would likely have destroyed each other long ago, however, while we cherish our own freedom, we lack the will to take it from others, to impose our way of thinking on those around us. Thus did we peacefully exist for centuries before your people came through the Portal."

T'arza's tone changed for the first time, as if he was trying to be careful in what he said to avoid offending Taylor. "Your people, on the contrary, are extremely susceptible to suggestion and driven to impose their will on others. Indeed, it is the primary reason we severed contact so long ago. Your people were known to mine long before you ventured to a Portal world. My race spent centuries on your planet, mentoring your ancestors, teaching them." T'arza spoke hauntingly, as if from personal memory. "We sought nothing in return, but the ancient humans began to regard us as gods, seeking out our favor in their own conflicts. We came to form the basis of many of your ancient religions, though through no effort or desire of our own."

T'arza paused. His tone was hard to discern, but Taylor thought he detected something there. Sadness, perhaps.

"Soon, some among your people began to use us to seek to control others. They waged wars in our names, and exhorted men to murder other men under pretense of appeasing us."

Taylor sat quietly and listened. He was skeptical, his mind unwilling to accept what this enemy was telling him. But he couldn't bring himself to discount what T'arza was saying either. It felt somehow…true.

"So we left your world, fearing the damage we might cause to your then-primitive forefathers. We resolved to guard the Portals and wait for your people to mature…and to join us." He stopped speaking for a few seconds, giving Jake a chance to consider what he had been told.

"Indeed, we needed your race to step through the Portals. My people are a dying race. It has been many centuries since any have been born among us. We have never been able to determine the cause of this...perhaps we were only meant to exist for a certain time...or some ancient research of ours unleashed something terrible upon us. We are long-lived, vastly more so than your kind. Yet humanity shall outlast us."

Taylor found himself almost hypnotized, lost in what T'arza was telling him. His fear of the alien was draining away...and his hatred as well, leaving only confusion. The being speaking to him was so rational, so empathic. So different from most of the people Jake knew. His doubts began to crumble.

"We waited for your people to come, to take up the mantle as guardians of the Portals. But we saw what was happening on your Earth. Again and again, your people allowed evil, inferior men and women to lead them. They submitted themselves to be ruled by those unfit for such authority. They surrendered their judgment, their self-determination." T'arza looked at Jake unwaveringly as he spoke. "We began to despair, to fear that humanity would never mature, that we would have none fit to whom we could pass control of the Portals. We debated intervention, but we could not truly grasp the motivating factors of your behavior...nor could we discern any way to prevent it, save using force and imposing our own will on humanity. This is an option that has always been repugnant to us."

Taylor pulled himself up, propping his back against the cushions so he could look directly at T'arza as he spoke. The headache was subsiding, and he was becoming more and more focused on what he was hearing.

"We created the beings you call 'the Machines' to

replace us, to maintain the structure of our civilization as we dwindled. We had hoped they might become our free-willed successors but, alas, we were never able to achieve what we sought. They are little better than slaves, though it was never our intention to make them as such. We had the technology to create them, but not the knowledge or power to instill in them the spark of true life. We were never able to give them truly independent thought nor make them self-replicating, like a natural species. Every one of them that exists was manufactured. Every attempt at creating a reproductive capability in them has failed."

"So the Machines were not purpose built as soldiers?" Taylor finally spoke. His instinct still told him to doubt what T'arza told him, but the alien's words seemed so genuine, his skepticism was fading.

"Indeed, no." T'arza's tone changed again, sounding as though the very topic was distasteful. "My people are morally repulsed by the idea of creating a race of slave soldiers. The entities you call 'Machines' were intended to replace us when the last of us dies out, not to serve us in wars of conquest." He paused for a few seconds before cautiously continuing. "When the conflict with your people began, we had little choice but to employ them in a defensive role." T'arza's expressions were not easily readable, but Jake recognized sadness passing again over the alien's face. "My people are now far too few to wage a war of this size and duration. We were compelled to manufacture more of the Machines to defend the Portal worlds.

Taylor sat and listened. Again, the facts supported everything he was being told. The Machines fought competently, nothing more. He had no doubt that T'arza's race was capable of building better warriors if they so wished… if their ethical constraints would allow it.

He closed his eyes, trying to organize his thoughts.

He couldn't reconcile this gentle, intelligent alien with the atrocities committed on the first Portal worlds. With the savage race that turned man's first contact into a bloody crusade. "But why did you attack the first colonies?" Taylor's voice was strained, tense. "We didn't come to attack...we came to settle, to explore." Anger was creeping back into his tone, as the scenes from the early colonies ran through his mind. The Machines, slaughtering men, women... children. Burning down the tiny new villages. "And the Machines killed them...they killed them all." Taylor was practically screaming as he looked right at T'arza. "Why?" It was a cry of anger and a plea for understanding.

T'arza's expression changed again, though Taylor couldn't read the emotions behind it this time. "I do not know if you are ready to accept the truth, Jake Taylor, but I am about to provide it to you." He paused. "I fear you will find it...unsettling."

"What truth?" Taylor was angry, but confusion was once again supplanting rage.

"My people are not responsible for the acts that started this war."

Taylor was incredulous. "You murdered unarmed civilians! You massacred every human being that set foot on those worlds!" Taylor was shaking. "What did you expect us to do?"

"We murdered no one." T'arza spoke calmly. "The entities you call the 'Machines' murdered no one."

Jake stared back, his mouth open but silent.

"The events you describe, the horrors inflicted on your initial colonists...that was the work of other humans, Jake, not of my people."

Taylor felt a new rush of anger. "That is a lie! I saw it...I saw it all on the videos."

"I understand this is a profoundly disturbing revelation for you, Jake, however it is completely factual." T'arza hesitated, giving Taylor a few seconds to collect himself. "When humans at last came to the world you call New Earth, my people rejoiced. At last, we thought, the humans have found the Portals and come to join us. We had long considered your people, not as our children exactly, but akin to younger siblings. We welcomed your colonists, and we sent emissaries to greet them. We brought gifts, and we sought to share our knowledge of the Portals."

T'arza spoke slowly, with reverent respect for what he was saying. "Your colonists welcomed us. We were familiar with humans, and we had little difficulty communicating. Your ancient languages were still familiar to us, and your modern ones were simple to learn."

There was definite sadness in the Tegeri's commentary. It wasn't so much a tone of voice as an overall demeanor, almost a feeling. But Jake was convinced that the alien was speaking of something he thought of as a terrible tragedy.

"We spoke with your colonial leaders. As with all human social groupings, there was an obvious and rigid administrative hierarchy in play."

Taylor winced slightly, feeling a little defensive hearing T'arza characterize human behavior. He didn't disagree with anything the Tegeri was saying, but he still didn't like hearing it.

T'arza could see that Taylor was uncomfortable. "I do not mean to say anything that may offend you, Jake. I am not judging human behavioral norms, simply describing them." He looked silently at Taylor.

Jake nodded his head. "Please go on. I am not offended." Taylor was lying, but T'arza had his attention. He wanted to hear the rest of the story.

"We told your settlers about the true extent of the Portal network...something humans have still not discovered.

It is vast, and it leads to many places in the universe…to wonders you can only imagine."

Taylor was staring back, waiting for T'arza to continue. He didn't know what the alien was going to say, but he was starting to see shreds of it come together in his mind. He tried not to guess, to let his imagination run ahead of the facts. But he couldn't ignore the pit in his stomach.

"Then they came." Taylor could feel the ominous tone in what T'arza was telling him. "Soldiers, fully-armed and ready for battle. They attacked us and killed many before we fled. We tried to communicate, to tell them we had come peacefully, but they ignored all our entreaties." T'arza hesitated before continuing. "After we withdrew, we watched in horror as the soldiers turned their weapons on the villages." The Tegeri's mannerisms were different from human norms, but Taylor could tell how upsetting this was for the alien.

"Soldiers, what kind of soldiers?" Taylor felt his doubts again. What troops, he thought, could have attacked the Tegeri? There were colonies from seven different nations on those first two worlds, and all were destroyed.

"They came through the Portal. They destroyed the settlements, burning them to the ground. They pursued the few survivors, shooting them down as they fled. They murdered them all, even the children. My people watched in shock, in horror. Our race has had no live young born in uncounted centuries, and even in our oldest memories, children held a special place in our civilization. To see human soldiers butchering the colonial children was something none of my people will forget."

Taylor's mind was racing, wondering whether to believe what he was being told. Could it really have been some human force? Why, he wondered…what reason would other humans have for attacking the settlements?

The answer was forming in his head, slowly, hazily. It was something so terrible, so inconceivable, that his mind fought it desperately, not wanting to face it.

"Indeed, Jake…what I tell you is true. The attackers were humans, and they came through the Portal from Earth." T'arza was speaking, but Taylor was too consumed with his own thoughts to listen fully. The alien's voice sounded far off now, a distant whisper.

"What of the videos?" Taylor's voice was desperate, trying to think of any way to argue against what he had already begun to believe. "They showed us videos of the massacres."

"Any videos you saw were false, Jake." T'arza waved his hand and a screen on the wall flickered to life. "They had many dead Machines to model, and creating false video is a simple feat." He waved his hand a second time. "This is the true image of what happened that day."

The screen showed a small village, nestled in an idyllic valley. New Earth was a beautiful world, not a hell like Erastus. There were fields and forests…and deep blue rivers crisscrossing the landscape. But there was something wrong in the image Taylor was watching. Columns of smoke rose from the small cluster of buildings, and people were running, screaming…trying to escape the fiery death raining down on their tiny community.

There were soldiers attacking the town. They wore bluish-gray fatigues with black body armor. Those are pre-Consolidation UN troops, Taylor realized. He was sick to his stomach watching the soldiers bombarding the town, raking the peaceful hamlet with mortars and hyper-velocity rounds.

Small units detached from the main forces, pursuing the colonists who escaped the village. The terrified civilians ran for a nearby wood, but they were mowed down by automatic weapons fire. Not one of them made it 100 meters from the dying village. Taylor watched them die. He saw a child, no more than 5 or 6 years old, stumbling, fleeing…holding his own severed arm in his hand.

He wanted to weep, to give the victims the tears they deserved, but his mechanical eyes couldn't cry. He watched as the soldiers advanced, checking the bodies, finishing off any that were still alive. This wasn't a battle…it was methodical genocide. Taylor felt the sickness coming. He lurched forward, onto his hands and knees, emptying the contents of his stomach onto the polished stone floor.

"No," he spat out. "This isn't true…it is your video that is fake." He said it, longing for it to be true. But inside, he already knew. Everything T'arza had told him was the truth.

The Tegeri remained silent, clearing empathizing with the pain Taylor was feeling…the shock at the revelations he'd provided. "Jake…" He spoke softly, slowly. "…I understand this is a terrible discovery." He paused, giving Taylor a few seconds to focus on what he was saying. "You were chosen very carefully for this contact. We have examined many of your people before selecting you. I fear that I am laying upon you a great burden."

Taylor was silent. His mind was racing, but not a word came to his lips. He just stared at his alien companion, a numb expression on his face.

"We are prepared to offer you one more proof of our sincerity, Jake Taylor. Even as we speak, our forces are withdrawing from this planet. Within four planetary days, we will be gone from the world you call Erastus."

Taylor was shocked again. He sat quietly, trying to get some perspective on all he'd heard. He could hear the sound of his heart beating in his ears, feel the weakness in his legs. "What am I supposed to do?" His voice was weak, throaty.

"I cannot tell you that, Jake." T'arza spoke softly. "I do not know the answer. You must find this yourself…you must take what I have told you and decide how to proceed. Our peoples have fought an unnecessary and pointless war for far too long."

"But I am one man." Taylor's words were a plea. "What can one man do?"

"One man can do much. As I said, you have been chosen with great care. You are an extraordinary representative of your species, both in fighting ability and intelligence. You also have a number of less-easily defined qualities." T'arza walked closer. "You are capable of far more than you might imagine. And you inspire an especially potent form of loyalty from others."

Taylor looked up, staring at the Tegeri. He opened his mouth then closed it, once again without saying anything.

"There will be no more war on Erastus. You will have the opportunity to communicate with your fellow slave-soldiers, to spread the word…and formulate whatever actions you wish to take."

Taylor winced at T'arza's choice of words. He was about to object, but then he thought, he is right…what are we but slaves? "Actions? What actions? What can a few soldiers do?"

"You will have to decide that, Jake. It is only knowledge that I can offer you." T'arza paused. "It is important that you understand the truth in all of this. Do you still doubt anything I have told you?"

Taylor sat quietly for a few seconds, thinking, trying to get a grip on his emotions…to think rationally about what he'd been told. As he thought, he became more and more convinced. It all made sense to him. "No." He spoke slowly quietly. "I don't doubt any of it."

"I will give you a few solitary moments to collect your thoughts." T'arza moved toward the door. "Then I will return. I have more to share with you. I will provide you with my people's full knowledge of the Portal network. It is far more extensive than your people know. Your neural implant will retain the knowledge for your use. Perhaps one day it will be useful to you."

Taylor watched T'arza walk through the door. Then he bent over and vomited again.

# PART THREE
# REBEL

# Chapter 18

From the Journal of Jake Taylor:

Betrayal. It is a common story throughout human history, one all too familiar. Yet rarely has there been so shocking a revelation of perfidy as the one T'arza made to me.

It was a lie. All of it. Everything I fought for. All my men suffered and died for. A waste, a deliberate fraud perpetuated so a group of politicians and diplomats could seize power. It is all I can think about. It consumes my thoughts by day and through every sleepless night. I feel as if it will drive me mad at any moment.

The Tegeri didn't start the war...their Machines did not attack the human settlements. They had come in peace, to teach the colonists the secrets of the Portal worlds. And they had been attacked by secret UN forces. The whole thing, forty years of war and incalculable suffering...all to create a crisis, one the UN's leadership could use to annex the remaining independent nation states. Even worse, it was continued for decades. Why? Because it was useful to keep the masses in line? Because faced with an ongoing threat to mankind's existence, people will meekly accept whatever is imposed on them? It was a deliberate plot, a creation of minds so monstrous, I cannot comprehend such creatures. Or perhaps now, I can.

I felt empty, violated. My parents...my brother. The

family I lost. Beth, my sweet Beth. It was all for nothing. I was taken from those I loved and consigned to hell. Even my humanity was stolen from me. For nothing save to further base political corruption, the lust for power of a group of men not worth the life of even one of my soldiers.

The things I have done claw at me in the night, the horrors I have inflicted...on my own men...and on an enemy I have misjudged, one that didn't deserve my hatred. The Machines weren't an evil foe, seeking to destroy humanity. They were victims, unwilling warriors trying to defend the Tegeri against ruthless invaders...my men and I, and thousands like us. Their blood is on my hands now.

Ten years of war. A decade of bloodshed, of death. Ten years in hell, fighting an alien enemy, an adversary I long believed to be evil, ruthless. I have wronged the Machines, the Tegeri. My men and I, unwittingly, have become all we hated about our enemy. Our cause was the unjust one, not theirs; we were the aggressors, the killers.

The Tegeri released Taylor, just as T'arza had promised. He was dropped 10 klicks from the battlefield, with a canister of water and a day's rations. It was just after the small sun set, during the first twilight of the day. The second twilight, when the large sun passed below the horizon, was the coolest time, but it lasted less than an Earth hour. T'arza had carefully chosen the moment of Jake's release. Taylor was tired, and struggling to assimilate what he'd been told, but the effects of the Tegeri stun weapon were gone. T'arza wouldn't let him leave until the last of the symptoms had passed.

The transport carrying him had come in low, escorted by a dozen gunships. The Tegeri had gone to great lengths to choose Taylor, and they weren't about to get him shot down by his own people when they were trying to release him.

He started to walk slowly. He was really feeling the heat, even though it was far from midday. He'd been so confused, so disoriented, he hadn't even noticed that the room where he'd met T'arza was considerably cooler than normal for Erastus. It wasn't Gregor Kazan's air conditioning, but it was a hell of a lot more comfortable than the blasted rock and burning sands he was now traversing.

Ten klicks wasn't that far by most standards, but it was a long walk in the searing heat of Erastus. Unsure of his stamina, he moved deliberately, not wanting to tire himself out too quickly. Overdoing it early, exhausting yourself in the middle of the desert…that was the surest way to get killed on Erastus. He'd explained it a thousand times to rookies. They didn't all listen, but Taylor kept trying.

He could hear faint explosions…the sounds of battle in the distance. His men were still fighting. He was pretty far away, but the noise was random and sporadic. Whatever was going on at the front, it didn't sound very intense. He moved toward the noise, but he got less than a kilometer before he heard the antigravs moving toward him. The gunships were pretty quiet for aircraft, but when you knew what to listen for you could hear them coming from a distance.

He ran toward a small cluster of rocks, instinctively looking for a place to hide. He was halfway there when the sound of his com exploded in his ears.

"Jake!" The voice was immediately familiar. "Jake, is that you?" Taylor recognized Bear Samuel's slow southern drawl.

"Bear?" He stopped running and turned to watch two of the gunships land. "What the hell are you doing on a gunship?"

A team poured out of each of the antigravs, fully armed and equipped. They formed a perimeter around Taylor, weapons drawn and aimed outward, ready to defend their commander against any threat.

"I was looking for you…what do you think? We were almost ready to give up on you. Everybody but Blackie. He's got MacArthur's people out scouring the entire area for you."

Taylor saw his massive friend hop out of the gunship and run toward him. "Goddamn, Jake…I've never been so happy to see anybody in my life." Samuels threw his massive arms around Taylor and gave him a colossal hug.

"It's damned good to see you too, you big oaf." Taylor's voice was strained. "Now let me go so I can breathe."

Samuels took a step back. "What the hell happened, Jake? Everybody in the command post was unconscious when we finally got through those incendiaries. Nobody was seriously hurt, though. And you were the only one missing." The big man stared at Jake with a confused look.

"It's a long story, Bear." Taylor was looking past Bear, toward the battlefield. "But first, what's going on with the battle?"

"It's the damnedest thing, Jake." Bear put his hand behind Taylor, herding him gently toward the gunship as he spoke. He wanted to get his newly found commander to a secure location as quickly as possible. "The bastards just up and ran. They abandoned every position." Jake could hear the surprise in Samuels' voice. "It's the closest thing to a rout I've even seen." His face morphed into a bloodthirsty smile. "Blackie's got the boys hot on their heels…and the rest of MacArthur's birds will be hitting them in a few minutes. We're gonna blow them to hell, Jake."

"No."

Samuels stopped and turned toward Taylor. "No what?" He was completely confused.

Taylor stared back at him. "No pursuit, no air assault. I want all units to stand down immediately."

Samuels stood silently, a dumbfounded look on his face.

"Do you understand me, Bear?" Taylor's voice was cold and grim. "Immediately."

"Sure, Jake...I mean, yes, sir." Samuels yelled through the open door of the gunship. "Raise Major Black right away." The individual coms had a limited range, but the unit in the Dragonfire would reach Black wherever he was on the field. "Tell him we found Colonel Taylor." He paused for a second or two, a puzzled look on his face. "Advise him that the colonel orders all units to stand down at once. Repeat, all units are to cease attacks and stand down immediately."

Bear turned back toward Taylor. He looked completely lost.

"I'll explain it all, Bear." Taylor reached up and grabbed one of the handholds on the antigrav, pulling himself inside. "But let's go find Blackie and the others first." He smiled, an odd expression on his face. "I only want to go through this once."

No one said a word...they just stared back in shocked silence. Jake Taylor, Ten Year Man, Supersoldier...the invincible warrior of Erastus was telling them to let the enemy go. The Machines were withdrawing across their entire line, abandoning their entrenchments. Taylor's forces were ready to pursue...and MacArthur's gunships were rearmed and standing by to attack and annihilate the fleeing enemy. Everything was perfect...the entire army was ready to utterly destroy the Machines facing them. But Taylor was in command, and he said no.

"Jake..." Blackie's voice was strained. "...I don't know what's up with you, but do you realize the shitstorm we're gonna get if we let them get away?" He didn't want to push Taylor too hard. He didn't know what to do.

"Fuck it." Taylor's voice was cold, emotionless. "I don't give a shit what HQ wants." He turned and looked at Black with an icy expression. "My order stands. All units are to stand down." He was silent for a few seconds. "And I will shoot the first officer who disobeys."

Black stared silently at Taylor, trying to find his voice. He was Jake's best friend, but he felt like he didn't know him at all right now. What the hell is going on, he thought… what happened to him out there? Black had assumed Taylor got stunned or disoriented during the attack on the command post and wandered into the desert. But now he started to wonder what had really happened.

"Attention all units, this is Colonel Taylor." He was speaking over the open com, addressing every soldier in the army. "I have issued orders for all units to cease hostilities. All forces are to remain in current positions until further notice." His voice was imperious, commanding… as if he was daring anyone to disobey.

"Colonel, this is Major MacArthur." Taylor sighed. Here it comes, he thought. "What in hell is going on down there? My people are in position. I need to launch the attack now." MacArthur sounded angry and confused.

"No."

"Colonel, I don't think you underst…"

"What part of no don't you understand, Major." Taylor's voice was like death. "Your squadrons are to return to base at once."

"Colonel, my orders are to…"

"Your orders are whatever I say they are." Blackie and the other officers were standing around staring at Jake. They couldn't hear what MacArthur was saying, but they'd never heard anything like the menace in Taylor's tone. He wasn't shouting...not even raising his voice. But there wasn't a man present who would question anything Taylor said now. "If you disobey me, I will order every AA asset in the army to target your force." A short pause. "Do we understand each other?"

MacArthur was silent for a few seconds, but he scraped up the courage to come back at Jake one more time. "Colonel, I will not disobey your orders, however I intend to make a full report when I return to base." He cut the line.

Taylor stood still for a few seconds, the angry look on his face giving way, yielding to an amused smile. Pompous ass, he thought...if only he knew how much I didn't give a shit.

He turned back toward Black. "Don't look so glum, Blackie." He walked toward his oldest friend. "I know what I'm doing." He paused, noting the doubtful expression on Black's face. "Really, I do."

"Whatever you say, Jake." Black still sounded concerned...and even more confused. He'd been worried about Taylor for some time, and he was afraid his friend had finally lost it. Still, he wasn't ready to challenge him. "You know I'll do whatever you say."

"I know." He reached out and put his hand on Black's shoulder. "Just trust me, my friend. I'll fill you in on everything." He panned his head around, looking at the faces staring in his direction. "Just not here."

Chapter 19

From the Journal of Jake Taylor:

Back on Earth I was an obedient citizen. More or less, at least. I had the occasional gripe, as most people do, but basically I believed what I was taught and did what I was told. That began to change on Erastus. I saw things, not just the suffering all around me, but the gulf between the UN staffers and the lifers, like my men and I. I saw the injustice, the culture of superiority among them. I began to realize the inadequacy of the justifications we were given. I became bitter. I began to resent – and later hate – the system that sent me to this terrible place...without even the hope of coming home. I finally resolved to quit, only to be blackmailed into returning to my post...on pain of my closet friends being persecuted if I refused.

I long had my doubts about much of what the government and the high command did, the decisions they made and the often callous way they treated the soldiers fighting this war. But even in my angriest moments... even when Kazan was threatening to murder those closest to me...I had never perceived a shadow of the ghastly truth. No matter how upset I was or how much I chafed under the directives of UN Central, I had always believed, at least, that I was here defending mankind from an alien doom. Now, even that has been stripped away from me. My faith in our cause, and all the times I sought refuge in that belief...it all seems like the worst sort of idiocy now. Why was I such a fool?

Why are people so easily led? Why do we believe the things we are told, demanding no proof, no evidence? How do we fail, time and again, to think for ourselves? Why do we discover one fraud, only to willingly accept the next one without question? Because we're told to...taught to? Because our parents did...or, in the case of my father and I, because he didn't and I wanted to rebel against his constant tirades?

How much of what we are told is true? Government, teachers, family...how many are honest? How many lie? How many unwittingly pass on their own ignorance? The history we are taught…what of it is true, and what is fabrication? What ethical codes that we follow are truly just, constructed from our core beliefs, and which are constructs, created by evil men to control people's thoughts, their actions? The smarter, the wiser among us…those with the foresight and intelligence to see through what our world has become…do they languish and die in the reeducation facilities, ignored by the masses, who obediently write them off as crazy fools, menaces to society?

Is there even such a thing as "reeducation?" Or are those dark places simply death camps, where any who stand against the established order are sent to disappear?

I have changed in many ways since I was sent here to fight an unjust war. I have mourned the loss of my family and watched friends die in agony, terrified and far from home. There is almost nothing left of me, of Jake Taylor, the man. I have become soulless death.

But I have one thing left to live for, one force that drives me forward with relentless determination. I will have vengeance. For me. For the thousands who have died on Erastus and the other Portal worlds. For the men and women who fought alongside my father and saw all they loved about their nation stolen from them, for the billions forced to live under the yoke of UN Central. For the Tegeri, who sought only to be mankind's teachers, but became their victims instead.

I will destroy the creatures who have wrought this… and those who have come after them, filled their shoes and perpetuated this monstrous war for their own gain. I will tear down this unholy evil stone by stone, and I will see UN Central burned to ashes before these eyes close for the last time. This I swear, with all that remains to me.

Death to all who are complicit in this horror. To any who work to perpetuate it…for any who are part of this are stained with the guilt, as are those who offer them aid or succor. They must be eradicated from the universe, hunted down wherever they may seek to hide and utterly destroyed. Like an infection. There can be no pity, no mercy…and any who offer such are as guilty as those they comfort.

This is my oath, and I pledge to it my blood, and all of my soul that remains to me. Nothing shall stand in my way…and any who try will become my enemies. My victims.

The room was silent except for the faint hum of the ventilation system. Taylor stood in the center, staring down, moving his eyes over his seated friends. He'd just told them. About T'arza, the Tegeri, the war. Everything.

"So…" He broke the silence after a minute or two. "…you guys believe me? Or do you think I'm crazy?"

"Jake, you know we're with you 100%." Blackie spoke after another uncomfortable silence. "But this is a lot to absorb." His tone was confused, uncertain. Tony Black would never disbelieve anything Jake told him…but this was truly extraordinary. Black had already been worried about Taylor's mental state, and now this?

"Blackie…all of you…I know you guys have my back. You're the best friends I've ever had. And I know this sounds crazy." Taylor's voice was calm, focused. He reached into his pocket and pulled something out. "But it happened exactly as I said." He held up a small medallion hanging on a chain. It was silvery in color, but unlike any metal they'd ever seen. It seemed to be constantly changing its hue, giving it a shimmering effect. "T'arza gave me this before the Tegeri released me. The design is the sigil of his house." He paused, looking over toward one of the blank featureless walls. "But it is quite functional as well as decorative."

As he finished speaking, images appeared in front of the wall. Holograms...three dimensional video, depicting the first human colonies on New Earth. They were under attack...not by the Machines, but by heavily-armed soldiers. Human soldiers.

Every eye was on the projection, watching...wincing at the atrocities portrayed before them. No one spoke... they barely breathed as they stared in shock at the horrors Taylor displayed for them.

"This device is pretty strong proof I was with the Tegeri." Taylor spoke softly. "It's certainly nothing built by man." He took a shallow breath. "And the revelation they provided me was simply this...it wasn't the Tegeri and the Machines who started this war...it was UN Central. It was all a plan to facilitate the Consolidation."

"Jake..." It was Hank Daniels, sounding shaky, uncertain. "...how do we know this is real? I mean, we believe you, of course, but how do we know the enemy isn't playing all of us?"

Taylor walked toward his friend, taking a seat on the edge of the long sofa. "We don't, Hank." He looked over at the others. "The truth is, we have to decide what we believe."

"But you've decided." Karl Young looked over at Taylor. The excitable officer was uncharacteristically calm. "Haven't you, Jake?"

"I have, Karl. But you all need to make your own choices."

"Why, Jake?" It was Black, sounding skeptical. "Why do you believe this is true? It could all be a fabrication, an attempt to sow confusion in our ranks. If UN Central could make fake vids to show us, so could the Tegeri."

"You're right, Blackie." Taylor didn't argue...he just

nodded as he spoke. "I was skeptical too, at first. But the more I heard, the more sense it all made to me."

"This makes sense to you?" Bear spoke slowly, softly. "Could men really be responsible for this? Can we take an alien's…an enemy's…word for something like this?"

"No, Bear. We don't take anyone's word." Taylor stood up, the calmness in his tone giving way, showing a sliver of the suppressed anger. "For anything. We've done far too much of that already. We've accepted what we've been told…followed orders without question. We have aided this fraud in our own way, as have all Earth's citizens. That must end."

Taylor paused, looking around the room, seeing the uncertainty in his friends' faces. "You must each decide what you believe…and what course of action you will pursue." He hesitated again. "But think about all you know. Remember the way the UN staffers have treated you. The disrespect, the contempt. Think about the time before you came to Erastus. How much of your life was ruled by fear. Fear of penalties, of persecution…of ending up in a reeducation camp? How many of you went hungry? Blackie…how many nights did you sleep in the streets, just trying to find someplace safe enough to close your eyes. How many people went to reeducation camps and never returned?" He panned his eyes, looking at each of them in turn before he continued. "Ask yourselves…is Earth's government trustworthy?"

Taylor walked slowly across the room. "T'arza told me the Tegeri and the Machines would leave Erastus in four days." He stopped and turned back to face the others. "It has been two days. Have you seen a report of any enemy activity? You all saw the enemy withdrawing in front of us. Every one of you knows full well they had enough force there to give us one hell of a fight."

There was another long silence, everyone present deep in thought. Finally, it was Black who spoke first. "OK, Jake." His didn't sound convinced, but the skepticism was mostly gone from his voice. "Suppose we agree with you. What do we do about it?"

"We take our vengeance Blackie." Taylor's tone turned dark, ominous. "We destroy them...all those responsible for this abomination." He glared at the seated officers, his eyes on fire.

They all stared back at Taylor, stunned looks on their faces. Bear was the first to respond. "Jake, we'd follow you to hell...you know that. But how are the five of us supposed to take on UN Central?"

"A step at a time, Bear." Taylor spoke confidently. "First, we unite the forces on Erastus." His body tensed, his anger filling him with determination. "Let the revolution begin here...on this hell to which we were consigned."

"Some of the boys will follow, Jake...most of our guys probably." Black looked at Taylor, staring right into his eyes. "But UN Central will brand us as traitors...they will order all the other forces on Erastus to oppose us." He paused. "You know we will never convince them all. What do we do with the rest?"

Taylor stared back at Black, a pitiless cold in his eyes. "We fight them, Blackie. We kill them." His voice was unemotional, almost deadpan. "They must side with us... or become our enemies. Any who stand in our way must be destroyed."

The room fell silent again. Taylor gave them a minute to consider his words before continuing. "I know that is an upsetting prospect. But this is no time for half measures. There is no way to overstate the horrendous evil that has been perpetrated...upon us, upon all the citizens of Earth, upon the Tegeri."

Taylor began pacing across the room as he spoke, stopping to look intently at each man present. "Think about the scope of what has happened. Remember the families you left behind...those of all the soldiers on Erastus. Imagine your mothers – or sisters or girlfriends – looking up at the stars, eyes raw from crying, thinking of you, the pain of loss still fresh. All that suffering, all that sacrifice. And not just Erastus...but on 40 worlds. The thousands dead. Every bloody, scared kid any of us has held as he took his last rattling breath. All a waste...an endless parade of horrors. So a few men could make themselves the world's masters."

Emotion was creeping back into Taylor's voice. Anger, certainly, but urgency as well. He spoke like a zealot exhorting his companions to join a crusade. "Think of the Tegeri. You have fought them...been brainwashed to hate them, lied to and convinced they were genocidal creatures. But it is we, my friends, who have been the monsters. Our souls will bear that guilt forever, for what we have done, we have done, despite the false pretexts that drove us."

His voice began to crack slightly. Taylor had always carried guilt for the soldiers he lost; now he bore the burden for all those his people had killed as well...the thousands and thousands of Machines they had murdered in cold blood.

He could see the expressions change on the faces around him. His friends, his loyal companions...only now were they beginning to comprehend what he had told them, the true scope of what had been done to them all.

"We must destroy this evil...and nothing must be allowed to stand in our way. The shades of the dead scream for justice...for vengeance." Taylor was practically screaming. "Follow me, my friends...trust in me. We must act. For therein lies our sole hope for redemption...for absolution of the sins for which we all share the guilt."

He could see in their eyes. He was reaching them... digging, unleashing that pain they kept buried deep. Karl Young was the first. He stood up, thrusting his fist into the air. "Jake is right! We must set things to right...we cannot allow this to stand." He looked right at Taylor. "I am with you, Jake. Wherever this takes us...whatever we must do."

Taylor stepped forward, grasping Frantic's arm, turning his head, looking toward the others.

"Of course we're with you, Jake." Blackie rose, and walked toward Taylor. "Always."

Bear stood next. "Always." He moved to Jake, throwing his massive arms around Taylor, Black, and Frantic.

Hank Daniels sat, watching the other four embracing. He had an odd smile on his face. Taylor turned his head, looking at the last member of his inner circle. "Hank?"

Daniels' smile widened. "I'm just sitting here waiting for you to tell me when we start, Dog."

# Chapter 20

From the Journal of Jake Taylor:

I've tried for years to write about the feeling of battle, but every time I started, the words just wouldn't come. It's a hard thing to describe, especially to one who hasn't experienced it. I knew almost nothing about war when I enlisted. I was familiar with a bit of the history, at least the stuff on the approved list, but that's more of who fought who...not the actual experience of war. That part was a complete mystery.

The biggest surprise to me was the boredom. Actual combat is enormously stressful, but most of a soldier's life is spent on routine. In base, on patrol, doing maneuvers. In a place like Erastus, that routine is miserable, and long breaks between action can sap morale quicker than battle. If you sit in base long enough, you forget how terrible combat is...then you get into a nasty fight, and the routine doesn't seem so bad anymore. For a while.

Battle. How can I explain how that feels? You're scared, for starters. Even in a place like Erastus, even when your hope and your will to live seem to be gone... you're still scared shitless. Anybody who says he's been in battle and wasn't terrified is lying or crazy. Or both.

Surviving combat requires concentration...or luck. And luck never lasts. It's not easy to maintain a cool focus when your heart is pounding in your ears and sweat is pouring down your face. To make it through the battle-field you need to think about every step you take, every move you make. When you stop paying attention, even for a second, you do something stupid. And that's usually when you die.

That's the hardest part for the rookies. Most of them manage the fear...at least well enough. But they get rattled...they get distracted. They forget to keep their heads down or they get sidetracked, turned around. It's not easy to think straight, crouched behind a rock with hyper-velocity rounds tearing into the ground all around you. You can be sharp as a razor 99% of the time, but the other 1% will get you killed. It just takes one of those heavy projectiles moving at 3,000 mps to turn a large chunk of your body to red mist.

There's another feeling, one that's especially hard to describe. It's related to the fear, certainly, but it's more than that too. When you're in a firefight, or you're advancing across a field, you know you could take a hit at any time. You can almost feel the projectiles coming at you. Your body gets an odd series of urges, trying to somehow pull in on itself, get out of the danger zone. But there's nowhere to go. It's almost like the shakes, but not quite. When you've been in enough fights, you can more or less control it, but it never goes away entirely. At least it hasn't for me.

At its heart, combat is primal. Our primitive ancestors fought. Animals will fight if provoked. The basic impulse is in all of us, waiting for a flood of chemicals from the brain, calling the body to battle. Thinking, remembering your training, is something else entirely. It requires harnessing the wildness, controlling some of it and directing the rest.

Instinctive combat is a solitary affair. Your reflexes are designed for individual action. Your mind wants to fight alone...and to flee alone when advisable. A significant part of military training is learning to overcome this and operate as a team. We are soldiers, not boxers or street-fighters. Working together magnifies combat ability, and it makes it far likelier for each individual to survive... though that part must be forced into your brain...often by experience as well as education.

A great Gallic warrior would probably have defeated a Roman legionary in single combat. But a full legion would have shattered an equal number of barbarians in a pitched battle. The experience of combat for a soldier is a shared one. We are stronger as a whole. If a part of that whole falters, all are at much greater risk. When we don't work together, when we are not as one...that is when we fall.

"I've got the 213th and the 173rd dug in on the heights." Black was out of breath. He'd positioned the two strike-forces himself; then he'd run back the 3 klicks to HQ.

"Well done, Blackie." Taylor's voice betrayed an odd combination of emotions...determination, anger, confidence. He was fighting hard to keep his other feelings hidden. For all the anger and bravado about destroying any who stood in his way, Taylor dreaded firing on other units from Erastus. It was one thing to call for a crusade, to declare all who oppose you as enemy...but these were his brothers in arms. They had suffered the same injustice he had...their only difference from him was ignorance about what had been done to them. They were only here following orders, and they had no reason to doubt those commands. He was about to start a civil war...soon his soldiers would be killing men they'd fought beside. He was about to set brother against brother.

Taylor looked out over the terrain and sighed. He didn't fear defeat...he was certain he could win this fight. He'd set a trap, one he was sure would work. The approaching force was commanded by Major Simms. Taylor knew Simms well. He was a moderately capable officer, but nothing more, and he'd been promoted beyond his natural competency level. At best he would effectively, but unimaginably, manage his forces. But his chances of defeating a tactician of Taylor's ability were nil. Still, he was a good man, and Taylor was sick at the prospect of having to destroy him... and all the men serving with him.

"Jake, they're coming through the valley, just like you said they would." Young's voice was a little tense but, compared to his norm, it was downright calm. Like every soldier on Erastus, Young had been forced into the army. More than any of the inner circle other than Taylor, Young also wanted vengeance. He didn't relish the idea of fighting other Erastus units any more than Jake, but if they chose to stand with UN Central, Frantic was ready to send them all to hell. "I've got two drones up. Looks like 3 battalions...maybe 3,200 total strength."

"Thanks, Frantic." Taylor was having trouble keeping the lingering sadness out of his voice. "Keep me posted as you get new data." He wouldn't get much more info, Taylor thought...those 2 drones won't last. His forces had to preserve their equipment, at least until they found some source of resupply. So, unless something unexpected happened when the battle started, there weren't going to be any more drone launches.

Taylor stood silently for a few minutes, staring out in the direction of the approaching enemy. He couldn't see them yet, but it wouldn't be long. His own people were dug into a makeshift trenchline...all except the ambushing force up on the hills. He'd considered marching out of his defensive zone to begin the pacification of Erastus, but he knew UN Central would go ballistic at his rebellion, and he decided to take advantage of the predictability of their response. As expected, they'd thrown the first force they could assemble at him prematurely. He was anxious to get the war for Erastus over, but he wasn't about to interrupt when his enemy was making a mistake.

He started walking forward. "I'm going up to the line, Blackie. I want to get a closer look."

"Jake, this rebellion is over if we lose you. You know that."

"I'll be careful." Taylor was lying. He had something in mind, a bold move that was anything but safe. He'd rejected it when it first came to his mind, but the closer he got to having to start shooting at fellow-Erastus men, the better an idea it seemed. Now he'd decided. If it worked, he'd save thousands of lives and advance the cause. If it didn't, he'd be dead in half an hour.

Taylor peered over the trench. Here they come, he thought...it could be a diagram from the training manual. Major Simms didn't disappoint. His men were perfectly – and predictably – arrayed for an attack. They were going to march right into the ambush Taylor had set for them. And they were going to get massacred.

"Jake..." It was Blackie on the com. "...Lieutenant Davison is asking if he should commence fire." Davison commanded the heavy mortars...and the enemy was start-ing to move into effective range.

Taylor was silent, staring out at the approaching forces. He closed his eyes tightly, longing to shed the tears he was no longer able to produce. He'd been grappling with a choice. Should he give the orders...and watch his men slaughter their old brothers in arms? No...he'd decided on another option.

"Negative, Blackie." Taylor's response was tentative, uncertain. "Tell him to hold fire. All units are to hold fire until I order otherwise."

"Jake?" Blackie sounded confused. He was going to

argue, but he just sighed and replied, "Yes, sir."

Taylor stared out for another few minutes. It's now or never, he thought...Simms' people will start firing any second. "Once it starts, I'll never stop it," he whispered to himself.

He directed a thought to his implanted com, opening a channel to Major Simms. The com units were hardwired to link with each other, and neither side was able to shut out the other's communications. "Don, this is Jake Taylor. Are you reading me?"

He climbed up over the trench, the soldiers around him watching in horror as he stood straight up and started walking toward the enemy. Taylor's heart was pounding, but he kept his pace steady. To any onlooker, he was as calm as a man out for a pleasant stroll.

"I read you, Colonel." There was suspicion in Simms' voice, but curiosity too. "What do you want? Hurry it up. My orders are clear."

Taylor felt like a card player, shoving all his chips into the center of the table. He didn't know if he had a good hand or if this was a bluff, but he was damned sure it was the biggest gamble of his life.

Now, he thought...directing his com to expand the channel to every soldier present, on both sides. "We are not enemies, Major." Taylor's voice was firm, but friendly. "There is no reason for us to fight each other...today or any other day." He kept walking forward as he spoke. He was 50 meters ahead of his line now. Blackie was calling frantically on the com, but Taylor ignored it, remaining on the open line.

"Colonel Taylor, this is pointless. As I said, my orders are clear. Unless you are planning to surrender yourself along with your entire force, we have nothing to discuss." Simms didn't realize at first that Taylor was broadcasting to his entire army. "What is this, Taylor?" There was anger in Simms' voice now. "If you wish to communicate you will do so with me and me alone. Is that understood?"

"What I have to say is for every man here." Taylor's tone remained calm, friendly. He refused to take any bait... losing his temper would be disastrous now. "Many of you know me, have served under me. And the rest of you are familiar with me...with my reputation." Jake paused, taking a deep breath, trying to stay cool as he continued walking forward.

"I am no traitor. Certainly not to anyone on this battle-field today."

"Colonel Taylor...this is pointless. We have our..."

"Major Simms, allow me to finish. I am walking alone toward your lines. If what I say does not convince you, I will be exposed to your forces. You can end this fight before it begins."

Taylor was almost 200 meters from his own troops, and moving into effective assault rifle range of the opposing forces. He was making himself a sitting duck, risking all to make his entreaty.

"I did not take the actions I did for no reason. My officers and the men facing you here today did not take the actions they did for no reason." Taylor took a deep breath. OK, he thought, here goes.

"I was recently captured by the Tegeri." He continued to step forward, moving well into firing range now. He slowly slid his rifle off his back and let it fall to the ground. "I discovered something terrible...something that changes everything."

"Colonel, that's enough." Simms was getting annoyed, that much was obvious from his voice. "None of this has any bearing on why we are here. Now, are you going to surrend..."

"To the contrary, Major, it has tremendous bearing, and it is something everyone here must know before deciding how to proceed. But first, I will demonstrate my sincerity."

Taylor paused again. "Attention 213th and 173rd Strikeforces. Every man is to fire five shots straight up at the sky. Now!" There was a short pause before the fire started. It was sporadic, increasing with each second before peaking and tailing off. The whole thing took ten, perhaps twelve seconds.

"You all know what your orders were. Your entire force was going to assault my trench line...and you would have been attacked on the flank by those hidden strike forces." Taylor was practically screaming now. He'd gone all in, and he was working it with everything he had. "You would have been defeated, destroyed. You all know this now. I could have won this battle...but I sacrificed my advantage. I have done this to prove my sincerity to all of you. Because I did not want to harm any of you."

Taylor kept moving forward. He could make out individual soldiers now. A thousand assault rifles were aimed in his direction. He felt a shiver in his body as he took each step. All it would take was one soldier...one shot could end Taylor's rebellion before it even started. Keep going, he thought, forcing his feet forward.

"The Tegeri and the Machines did not attack the first colonies, as all of you were told." He shouted as loudly as his strained voice could manage. "It was a UN force that destroyed the settlements. It was done to create a crisis... one that would compel the remaining nations to yield to UN Central's control."

Taylor's hand moved to his neck, fingering the talisman T'arza had given him. He touched it as he spoke. "I will..."

"This is enough, Colonel." Simms was angry, though

Taylor could hear the uncertainty in his voice as well. "This is my last warning. Surrender now."

Taylor pressed the button on the talisman. "See for yourself...this was given to me by the Tegeri, who then departed from this world as they promised me they would." The images appeared behind him, the same ones he had seen in T'arza's lair...the ones he'd shown his own people. The image expanded, towered 30 meter over Taylor's head...scenes of murder and destruction, carried out not by Machines or Tegeri...but by other humans.

"This is what truly happened to the first colonies." There was silence, save for Taylor's voice, every eye riveted to the video projected behind him. "These soldiers you see are pre-Consolidation UN special forces...troops the Tegeri should never have seen. This war is a terrible fraud...a lie perpetrated by a small group of people so they could make themselves rulers over us all."

Taylor stared out at the entrenched forces deployed before him, eyes still focused on the graphic images behind. "It is corruption, deceit...murder. Your brothers who poured their lifeblood into the sands of Erastus, your families left behind, the thousands of men who will follow us through the Portals to their deaths...all for lies. For the base greed and lust for power of those who would be our masters."

Now, Taylor thought...make your play. "It must stop! This unholy evil must be destroyed." He was shouting into the com, struggling to keep him voice firm, confident. "My forces have sacrificed their surprise, their guarantee of victory because you are all our brothers." He took a deep breath and balled his fists in a mighty scream. "Join us, my brothers. Stand up with me, with all of us..." He held his arms outstretched, gesturing toward the forces deployed before him. "You are our brothers, all of you. You have shared hell with us, and now we will march out together."

Taylor took a few steps forward, flipping the latches on his armor and letting his breastplate and exos fall to the ground. "Join us!" He held his arms out, exposing his unarmored chest. "Or shoot me now...kill your brother and serve those who have made you slaves."

Taylor stood stone still, staring at the helmets peering out over the trenches in front of him. There wasn't a sound...nothing. All Taylor could think about was Blackie going crazy back at the command post.

The silence continued, seconds feeling like hours. Then he heard it...a scream, and the glimpse of an assault rifle flying through the air as a single soldier climbed up over the trench and ran toward Taylor. The whole thing was surreal, slow motion. Taylor was transfixed on the solitary figure moving toward him. Then, slowly, another...and another. Then hundreds...a tumultuous surging mass running toward him, cheering, screaming. "Taylor...Taylor...Taylor!"

# Chapter 21

From the Journal of Jake Taylor:

I hated the Tegeri...at least I thought I did. They had attacked us for no reason, murdered my people in cold blood. Destroying them was a cleansing, the one thing that made my consignment to hell bearable. Until my encounter with T'arza, my hatred was resolute. Whatever gripes I had against UN Central were subordinated to the crusade against the alien enemy.

Still, now that I look back, I realize there was always a sliver of doubt. They are aliens, I told myself in my most introspective moments...their perceptions are different from ours. Perhaps we unknowingly offended them. Could we have destroyed sacred religious sites or hidden nesting grounds? They had been there before us, after all. How would humans have reacted if an alien raced swarmed onto worlds they had long occupied? Could there be a reason for the hostility, one more justifiable than pure xenocide?

Such meanderings tended to end abruptly for me, usually accompanied by the scenes of dying colonists. No, I would say to myself. There is nothing that could justify what they did. Nothing. And yet that tiny doubt remained, surfacing again every so often.

Now I know it was all a lie, that the Tegeri were blameless. In their place I have a new enemy to hate...and for them there is no doubt, however small. The men who ordered the deaths of the colonists – who lied to the world and sent me and thousands like me here to fight and die on an alien hell far from home – there is no misunderstanding about them. They are human monsters, hideous creatures devoid of morality. They crave only power and dominion over others. No lie, no atrocity, is too much for them to employ in their foul and base schemes.

They are men who consider themselves above me, more worthy than the soldiers who fight at my side and the families we left at home. The suffering they cause is of no concern to them as long at their lust for power is satiated. There is no sacrifice too great, in their estimation, to demand of the people to sustain their grotesque, self-proclaimed elite.

Yes, I have a new enemy, and one who will see no weakness from me, not even those few doubts I afforded the Tegeri. I will not listen to their lies, to their schemes, to their frauds. I will be blind to their pleas for mercy. I have only one purpose...to visit death upon them. To hunt them down to the last, down whatever rathole they may seek refuge. I will kill them all. Every one of them, so help me God.

Keita slammed his fist hard onto the dark walnut desk. "Do you have any idea of the problem we have on Erastus now, Kazan?"

Kazan was standing in front of the desk, noting Keita's lack of an invitation to sit. He'd been named Under-Secretary just days before all hell broke loose on Erastus. Admittedly, that was considerably better timing than a few days later would have been, but he didn't fool himself. Keita could strip him of his position in a heartbeat if he wished. And if making Gregor Kazan a scapegoat for what was already being called Taylor's Rebellion was expedient, that is exactly what would happen. Kazan knew he could find himself shuffling papers in some clerk's office at any moment...or worse. Maybe even a reeducation camp. And he knew exactly what went on in those facilities.

Kazan nodded, keeping his mouth shut. He knew Keita wasn't even close to finished yet. The longer Keita ranted and the more he said, the better a chance Kazan was going to get some kind of chance to deal with the situation. If Keita – or the Secretariat – had already decided to scapegoat him, he'd be in shackles by now.

"The Supersoldier program brought you to the Under-Secretary's chair, and you allow this to happen?" Keita normally controlled his emotions like a razor, but this time his anger was getting the better of him. "You allow a soldier, one who had already proved to be insubordinate, to rally support and raise a rebellion...a challenge to UN Central itself!"

Kazan could see the large vein bulging on Keita's head. He began to wonder if he was going to get another chance after all, or if Keita just wanted to slap him around a little before he was dragged away. He struggled to hold himself upright, but he could feel his legs slowly buckling. Kazan was a bully and, like most, he was a coward at heart.

"Then you sent other Erastus army units to face this man...the most famous soldier on Erastus, the first Super-soldier...with no support, no external supervision?" He stared right into Kazan's eyes. "So, of course, he sweet talks them and they spread their legs for him. He doubles his strength in a few minutes, thanks to you." He paused. "What kind of fool are you?"

Kazan parted his lips, still unsure what to say. "Mr. Secretary, I assure you, I had no idea that General Hammon was planning precipitate action against Colonel Taylor." That wasn't true...Hammon had asked for Kazan's orders before sending Major Simms against Taylor. But

Kazan was pretty sure he'd erased all records of that communication or his subsequent instructions. It had been his stupid mistake, but General Hammon would hang for it in his place...he'd make sure of that much, at least.

"So, your defense is merely that you were neglecting your duties and General Hammon is the fool? That you are simply a lazy imbecile and not criminally negligent?"

Kazan took a breath. "I assure you, Secretary Keita, that if you allow me, I will take full control of the situation and deal with this crisis."

Keita looked back, undisguised disgust on his face. What a spineless creature, he thought...he will take any abuse I hurl at him and then kiss my feet for another chance. It didn't occur to Keita that this was how the entire system functioned, with officials groveling to their superiors and scapegoating their subordinates. The battle cry in UN Central headquarters was, "It's not my fault." And Anan Keita was no different than any other. His anger was fueled not because he demanded excellence from his subordinates. He didn't care how much of a fuck up they made of things, as long as it didn't blow back on him...and this mess was splattered all over the place.

"You will take full control? What does that mean? You will eradicate the rebellion on Erastus? Will you do so as effectively as you did with your first effort? Because all that served to do was swell the size of the rebel army." He glared at Kazan. "No, we must assume that Taylor has taken full control of UNFE by now. There is no reason to suspect that the other lifers would be any less susceptible to his manipulations than Major Simms and his people."

Keita sighed loudly. "We do not have sufficient trained troops available in the Military Affairs Department to handle this situation, not while maintaining force levels on the other worlds." His voice was raw. "I will have to go to Secretary Samovich now, and request internal security forces to invade and retake Erastus." Keita was glaring across the desk with murder in his eyes. "Do you know what an embarrassment that is for me?" He let out a deep, angry breath. "Do you have any idea how costly it will be... especially since it must be rushed? There are no more warring armies on Earth, you stupid fool, no easy place to pull the soldiers we need. By losing control of the situation on Erastus, you have created a problem beyond the scope your infantile mind can grasp. Samovich will have to strip every internal security unit of its heavy forces in order to field the expedition we need." Keita paused again. "He will take it out of my hide." His eyes zeroed in on Kazan's again. "And I will take it out of yours."

Keita sat quietly, respectfully. He was on the other side of the desk now, about to face the same kind of tongue-lashing he'd given Kazan. Keita was more than willing to sacrifice his terrified under-secretary as a scapegoat...and he was well aware that Anton Samovich would do the same to him if it was expedient. Keita was smarter than Kazan, and he figured he had a good chance to survive the storm if he was careful. Very careful.

The room was dark, one side of Samovich's face dimly lit by a small lamp in the corner. It was late outside, a dark cloudy night, threatening of rain. "Secretary Keita, as you are well aware, I sponsored and actively supported your candidacy to the Secretariat." A half-smoked cigar sat neglected in a silver ashtray, small wisps of smoke rising slowly into the gray darkness.

"You and I had not been close allies before your candidacy; I made my choice to support you based predominantly on my perception of your competence. Indeed, you had essentially been doing the job for several years, as Raj

Patel sat in a hospital bed and drooled on himself." Patel and Samovich had not been fond of each other, but Keita hadn't realized how strong their rivalry had been until he'd become a member of the Secretariat and started hearing stories.

"You can imagine, Mr. Keita..." His use of mister instead of Secretary was deliberately disrespectful. Everything Anton Samovich did was deliberate. "...my dismay to have a full-blown disaster exploding on my desk just weeks after your confirmation."

Keita sat perfectly still, trying to decide if he should respond or stay silent. He was just about to open his mouth when Samovich beat him to it.

"I would ask you to explain yourself, but I really don't care about whatever imbecilic argument you have fabricated in an attempt to obfuscate your own guilt. I am not one to waste time with excuses. They are meaningless, insincere, and a waste of time."

Samovich remained almost unmoving, sitting in the shadows, hands clasped in front of him on the desk. He hadn't raised his voice nor spoken a phrase in apparent anger...yet Keita had never felt more exposed or vulnerable. This is a dangerous man, he thought.

"Unfortunately, I have just gone on record supporting your candidacy, and your unanimous appointment was the result of my efforts." He angled his head slightly, staring even more intently at Keita. "Unfortunate for me, at least. For you it is, perhaps, a bit of luck you do not deserve. Were I not covered in your stink already, I can assure you we would not be having this discussion."

Keita had been fearing the worst, but now he felt a spark of hope. Perhaps he'd wiggle his way out of this after all. "Mr. Secretary..."

"Silence, Keita." The tone was still neutral...no shouting, no anger. But the menace was unmistakable. "You are here to listen, not to offer your insights. I will tell you when I am finished."

Keita felt his body sink back into the chair. He tried to hold himself steady, but his head nodded slightly in acknowledgement.

"This entire sorry episode will be disruptive enough. I do not intend to compound matters by affording Chang Li a greater opportunity to embarrass me for my misplaced faith in you." Keita had begun to realize that the struggle between Chang Li and Samovich was more than the usual political rivalry. They both saw themselves as the next Secretary General, and neither intended to let the other interfere. It was a battle to the death between the two...the ascension of one would almost certainly encompass the destruction of the other.

Keita wondered, for a fleeting moment, if it might be worth his reaching out for Chang. Perhaps Samovich's rival would offer him a better deal to humiliate his rival. No, he thought, almost immediately...he was too closely aligned with Samovich already. Chang would never risk it. Especially not now. Chang and Samovich hated each other, but neither one wanted to allow a rebellion to get out of control. They disagreed on most things, but neither one of them wanted the masses forgetting their place, and especially not when they were armed, trained killers.

Samovich slid his chair and stood up, turning his back to Keita and looking out the window. "Here is what we are going to do." He stared out at the swirling, gray night. It was just beginning to rain lightly, droplets finding their way slowly down the heavy glass of the floor-to-ceiling windows. "I will provide you with sufficient forces to crush this rebellion." He paused. "The current strength of the armed forces on Erastus is, what, 12,000?"

"Planetary regulars were at 11,987 as of our last reliable report approximately eleven days ago. Of course, we cannot know that all of these forces have rallied to the rebel side." He hesitated. "There are also approximately 1,743 auxiliaries deployed...engineers, antigrav crews, and similar forces...as well as 872 headquarters staffers. These are rotational troops who would be unlikely to sympathize strongly with the lifers. Whether they are still holding out... or whether they have been killed or captured...we cannot know."

"You are certain they would not join the rebels?" There was doubt in Samovich's voice. "Admittedly, they enjoy a higher social standing and superior benefits, but I fear you fail to fully comprehend the power of a charismatic leader." He paused and turned to face Keita. "Do not underestimate this Jake Taylor. He is precisely the kind of leader who is capable of rallying disparate forces to his side." Another pause. "He is a serious danger, and we must eliminate him now. Indeed, I am surprised his behavioral traits weren't identified at a younger age. We are typically quite effective at targeting problem personality patterns in youth. This Taylor should have been sent to a reeducation facility a long time ago, probably in childhood. I can only assume his own particular latent abilities failed to surface until he was subjected to the crucible of war on Erastus. It is regretful that we will not have the opportunity to study him in detail. It could prove useful in developing methods for more effectively culling out such problem individuals from the societal pool."

Keita found it hard to be overly scared about some lifer on Erastus, though he played along with Samovich's concerns. It was the cost and the embarrassment of the whole thing that troubled him, not some fear that Taylor's band of flag-wavers could actually win.

"Such musings are immaterial at this point, however." Samovich turned back toward the window. "I would indeed be interested in studying this rebel leader, but it is too risky to even try. This cancer must be eradicated immediately." He paused, thinking quietly for a few seconds. "I will provide you will 50,000 internal security troops from the paramilitary teams. You will send them through the Portal to reclaim Erastus. They will have orders to terminate everyone on the planet."

"Yes, Secretary, but the headquarters staff is certainly not…"

"Everyone, Secretary. Is that understood? Erastus is to be swept clean. No trace of the infection must remain."

Keita hesitated for an instant. "Yes, Secretary Samovich. Understood."

"Good." Samovich clasped his hands behind his back. "The forces will be assembled in two weeks. You will be ready when they arrive." A statement, not a question. "I would tell you to go through the Portal yourself, but that would be highly unusual for a Secretary, drawing far too much attention."

"What about Gregor Kazan?" Keita just blurted it out, wishing almost instantly he'd kept his mouth shut.

"Perhaps." Samovich thought for a few seconds. "Mr. Kazan has every incentive to attempt to save himself. There may be some use in that."

"With your permission, I will order him to assume overall command of the expedition." Keita paused. "He is of no use militarily, but his interests are aligned with ours, and his motivation is beyond question."

"Indeed, Mr. Kazan finds himself in a very undesirable position. I can think of no one with greater incentive to swiftly destroy the rebels." He paused for a few seconds, thinking. "Very well…Gregor Kazan shall accompany the expedition, and he shall have full vice regal authority on Erastus." Samovich turned again from the window and sat back in his chair. "Perhaps if he is thorough enough in eradicating all trace of this rebellion, he can even save himself."

# Chapter 22

From the Journal of Jake Taylor:

Fourteen years. I've been in this miserable hellhole fourteen years. Some days it seems like an eternity, others I wonder where it all went. Home seems like a distant dream to me now. I don't even miss it anymore, not really. It's just sort of a dull ache, a numb spot in the back of my mind. Something that was part of me once, but isn't anymore.

I guess time passes the same way for most of us. If you don't get wasted as a rookie, which most do, you go through a sweet spot. You've learned how to survive, but you still have something left of who you were before you were sent here. You cling to ceremonies and traditions, still mimicking the ways of life you left behind, but you also adapt to your new reality; you get used to the routine. The pain of losing home isn't as keen as it was, but the memories are still clear.

It usually starts when you've been about two years onplanet, and it goes on for a few good years, before exhaustion and hopelessness really start wearing down your soul. Sooner or later we all become too tired, too grim, too used up to do anything but move through every day like a zombie. We start off remembering exactly when we came through the Portal, and most of us commemorate it for a while, sort of like a birthday. But eventually it gets too hard to care about anything, and another year on the calendar doesn't seem like such a big fucking deal anymore.

Back when I first got here, the idea of being on planet fourteen years would have been unthinkable. Men just didn't live that long on Erastus. Five Year Men were iron veterans, admired and respected. Ten Year Men were more legend than reality. I think there were two onplanet when I got here. And neither one of them made fifteen.

Things have changed, though, and the last five or six years have been different. The rooks still died like flies... the same as always. No matter how hard we tried to teach them, it just took time...more time than most of them had. But the ones who survived long enough to get their mods lived longer, much longer. Five Year Men became less of a rarity. A lot of the troops even knew a Ten Year Man or two, perhaps one of their officers.

Longbow was the only one of my close companions to die after we got the Supersoldier mods. Blackie, Bear, and the others...and me too...we've all been wounded, mortally by the standards of normal men. But the mods saved us. It turns out cyborgs are a lot harder to kill than men.

There's a price to pay for everything, and survival is no exception. With longevity, I discovered a new kind of fatigue...a bone-deep weariness that grows with each passing year. It becomes harder and harder to care about anything...at least until the lust for vengeance filled the empty place in my soul.

It's been years since I did anything to celebrate my Portal day, but I still remembered it every year...and gave a silent nod to my resilience. Every year until this last one. For the first time, I completely forgot. It was days later when I realized, and it was Blackie who remembered, not me. I'm not sure what to make of it. For better or worse, I am newly embarked on a road vastly different from any I have traveled. I am still on Erastus, but my mind has

*moved on to a new chapter. The road ahead promises*
*no less suffering or bloodshed...but now, at least, I will be*
*fighting the right enemy.*

"Not many people surprise me, Major." Taylor stared
across the table at MacArthur. "But you have." For perhaps the first time, Taylor looked at the antigrav pilot with
something approximating admiration. "Are you sure?"

Jake Taylor was about to embark on a fight to the death.
He wasn't going to defeat his enemies; he was going to
exterminate them like vermin. Or they were going to do it
to him. This conflict would have no prisoners, no rules of
war, no blathering diplomats arguing over etiquette while
men died in the front lines. Taylor had no pity, no mercy
to offer his enemies.

The auxiliary services on Erastus weren't in the same
situation as the footsoldiers. They had been better treated
than Taylor's people, and many of them had behaved
poorly toward the lifers, displaying an arrogance born of
their different status. But they'd fought alongside Taylor's
men, and they'd suffered their own losses in battle. Taylor had some resentment against this privileged group,
but they weren't the enemy, and he knew it. He'd gone to
MacArthur to offer safe passage through the Portal for his
survivors and the other auxiliaries.

"I know we've had our differences, Colonel." MacArthur's voice had an odd tone to it, like the pilot was still
trying to figure out exactly how he felt. "But what UN
Central has done transcends any of that. We may have
argued, but we were always on the same side...and we have
all been used in the most horrendous manner." There
was heavy emotion just below the surface...MacArthur
was barely restraining his anger. "I believed I was here
defending Earth, just as you did. Do you know how many

thousands of Machines my gunships have slaughtered?" He was staring plaintively, desperately looking to Taylor to make some sense of what he was feeling. Jake's retelling of T'arza's description of the Machines had hit MacArthur hard. He'd always considered them almost as robots, created solely to fight. Now he realized they were much closer to sentient beings than he could comfortably accept, that they'd been created to live something like a normal life and only turned into soldiers when mankind attacked their welcoming parties and started a war. "I was a soldier, Jake…" Taylor blinked in surprise as MacArthur used his first name. "…at least I thought I was. But I'm nothing but a mass murderer, am I? That's what we all are."

Taylor took a deep breath. He didn't know what to say. He found himself wanting to reassure MacArthur, but he wasn't sure his own opinion was all that different. It was easy to tell yourself you were misled, that you didn't know what you were doing…but the blood on your hands was still there, and the thousands you massacred were still dead.

"John…" Taylor hesitated, still not sure what to say. "I don't have any wisdom for you. We're all going to have to learn to live with what we've done. One way or another." Taylor looked down at his feet for a few seconds before meeting MacArthur's gaze again. "But now isn't the time to sink into remorse and self-pity. We can't undo what we've done, and some crimes are beyond atonement." Taylor's gaze narrowed, and a firmness returned to his voice. "But we can avenge the dead…and punish the guilty. We can put a stop to this insanity before it drags on for decades on the other Portal Worlds. We can cleanse Earth. We were unwitting parties to this great crime, but not those back at UN Central. They knew…they did this intentionally. They are truly those who bear the monstrous guilt. If we allow them to escape judgment, we will compound what we have done. This is our mess to clean up."

The anger was rising again in Taylor's voice. It was never far below the surface anymore, a bubbling rage ready to escape at the slightest instigation. "That is my purpose now, John. Nothing else matters to me, and there is nothing I will not do to achieve what must be done." His expression softened slightly as he gazed into MacArthur's eyes. "And if you and your people are truly willing to join us, I for one, will be very grateful."

MacArthur nodded his head slowly. He was silent for a moment, but his face looked calm, settled. "Like I said, Jake, I'm with you." He paused briefly. "But it's not just me. We're all with you. My aircrews, the engineers, the transport teams. Everybody." He extended his hand toward Taylor, even managing a thin smile. "Now let's make the bastards pay."

"Jake, you're wrong this time." There weren't many people with the balls to tell Taylor to his face he was wrong, but Tony Black was one of them. "We're better off spreading out, manning all the strong points. Make the bastards run all over, sweating their balls off trying to dig us out." Black's voice had a vindictive edge to it. Clearly, he relished the thought of unacclimated UN enforcers trying to assault strongholds under the burning Erastus suns. "The troops they send through are probably going to be inferior on a man for man basis, but you know they're going to outnumber us. Probably by a lot. Why not let the planet wear them down as much as possible?"

Taylor sat quietly, listening to what his second in command had to say. Finally he waved for the short, stocky officer to take one of the seats next to him. He trusted Black's judgment, and he knew there was sense in what his friend was saying. But Taylor had decided exactly what he wanted to do. His anger had cleared his mind, and his focus was razor sharp.

"You're right, Blackie." Taylor wiped the back of his neck with a small white towel as he spoke. They were down in the equatorial zone, gathering equipment and supplies from the garrisons moving north. Years in the desert had weakened his acclimation to the extreme humidity, and he was really feeling it. "Or at least you might be if I wanted to fight a conventional campaign. But that would take too long. Besides, if they were smart they'd just mask our strongpoints and wait us out. Our supplies are limited; theirs aren't. Not if we hole up in our bases and give them unchallenged access to the Portal. If we let them pin us down we're screwed."

Black dropped hard into the chair, letting out a deep breath as he did. "OK, Jake." There was partial capitulation in his voice. "Maybe you're right...maybe we'd just end up besieged. But then why not defend the Portal, hit them as they emerge? Why let them come through and deploy? Do we need to give up all that advantage when we can be waiting just this side of the transit point and hit them as they come out?" Black wasn't arguing with Taylor. He was genuinely questioning, his tone one of confusion, not debate.

"I don't want to hold them back, Blackie." There was a confidence and a coldness in Taylor's voice that sent a chill down Black's spine. He couldn't tell if Jake was sure he was right, or if he just didn't care enough about surviving to worry about it. "If we defend the Portal, we'll bottle them up. They won't get a fraction of their total force through."

"Isn't that the point?" Black sounded even more confused. "Doesn't that give us an edge, balance out their numerical superiority?"

"Conventionally, yes." Taylor's voice was cold, analytical. "But I don't want to defend against them, Blackie." There was a short pause. "I want to annihilate them. I want to kill every soldier they muster to send here." There wasn't a shred of doubt as he spoke, just icy determination. "If we hold the line at the Portal, the fighting will drag on forever. But there's a limit to the force they can put together on short notice, and the arrogant bastards will send it all through at once if we let them...I'm sure of it." Taylor paused for a few seconds. "I intend to let them transit every man they can assemble. Once they're all through, we'll retake the Portal and cut them off." Taylor looked right into Black's eyes as he spoke. "Because I'm going to let them in..." His words were pure venom. "... but not one of them is getting out."

# Chapter 23

From the Journal of Jake Taylor:

I thought I hated the Machines. I despised them for what I believed they had done, and for more than a decade I gleefully gunned them down. I don't know how many I personally killed, but it must have been dozens...if not hundreds. And the men I led killed thousands, tens of thousands. Whatever else I felt, whatever questions I had about UN Central and the way my men and I were treated, my anger for the Tegeri and their bio-mechanical soldiers always flared hot.

I thought I hated them...until I experienced true hatred. Alien creatures, served up by Earth's best propagandists, reach down into a dark place inside us all, stirring up anger, fear, righteous indignation. But it is human monsters who have tapped into the true veins of boiling, surging, molten rage deep inside me. Traitors who betrayed their own people and massacred thousands of innocents...all so they could enslave the rest of mankind.

Now the real battle is about to begin, the fight against the hideous evil that rules mankind. They turned my men into cyborgs, soulless killing machines to serve their own purposes. Now they will taste irony as that force is turned upon them. My soldiers shall be avenging angels, cleansing the universe of their filth.

I am ready. I am anxious, almost gleeful at the chance

to destroy these soldiers my enemies have sent to murder my people. I feel the rage day and night, making my body shake with such force it is all I can do to hold myself still. Now I know what real fury is. Anger so profound, so primal, it scares me to my core. I don't know who or what I am anymore. I feel as though my soul has been possessed...consumed...by some force, some demon. The hate I felt for the Tegeri served me, it gave me strength in my fight, drove me on. But it is I who serve this hatred, this terrifying lust for vengeance. It is the master, I the willing slave.

Am I sane? I don't know. But I am sure of one thing. I don't care.

John MacArthur lurched hard to the side as his Dragonfire gunship loosed two Ripper air-to-air missiles. The sleek weapons zipped over the scrubby hills below, homing in on the light fighter he'd spotted. They swung wide, each looping around and approaching the target from a different side. The fighter pilot banked hard, trying to evade the fiery death zooming in on him. He zigzagged past one of the missiles, a temporary respite, as the Ripper arced around to make a second pass. His efforts were in vain anyway. The second missile slammed right into his small craft, practically vaporizing it.

"All ships, shout out those sightings as soon as you have them." MacArthur's birds were deployed on combat air patrol around the Portal. The UN forces had been pouring through for two days. They outnumbered the Erastus forces 3-1, and they were still coming. On the ground, Taylor had positioned only light forces near the transit point...snipers and small, fast-moving teams. He didn't want to stop the enemy's advance, or even seriously hinder it. He was just looking to pick off as many as he could, and put up a show of some sort of defense. Enough, at least, not to arouse any suspicion that might instill caution in whoever was commanding the UN force.

The air battle was a different story. Taylor wanted all those invading ground troops to transit onto Erastus, where he could engage and destroy them. But he was determined to keep the enemy air power contained, and prevent as much of it from transiting as possible. He had the Dragonfires patrolling in shifts, keeping constant pressure on anything that flew through the Portal. He'd suspected the UN force wouldn't anticipate the Erastus air units would have rallied to him, and he turned out to be right. The waiting squadrons had quite an element of surprise.

The enemy air units MacArthur's people were battling were lighter...small antigrav fighters that were no match for the massive Dragonfires. Gunships and other heavy craft had to be brought through in pieces and assembled on planet, and MacArthur and his birds were keeping the transit zone way too hot for anything like that to succeed. Taylor didn't know how much airpower UN Central would be able to muster on short notice, but he was determined to keep most of it pinned back behind the Portal.

"I've got two bogies just through. They're climbing hard." It was Lieutenant Stewart, skipper of Condor 06. A good pilot, and probably the best spotter in MacArthur's entire force.

"Condor 01 and Condor 02, move to support Condor 06." MacArthur snapped the orders into the com. He didn't want those enemy birds slipping through. The fight around the transit point was different than any air battle he'd ever seen. The immense energy pumped through the Portal to sustain matter transmission gave off extensive interference, rendering normal detection equipment inoperative. Even old-fashioned radar was useless. The only thing that worked was eyeballing targets, and that meant getting a lot closer than normal.

"Bogie one intercepted." It was Condor 06 again. Stewart got the first one himself.

MacArthur was happy with his crews. They weren't used to fighting almost blind, but so far not an enemy antigrav made it past them. And he was determined to keep it that way.

"Bogie two down." Stewart again. His bird had gotten both kills before the support even got there.

MacArthur smiled.


"The resistance we have encountered is extremely light, Mr. Kazan." Laurence Graves was an imposing figure, at least 10 centimeters taller and 20 kilos heavier than Kazan. "The enemy antigravs have been attacking our fighters and supply shipments incessantly, but we have faced minimal ground forces so far."

Kazan stood outside his command vehicle, sweat pouring down his cheeks. There was an angry scowl on his face, a mask of arrogance he wore to cover his fear and insecurity. He had absolute power over the forces invading Erastus, but he had no illusions about what he faced back home if he returned with anything short of total success.

"They are a rabble, Colonel Graves." Despite his position in the Department of Military Affairs, Kazan understood remarkably little of the realities of war. "Your forces should have no difficulty sweeping them from the field."

Graves was uncomfortably silent for a moment. His career had been spent putting down protests and riots, not fighting veteran armies. He wasn't sure what to expect from these Erastus soldiers, but he suspected they were going to be a lot tougher than Kazan suggested. These weren't civilians armed with clubs and knives, rioting for food...they were seasoned soldiers defending a battlefield familiar to them and unrelentingly hostile to his own troops.

"Sir..." Graves had enough experience dealing with government officials to know he had to tread carefully with an arrogant ass like Kazan. "...I strongly advise caution, at least until we can get a good idea of what we face. We don't want..."

"What we face are criminals, Colonel." Kazan interrupted, his voice heavy with arrogance. "Nothing more. And we will not delay any further."

"Secretary Kazan..." Under-Secretary was a cumbersome title to keep repeating, and Graves figured the informal courtesy promotion would only stroke the vain fool's ego. "...I remind you that we did not expect the air units to rally to the rebel forces." He paused for an instant. "Yet, it appears they have, and in significant numbers." He could tell he wasn't getting anywhere with Kazan, but he wasn't ready to give up yet. "Do we know if the engineers have also joined this Colonel Taylor and his troops?" Graves paused, but Kazan just stared at him. "Sir, I am only suggesting that we hold some units in reserve back on the Earth side of the Portal. Just to be cautious."

"I want the entire force together, Colonel. That means every man is to transit as quickly as possible." Kazan's voice was all bravado, but beneath there was a shakiness he was trying to hide. He wasn't sure if Graves' concerns were reasonable, but he did know that he was under considerable pressure to produce results on Erastus. Quickly. If he moved slowly, if no progress reports made it back to UN Central, it was only a matter of time before Keita – and Samovich – lost what little patience they had. That would be a bad day for Kazan...he was sure of that.

He turned toward Graves and stared at the colonel intently. "As quickly as possible. Do we understand each other, Colonel?"

"They're pulling back, sir. We've secured the western half of the headquarters complex." Captain Shinto was excited, but all his parched throat could manage was a hoarse croak. The heat on Erastus was like nothing he'd ever experienced. At least half his troops were down with hyperthermia, and the rest were barely effective. He'd expected to encounter a significant enemy force defending the HQ complex, but there couldn't have been 200 in total, and most of those pulled back after a nasty firefight.

"Very well, Captain." Colonel Graves' voice was crisp and clear, but then he was in a climate controlled command vehicle while Shinto and his people were out in the blazing sun. "You are to push on and take the remainder of the complex."

Shinto almost groaned out loud. He'd started his assault with 1,100 troops, but he doubted there were more than 300 left standing. Most of his losses were from the heat, but the Erastus forces had taken down at least 200 of his men before they pulled back. He had no idea how many casualties his forces had inflicted, but he was sure it was a lot fewer.

He'd never seen anything like these Erastus soldiers. They ran far faster than his troops, and they did it at high noon under the blazing light of both suns. Their aim was uncanny, and they functioned together with inexplicable fluidity. There was no way his people were going to be able to clear the rest of the objective.

"Colonel Graves, sir, I must advise you that my forces have almost no chance of completing your orders." He was nervous, trying to speak with as much false confidence as he could muster. Officers in the UN Internal Security forces didn't prosper by questioning the orders of superiors…especially in the elite paramilitary units.

"There is no alternative, Captain." Graves wasn't angry. Shinto was just telling him the truth. But Kazan was on the com every twenty minutes, pushing for faster progress. Graves was starting to get pissed about being pushed so hard to pull the bureaucrat's ass out of the fire, but there was nothing he could do about it. "Launch the assault immediately." Graves took a short breath, running through his OB quickly in his mind. "I'm sending you Lieutenant Garcia and his men as reinforcements. That's another 550 troops, Shinto…don't you ask me for any more. That's all you're getting. Now, just take the rest of the objective."

"Yes, sir." Shinto's voice was still tense, but there was relief there too at the prospect of support. "I will launch the attack in ten minutes."

"Very well." Graves cut the line.

Shinto activated the unit-wide com. "Attention, all personnel. We will be advancing in ten minutes." He could practically here the groans among his exhausted troops. "We have reinforcements incoming to support the assault." He had no obligation to let the men know, but he figured it would help morale.

He walked up to the edge of the trench, peering out cautiously at the enemy-occupied buildings on the eastern edge of the compound. What, he wondered…what is waiting over there?

Carson Jones lay perfectly still, his cybernetic eyes fixed on the jagged edge of the enemy trench. He'd been stalking his target for over an hour. An enemy officer, the one commanding the whole attack in this sector. He was confident about his ID on the target, but the bastard hadn't shown himself enough to give a good shot. Jones was more than four klicks away. He could make the kill, but he needed a decent opening.

They called Jones "The Surgeon." It wasn't so much because he was a great sniper, but because he was a great sniper with an uncanny ability to get a fix on the highest value targets in a formation. His list of kills included a roster of Machine officers and two Tegeri. And over the last few days, 14 UN Internal Security unit commanders.

His NIS was linked to the SK-11 computer-assisted sniper's rifle, providing him with real time adjustment to wind conditions and other variables, all controlled through the direct neural connection. All Carson needed was the raw marksmanship and the patience to wait for his shot, both of which he had.

He was lying in the rubble of a wrecked storage shed on the outskirts of the UNFE headquarters complex. The invading UN troops had taken the western half of the compound, and now they were massing to assault the eastern perimeter. The Erastus troops weren't really defending the place; they were falling back slowly, bleeding the attackers. Taylor had been clear…the orders were to inflict as much damage as possible and withdraw before taking serious losses. Those orders had been carried out to the letter. The enemy had taken at least 300 casualties so far, in addition to half their strength incapacitated by the heat. The defenders had 7 KIA and about 25 wounded.

"C'mon you SOB…" Jones muttered softly to himself. …show me some skin, baby." Jones had immense patience, but he knew he was running out of time. The Erastus forces would start pulling back once the attack began, and that meant he'd have to retreat too. If he didn't take his target down by then, he'd lose the chance.

He was listening intermittently to the chatter on the unitwide com. The enemy had already advanced on the far flank, and there was a sharp firefight developing. The

Erastus forces were dug into strong positions. They'd probably repel the first assault, but then they'd pull back while the enemy regrouped.

Jones was thinking, analyzing, trying to figure how long he could stay where we was...how far he could stretch his orders without actually breaking them. Then he saw it. It was almost pure instinct. The target was moving, raising his head to peer over the trench. Jones flashed a thought to the NIS, making a last second adjustment. His cybernetic eyes focused intently, peering through the targeting scope. There it was...the top of his target's head...moving slowly up. Forehead, eyes...up over the edge of the trench.

Snap. Jones depressed the trigger, loosing a single hyper-velocity round. The target's head exploded as the projectile slammed into it at 3,000 mps, sending the lifeless body careening up and back before falling to the ground inside the trench.

"Gotcha." Jones had the same feral bloodlust as any great sniper. He believed in the cause...and even more, he had unshakeable faith in Jake Taylor. But once he was in the field it was all about the kill. Politics didn't matter, nor grievances. He would track his prey with unrelenting determination.

He scooped up the sniper's rifle and rolled to the side, out from under the pile of debris and behind a heavy chunk of broken masonry. He pulled himself up prone and slung the rifle over his back. Time to find another target.

"He's dead, sir." Lieutenant Smythe was beyond edgy...he was nearly in a panic. "One second he was giving me orders, preparing for the assault...the next he was dead." Smythe was covered with blood and gore...all that remained of Captain Shinto's head.

"Control yourself, Smythe!" Graves voice was tense

on the com…he was getting overwhelmed, panicked calls coming in from units all over the field. His forces were advancing on all fronts, breaking through every defensive position. But he was besieged with frantic communiques from his officers. Casualties were high, much worse than expected, and the troops were dropping by the thousands from the heat. Even worse, the enemy snipers were picking off his officers everywhere. The last thing he needed was widespread panic among his commanders.

"Take charge immediately, and lead that assault in." His voice was harsh, commanding. He didn't have the time or patience to wipe every junior officer's nose. "Lieutenant Garcia will take command when he gets there." Garcia was the senior of the two, plus he had a calmer personality than Smythe. And Graves was desperate for officers he could trust.

"Yes, sir." Smythe was starting to get a grip on himself, brushing Shinto's remains off his shoulder the best he could. "Launching the attack now."

Smythe flipped his com unit to his unit frequency. "Bombardment teams, commence firing." He was shouting into the com, using volume to cover up his fear. "All units, prepare to advance in five minutes.

The whoosh of the light rockets whipping overhead made Smythe feel better. At least his forces were striking at the enemy, hopefully softening them up before lunging out of the relative safety of the trenches and charging.

He trotted over toward the center of the formation. He found himself flinching self-consciously as he moved around. The sniper's shot that killed Shinto had come out of nowhere, and Smythe felt like he was in the crosshairs every second.

"Prepare to attack." Smythe dredged up all the courage he could muster and spoke clearly and firmly into the com.

He rubbed his hands on his pants, wiping off the dripping sweat, and he pulled his pistol from its holster. "Charge!"

He climbed up over the trench as he shouted, running forward as quickly as he could. He glanced behind, seeing his troops following, yelling as they ran, and firing forward, more for the morale effect than any real chance of scoring a hit.

Men started dropping, slowly, sporadically. The fire was light, but it was extremely accurate. Smythe's troops could cover most of the ground under cover of a low rise, but there were a few spots where they came out into the open...and they paid a price each time.

Running in the heat was almost as much as he could bear. His chest was heaving as he gasped for air, his uniform drenched in sweat. The men he still had with him were the ones who'd withstood the heat best, but now they too started dropping. Men simply fell to the ground where they were, unwounded, but no longer able to stand or walk another step.

Still, Smythe pushed himself forward. He didn't think he had more than 70 or 80 men still moving, but he could see on the tactical display that Garcia's fresh troops were less than 1000 meters behind. That gave him the morale boost he needed. He was almost to the objective, and he could see the enemy forces withdrawing. He'd though he was facing at least a strikeforce, but there were only a dozen or so enemy troopers scurrying away as his forces reached the first row of buildings.

A dozen, he thought...that was only a dozen troopers we were facing? He watched as they ran, moving at least 3 or 4 times the speed of his troops. He was overwhelmed by the accuracy and the physical capabilities of these Erastus soldiers. What the hell are we fighting here? He was focused on that thought when he felt the projectile slam into his neck. He didn't feel pain, just a sort of numbness...then he was floating. It went on, seconds dragging out, feeling like much longer. Than dimness, cold, blackness.

Bear crouched down near the mouth of the cave. The network of tunnels was on every tactical map of Erastus, but the enemy zipped right by without even scouting them. Just like Jake had predicted. He moved his hand behind him, giving the prearranged hand signs. The men lined up down the cavern relayed the signals back, giving the word that the attack would begin in one minute. Bear wasn't going to risk detection, not with a transmission, not even with a shout. His people were less than a klick from the Portal, and his operation's success depended on speed and surprise.

He counted down in his head, reflexively checking his rifle as he did. Normally, he'd be on the com right now, reminding the rookies to check their weapons and ammo. But he was on radio silence, and there wasn't a newb to be found in the force crouched down behind him. Every man was a veteran with Supersoldier mods. Not one of them had been on Erastus less than three years, and none of them needed to be reminded to load their guns.

Bear waved his rifle in the air and lurched forward, out of the cave. He knew he shouldn't be the first one out, but it would have taken a direct order from Taylor to push him farther back. He ran quickly, his enhanced leg muscles powering his massive body over the scrubby grasslands at 30 kilometers per hour. He didn't have to worry about leaving anyone behind since all his men had the same mods.

He ran toward a small rock outcropping. That was the signal point. When Bear passed the rock, the unit would lift radio silence, and the section and team leaders would organize their attacks. It was halfway to the objective, which would give them about 90 seconds before they hit the outer perimeter of the Portal complex.

The enemy still hadn't started firing, though Bear figured they would any time now. There was no way they hadn't spotted his people yet. Still, every second got them closer, and cut down on the losses his guys would take going in.

Bear zipped past the 2 meter high sliver of rock, blasting a thought to activate his com as he did. "Alright, boys, let's go. Form up your attacks."

Then the enemy started firing.

Taylor stood in his command post, listening to all the reports coming in. He was mostly concentrating on the chatter among Bear's people. They had the toughest job. Taylor could only hide two strike forces in the caves, so Samuels had to take the Portal with fewer than 300 men. The UN forces had been careless about their defenses, but they still had at least 1,500 troops deployed in the immediate area. Bear had a hand-picked crew, Supersoldiers and veterans all. But it was still a tough fight.

"Let's go, 1st Section." It was Samuels' voice on the com. His people had just made it to the Portal itself, the UN units in full flight, leaving at least 200 dead behind them. "I want that defensive perimeter up NOW." There was a short pause, then: "HHVs there, there...and there."

Taylor had total faith in his closest friends, but it still surprised him sometimes listening to their cool competence. His people had spent their time on Erastus battling the Machines. This was the first time they were fighting against other humans...and it struck Taylor just how good his veterans were. These UN troops were well trained and equipped, but they were glorified bullies and secret police, not soldiers. The Erastus forces were tearing them apart everywhere they fought.

Bear's people had drawn the hardest duty, and they'd taken the heaviest losses. One in five of Samuels' men were down, but that was far less than Taylor had feared. They'd taken the Portal. Now, they'd have to hold it against the inevitable counterattacks. The UN command would freak out when they realized they'd been cut off from the Portal. But that was about to become only one of their problems.

Taylor moved toward the command console and activated the main com unit. "Attention, Army of Erastus…" That was the first time he'd called his forces that. He'd never considered a designation, but he sure as hell wasn't going to call them UNFE, with or without UN Central's blasted colon. He didn't know it then, but the name he gave them would stick. "…Objective Z is secured." He paused and took a deep breath. It was time. "Execute Plan Alpha-Omega."

# Chapter 24

From the Journal of Jake Taylor:

A crusade. Many struggles have been so called, yet few, I suspect, have lived up to the purity of purpose implicit in the name. Our war will be a true crusade, and we shall not rest until our enemies are vanquished and the terrible wrong they wrought has been eradicated. My devotion is pure. I don't seek permission or approval, and I will not be deterred by apologies and pleas for mercy. I am what I am, and I have made my peace with that. I am ready to do whatever I must.

If the wrong done to you is bad enough, the primal need to seek some sort of redress can be overwhelming. Sitting and thinking about grievances, planning and devising the means of your enemy's destruction...it all feeds the beast inside. But when it is time to actually do it, to deal out massive death and hideous suffering, to make the decisions that threaten your very humanity...that is when we encounter the greatest test of our resolve.

But there is another aspect of zealotry, of the insatiable need to attain victory at all costs...one that can be the hardest to live with. You must give all to the crusade, holding nothing back. Risking your own life is easy, but sacrificing a friend...that is the hardest thing to live with. And it is just such a friend who is likeliest to be the one you can rely upon in the most vital, the most desperate situation.

**The closest I have come to abandoning my calling, of giving in to my own desires over the needs of the crusade was when I was trying to save a friend...a brother who walked into a firestorm because I asked him to.**

"Pour it into 'em, boys!" Sergeant Harrigan was firing as he encouraged his men. "Don't let the fuckers breath."

The 45th Strike Force had the enemy battalion – what was left of it – pinned. The ridge was high and steep, much too rugged for the panicked UN troopers to retreat over, and every other avenue of escape was over flat, open plateau. Perfect killing ground.

Harrigan's forces had been attacking all day. He was part of the force driving hard toward the Portal, trying to reach Captain Samuel's forces before they were over-whelmed. There were four pincers, approaching Bear's beleaguered survivors from every direction. Taylor was on the com every few minutes, pushing Harrigan and his people, urging them to make the absolute maximum effort. No one had ever heard Jake so determined. Taylor was going to get through to Samuels' people if he had to smash the entire army to bits to do it.

The battle plan had been a success so far...the entire UN force was onplanet and cut off from the Portal. When they realized what Jake's people had done, they launched massive counter-attacks, seeking to retake the transit point. Samuels and his small force had been fighting like ban-shees against 20-1 odds, beating back every charge. But they paid a price each time, and fewer than a third of them were still in the line.

The unit facing Harrigan's forces began to melt away under the murderous fire. They weren't even fighting back anymore, nothing but a few sporadic shots. A lot of them were down from the heat, and the ones still standing were routing, trying desperately to escape the 45th's trap.

"This is Sergeant Harrigan." He was shouting into the com, his excitement boiling over. "Lieutenant Nguyen, Sergeant Harrigan here…the barn door is open, sir." He turned back toward the disintegrating enemy formation and added his fire to that of his men. They'd opened the way for the 111th Strike Force to move through the gap and reach Samuels' perimeter. All he had to do now was make sure none of these troops regrouped and hit the 111th on the flank. He gritted his teeth and slapped a new clip into his magazine. He knew just how to make sure of that.

The fighting had been brutal along the curving ridgeline just east of the Portal. The dead were piled up everywhere, and the advancing troops had to climb over the bodies to push their way forward. Samuels' troops had performed wonders along this line, holding the outer perimeter against 11 charges. By the time the enemy launched number 12 there only 8 men left manning the position.

There wasn't a lot of doubt…this time the enemy was going to get through. There was no military reason for Corporal Sebastiani and the 7 troopers under his command to stand…they didn't have the slightest chance of holding back the 1,200 enemy soldiers formed up for the final push. But all 8 of them were of one mind. There was no way they were pulling back. If the enemy wanted to take their position, they were going to have to take it. Not one of them was ready to give it away for free.

"Well, Private Ramirez, we've earned our pay these last few days, haven't we?" Sebastiani had walked up behind Ramirez. The private had been part of an HHV crew, but his teammate and the weapon itself had been blasted to bits a few hours earlier. Now he was crouched down with his assault rifle. He didn't have the firepower he'd had before, but that didn't matter. He'd be standing here with a knife if that was all he had.

"Yes, sir." Ramirez was focused, ready. Somehow he had mastered the fear, at least for the moment. He knew just as well as Sebastiani that they all had about ten minutes left to live. "I think Colonel Taylor will be pleased with us." There was an almost eerie contentment in his voice.

"Yes, private." Sebastiani's tone had become thoughtful, almost serene. "I think you are right. We did our duty for the colonel." He looked out across no man's land, but he wasn't seeing anything...at least nothing on Erastus. He saw images of home, memories he'd long since thought were lost to him. The rolling hills of Tuscany, the small town where he was born...the place from which he'd never traveled more than 20 kilometers before they came and made a soldier out of him. He knew he was going to die, but he'd made his peace with it. The fear was gone.

Perhaps it would return at the instant of death, when he was staring at the advancing enemy soldiers...when he was lying in the hot sand, feeling his life slip away. But for now he was satisfied. He'd done his duty...for his comrades and for Taylor. There were worse ways to die.

"Corporal, there's something going on over there." It was Private Vick on the com. "Look." His voice was rising in pitch, becoming excited. "It's us, corporal. I mean Erastus troops. They're attacking the enemy from the rear."

Sebastiani snapped out of his daydream and stared out at the enemy lines. Vick was right. The enemy was falling into complete disarray. Then he heard it, a series of low rumbles...explosions all along the enemy rear.

"They're here." Sebastiani shouted into the com. "The relief column is here."

Vick was the first one to start cheering, but it was only

a few seconds before all 8 of them were shouting joyously. Sebastiani let it go for a minute…they deserved it.

All they had to do was hunker down and wait. The relieving force had caught the enemy in a difficult position. There wasn't a doubt in Sebastiani's mind that the forces coming to their aid were going to defeat the units facing them. But sitting around and watching their saviors fight it out wasn't how he was wired.

"Alright boys. This isn't over yet." He grabbed his rifle and cautiously moved forward. "Let's move up and help our boys out. What do you all say?"

He was shocked how loudly seven men could cheer.

The Surgeon had been at work all day. Jones was ranging all along the front lines, scouring the enemy position for choice targets. Conditions were perfect…Taylor's forces were attacking the enemy at every point, driving them back in utter disarray. Nothing made officers more careless than panic and disorder in the ranks…and Jones only needed one slip up to put his target down.

He was back near the old UNFE headquarters complex. There wasn't much left of the buildings but, even though it was militarily useless, Taylor figured it would be a psychological strongpoint for the UN forces. As usual, Jones thought, he turned out to be right. There were at least 10,000 enemy troops trying to rally in the area, half without weapons, all in complete disorder. A perfect environment for hunting.

Jones was after a very special target, and he figured this was where he'd find him. Taylor's army didn't have any real intel on the enemy OB or command structures. But Jones had done some research…mostly with a notched blade and a few carefully selected prisoners. He was pretty sure he was hot on the trail of his prey.

He was crawling very slowly, concentrating hard on staying concealed. Carelessness could be as deadly to him as his target. He pulled himself just behind the crest of a small rise and peered over cautiously.

There it was, just as he expected. The command post was small, maybe half a dozen vehicles parked around a series of portable shelters. The area was clogged with soldiers, mostly wandering around, trying to find their units... or just walking in stunned shock. There were hundreds on the ground too, those who'd succumbed to the heat. Jones knew from his own experience, some of them would recover after a short rest and a few gulps of water...and some would never get up again. Indeed, he could see the burial details moving about, scooping up the bodies of those who had died from heatstroke.

His enhanced eyes peered through the scope of his rifle, panning along the confused mass. It was hard to get a view through to the central area past the crowds. There were a number of officers in his sights, but Jones was after one target, and he was determined to get his man.

"That's the main command post," he whispered to himself. "That's where he'll be."

He watched, slowly moving from one figure to the next. He couldn't just start dropping officers. He'd get one shot, maybe two, then all hell would break loose down there. He needed to spot his target first, and he would stay at it however long it took.

Then, just a few seconds later, his eyes locked on a figure. The uniform was right. He felt his heart beating faster, excitement building along with realization. He focused harder, bringing all the power of his upgraded eyes into play. The insignia looked right too. Suddenly, it all clicked...he was sure. It was him.

He stared intently, waiting for a cluster of soldiers to

pass, opening the field of view. There it was...the shot.

He slowly tightened his finger over the trigger. "Say goodnight, Colonel Graves..."

Taylor stared out over the mass of miserable prisoners milling around behind the makeshift fencing. They stretched over a kilometer, huddled together and guarded by a dozen strikeforces. These men had been enforcers on Earth, privileged bullies who persecuted helpless citizens, but now their arrogance was gone. They were utterly beaten...broken and terrified.

"Jake, come on..." Blackie wasn't quite pleading, but he was trying hard to convince Taylor. "...we're not murderers. That's the whole point of this, isn't it? That we're better than they are."

Taylor was trying to show respect for the feelings of his best friend and second-in-command, but he was utterly unmoved. These men might not share the degree of guilt that Gregor Kazan had, but they were part of the same cancer and, as far as Taylor was concerned, they had to be cut out the same way. It was all well and good to aspire to loftier standards of mercy, but first they had to win the war.

Kazan had already been dealt with. Taylor's men had dragged the whimpering bureaucrat from his hiding place and thrown him on the ground in front of their victorious commander. Some of them had probably expected Taylor to gloat to the pathetic fool, and others expected to see him mete out a horrible, lingering death to the UN leader, but Jake hadn't obliged them. He simply walked up to Kazan and looked at him for a few seconds, though he didn't share what he was thinking with anyone. Then he pulled out his pistol and shot the crying prisoner in the forehead without a word. "We are revolutionaries, not sadists," was all he had to say afterward.

The army had expected Kazan to pay the ultimate price, but no one knew what to expect for the masses of enemy soldiers who had surrendered. More than three quarters of the enemy forces were already dead, slain on the battlefield or done in by the relentless heat. There wasn't a live enemy soldier anywhere on Erastus outside this prison camp, Taylor was sure of that. Soon there wouldn't be one anywhere.

"I'm sorry, Blackie. There is no choice." He was a little annoyed by Black's hesitancy, and yet he understood in a way too. "Those men out there...they are not like us." He was looking at Black, but speaking to everyone present. "They were not yanked from home and family and conscripted to fight. They pursued careers as Internal Security troopers. For God's sake, most of them probably needed some sort of influence to even get the job."

Taylor took a breath. He was starting to get angry even thinking about the Internal Security forces. "We were all fools once, perhaps, but now we understand how Earth's government works. And we know exactly what these men are."

He stared around the room, seeing a mix of agreement and doubt. "How many people suffered and died in reeducation camps, dragged there by these thugs? How many were shot down in street riots and demonstrations because they had the temerity to pour into the streets and demand food?"

Taylor stopped. He was willing to try and convince his officers...to a point. But he was in command, and that was just what he intended to do. Command.

"It doesn't matter what anybody thinks about this anymore." His voice was like steel. "The decision's been made."

Taylor had other motivations too. His forces were short on supplies. There was no way they could sustain another 12,000 men, and even if they had the logistical capacity, there were no soldiers to spare to guard them. Dragging along hostile prisoners was a security risk Taylor wouldn't have considered, even if he'd had the resources to do it. The only other alternative was to send them back to Earth…and that was out of the question. Taylor was determined that any force the Earth authorities sent after his people would disappear without a trace. There would be no survivors to tell the tale. He wanted the UN authorities to know fear.

He turned toward Daniels. "Captain, the prisoners are hereby sentenced to death, to be carried out immediately. Assemble the forces you require, and see that it is carried out."

Daniels snapped to attention. "Yes, colonel." His answer was crisp. Taylor hadn't designated the duty randomly. He knew that Daniels agreed with him completely. He didn't make a habit of excusing soldiers from duty they considered upsetting, but he knew the magnitude of what he was ordering, and his people had lost enough of their souls already. Daniels would handle it better than Bear or Blackie or any of the others.

He watched as Daniels saluted and trotted out of the room. Then he took a quick look at the others and turned to leave himself. "Dismissed."

# Chapter 25

From the Journal of Jake Taylor:

Victory. Erastus is ours, the enemy army utterly destroyed. Yet there is no joy, just a grim satisfaction. Our war is just beginning, and we face an enemy vastly stronger than ourselves. We fight to destroy a tyranny, to free a world that looks at us as traitors. Those we would liberate are under the thrall of our enemies, too beaten down and blind to see the truth.

My soldiers have come far already, and suffered much. Yet I must ask so much more from them. Few, perhaps none, will survive this final war. But if I must ask them for their lives to right this horrific wrong, then that is what I will do. Just as I will willingly give my own.

Hatred is a more complex emotion than I'd imagined. I ordered the execution of 12,000 helpless prisoners yesterday, and I feel no doubts, no remorse for what I have done. There is no question Gregor Kazan was a willing participant in the great evil we fight, fully deserving of the death I gave him. The troops he led to Erastus, the 50,000 who now lay dead on the rocky sands of this inhospitable world – 12,000 of them shot along a stone wall by my command - they are more difficult to judge. Their culpability in the crime is more ambiguous, less straightforward to judge.

Surely, the jackbooted enforcers of a despotic government bear some of the guilt for the system they serve.

These men spent their lives terrorizing helpless civilians and dragging people to reeducation facilities. They didn't create the policies they imposed, but they were part of the machine that stripped freedom from the people. I cannot imagine the thousands these men beat and killed...how many they dragged from their homes in the night, never to be seen again by distraught families.

But was it really necessary to kill them all, to wipe them out to the last man? Certainly we sent a signal to our true enemies. The disruptions and panic on the Secretariat will almost certainly erode their efficiency. Fear will make them dither and argue, giving us more time to prepare, to move forward.

Yes, these soldiers had to die. All of them. I know not all my people agree, but I am in command and, as long as I am, I will do what I believe right. I will not allow misplaced sympathies, undeserved pity to stand in the way of our righteous fire.

My officers have doubts...I know that. Probably not Hank Daniels...he is as determined as I am that nothing be allowed to defeat us, nor divert us from our crusade. Blackie and the rest are loyal; I know that as surely as I know anything. They will follow me wherever I go. But they are conflicted, uncertain about the means we must employ. They will do what I command, but they will suffer for it, consumed by doubts, by pointless guilt. I am sorry for this pain added to all they have suffered, but if they insist on torturing themselves, so be it. The crusade transcends us all. Our own suffering, our pain, even our deaths...they are nothing next to the importance of victory. And that victory may well cost us all we have to give...all that is left of us.

I will have to stay close to my troops in this war, lend them support. They will be fine when the battle is raging and they are fighting as soldiers. But when victory is near, and they are chasing down panicked survivors, gunning them down in whatever ditch they crawl to for refuge...that is where they will need my strength.

**The struggle is all. We have won nothing yet. War has just begun, and it shall not end until the last of those stained with the guilt of this crime are crushed beneath our boots, never to rise again.**

Taylor stood on a small rise, watching the heavy diggers tear into the rocky sand. He was focused, staring intently at the excavation machines, flashing a thought to his aural implants to lower his auditory response. The damned things were loud.

Taylor was just glad he had them. They had to dig 40 meters, and that was a long way to go with shovels, even with cybernetically-enhanced muscles wielding them. It was expensive to transport and reassemble heavy equipment. When Jake got the loyalty of the engineers, he also got their machines. And that included these two plutonium-powered heavy excavators.

He knew there were more Portals here, buried near the recently exposed one the Tegeri had used to withdraw from the planet. T'arza had told him, and the alien had been true to his word on everything else. Taylor doubted most things, but not those the enigmatic Tegeri had shared with him.

UN Central never knew about the other Portals on Erastus. They probably assumed there were some, Jake thought, but they had no idea where they were. The Tegeri had buried them, practically rearranging the entire landscape to keep them hidden.

Now they had shared their location with Taylor, and he was going to use them to lead his forces off Erastus. Marching through the Portal to Earth would be a fool's game. His troops didn't have the strength to take on all of UN Central Earthside. Taylor would have loved nothing more than to end the war in one great battle, but he knew that was impossible. Their quest would be a long one, down roads he was sure he couldn't imagine now.

Blackie had argued for standing firm on Erastus, digging in and defending against every attack the UN forces launched. But that strategy would fail as well. Taylor's troops had decisively defeated a much larger enemy force, but when UN Central truly marshaled its resources, as it would certainly do now, they would dwarf the just-defeated army. The Erastus forces would draw their price in blood, but if they stood firm, sooner or later they would be overwhelmed and destroyed.

No, Taylor knew the only hope was to march on to other Portal worlds. Erastus was far too hostile an environment to support the army for the long term without resupply from Earth, but many of the other worlds were lush and green, unspoiled paradises that would provide food and water and other essentials. There were troops on many of those worlds too, not Supersoldiers, perhaps, but lifers like Taylor and his men. They didn't know the truth on those worlds, not yet, and they hadn't lived in the burning crucible Taylor and his men had, but perhaps they could be recruited to the cause, swelling the forces of the crusade. Taylor saw no other option, but whatever the pros and cons, the decision had been made. They were moving forward,

The Army of Erastus. That's what they were calling themselves. Taylor was amused by the irony. Erastus was where they were all sent to fight...to die. A hell world the first expeditionary forces had dubbed Gehenna. A place where they had suffered, where their friends and brothers had died. Its name was spoken most often as a curse. But it was different now. It had become a source of pride as well, of élan. These men had survived the worst place men had ever been sent to fight. They endured betrayal and unimaginable hardship, and they had come together to form the most effective army in human history.

They faced a long march and many battles ahead. They would be vastly outnumbered by the forces they would face, but they were ready. There was guilt and uncertainty among them, but all agreed they'd been betrayed, as mankind itself had been. They were united in their determination to punish those responsible, though some were more prepared for the grim choices ahead than others.

Taylor stood on a small rise outside the old Firebase Delta, watching the large sun set. He was struck by the deep hues of red and pink in the sky, stretched out in long, gauzy ribbons. He'd seen it thousands of times, but this was the first time he really noticed the beauty of it. He'd been on Erastus for fourteen years, and he'd never expected to leave. Now that the army was preparing to depart, he was noticing all sorts of things he never had. He'd hated Erastus since he first stumbled through the Portal, but now he realized, it had become home to him in ways he could never have foreseen.

He didn't know if any of the other guys had similar thoughts. He was too embarrassed to admit his own wistfulness to talk about it. Besides, they were just passing feelings, he thought, nothing more. Overall he was anxious to begin the next chapter in the crusade…and his mind raced with curiosity about what another world would be like. A new world. Something Jake had long ago ceased to imagine.

The army was elated by the magnitude of its victory. The men had been celebrating for days. They knew the grim realities of what lay before them, but they believed in what they were doing…and they had a new confidence in themselves.

Taylor knew many of them had begun to idolize him as well. The legend of Jake Taylor was growing, taking on a life of its own. Taylor the man was uncomfortable with it, feeling it was wrong. But General Taylor, the revolutionary leader knew how useful it could be. In the end, he indulged it, even encouraged it. The cause before all else.

He heard the footsteps behind him. People didn't sneak up on soldiers with the mods. His electronically-enhanced ears tracked them all the way from the base...four sets of footsteps.

He turned slowly from the fading sunset to face his four closest friends. The all had thoughtful looks on their faces, just as Taylor did. "Come to enjoy one last Erastus sunset, gentlemen?" Jake had become a grim and serious creature, but he managed a smile for these four brothers.

They all returned the smile, but it was Black who spoke first. "I can't say I'm going to miss this place, Jake, but it still feels strange to be leaving." The others offered a ragged series of nods.

"Yes, it certainly does." Taylor let his smile morph into a pensive expression. "Well, boys, whatever happens next, we accomplished something here."

They nodded again, but Jake continued before any of them spoke. "And I don't mean the battle, though that was as brilliantly executed as anything I've ever seen." He paused. "I mean the way we united the forces on Erastus...without firing a shot. The troops who came through the Portal were our enemies; we knew that going in. But it could have gone differently with the other Erastus forces." He hesitated again and then continued. "And killing them would have only added to our crimes." He was quiet again for a few seconds, looking thoughtfully out over the rocky desert. "If we are to prevail in this war we will have to make new allies, convince others to come over to our side. Destroying those who fight us...that is the easiest part of what we must do. Finding friends is always more difficult than finding enemies."

They all stood quietly, pondering Jake's words. There were a few silent nods, but finally, Hank Daniels was the one who spoke. "Jake, we all wanted to come out here and tell you what it means to us to serve at your side. You've saved every one of us, and some of us more than once. You're the best commander soldiers anywhere could ever have." Daniels wasn't normally emotional, but his voice was halting, cracking. "We want you to know we're with you to the end...wherever and whatever that may be."

Daniels extended a hand, and the others quickly reached in, stacking their palms on top of each other. Taylor looked at them for a few seconds. He opened his mouth then closed it again. There were no words that could express what he was feeling...and none that were necessary between these five friends and comrades. He smiled again and reached into the center, grasping hands with the others.

"To victory."

# Also By Jay Allan

Marines (Crimson Worlds I)

The Cost of Victory (Crimson Worlds II)

A Little Rebellion (Crimson Worlds III)

The First Imperium (Crimson Worlds IV)

The Line Must Hold (Crimson Worlds V)

To Hell's Heart (Crimson Worlds VI)

The Dragon's Banner

www.crimsonworlds.com

www.jayallanbooks.com